HORNED OWL HOLLOW

By

Karla Brandenburg

D1607923

Foster Family Tree

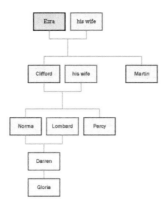

Mansfield Family Tree

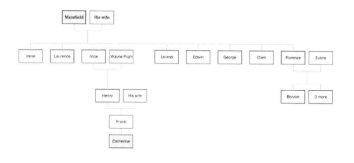

HORNED OWL HOLLOW
Karla Brandenburg
Copyright 2023 © Karla Lang

For questions and comments about the quality of this book, please contact Karla@KarlaBrandenburg.com

Welcome to ***Whimsical Collectibles***
Shop hours: Monday - Wednesday by appointment
Thursday - Sunday 12-5pm
Elspeth Barclay, Proprietor

Chapter 1

Everyone in Longhill, Illinois, knew who the Lombards were. My heart fluttered when they'd offered me the opportunity to go inside Horned Owl Hollow, their stately mansion. They'd stopped hosting fundraisers a few years back, when Norma Lombard was rumored to have become infirm. The newspaper had reported her death a month or so ago.

Had she died in the house?

A chill raced down my spine at the thought the beautiful old place might be haunted.

As I drove my younger sister past the spiked iron perimeter fence of our destination, large gray and white clouds floated over the sun, casting shadows over the three-story house, threatening an impending storm.

Laine leaned forward to look through the windshield. "Not quite the showplace it used to be."

"What makes you say that?" I asked. "It looks to be well-maintained." I turned at the corner and drove between the ornamental pillars that marked the driveway, to the carriage house behind the mansion.

"Maybe, but there's a vibe, you know? I have to wonder if it's haunted."

Her thoughts echoed mine. Laine didn't share my sensitivity, but she'd had enough validation of my experiences to trust I could see things she couldn't. "We aren't here in search of ghosts. We're here to evaluate the collectibles for consignment." I stopped in the parking area the owners had described to me, got out, and glanced at the third-floor dormer windows.

I shivered in the early March morning and grabbed my tote bag from the back seat of the car. While Laine and I started along the circular gravel drive toward the front door, a cool breeze teased my hair. The beautifully manicured lawn was a verdant green, bordered by woods on the other side of the house. A bench marked a winding path lined by daffodils and bluebells.

The driveway passed a sidewalk to a small bungalow—a caretaker's cottage?—and beyond that, a Tudor house on the corner of the property by the perimeter fence. As we neared the main house, an older couple came into view on the stone terrace, seated at a round table. The woman rose from a wrought-iron chair and leaned across the marble railing.

"Elspeth Barclay?" she said. "I'm Faith Lombard." She had faded blonde hair cut into a smooth bob and was dressed in designer capris paired with a nautically themed blue and white striped shirt.

"You can call me Elle. This is my sister, Laine." We crossed to the terrace and climbed the stone steps. "Pleasure to meet you." I reached out to shake her hand.

"And this is my husband, Darren," Faith said.

He rose to shake my hand, as well. Darren had a full head of silver hair and baby blue eyes. He wore neat khakis and a royal blue Ralph Lauren polo.

"Pleased to meet you, Mrs. Lombard. Mr. Lombard." I handed Darren my card for the business I owned with my sister, *Whimsical Collectibles.*

"Please. It's Faith and Darren," he said.

Aside from the designer clothes, neither of them gave off "rich people" vibes. Old money rarely did. The nouveau riche were more likely to make sure you knew how well-off they were.

Darren extended an arm. "Shall we go inside?"

A dark cloud blocked the sun, casting long shadows across the yard. In spite of the warm welcome, a shudder of apprehension held me back. I shook off the sensation. If I was going to appraise their collection of figurines, I'd have to go inside at some point.

Laine and I followed Darren to the terrace doors, which were bordered on the outside by wide shutters on hinges.

"I don't normally see shutters on hinges other than in the South," I said. "Do you close them?"

"No, we never have," Faith said. "I suspect they were a feature brought over by the original builder. Generations of Darren's family have lived here, but they originally came from Louisiana, as I understand it."

Two sets of French doors and transom windows provided natural light from floor to ceiling. As I stepped inside, the energy in the room engulfed me. Someone had died in this house. Goosebumps rose on my skin. Encountering spirits always creeped me out, even the friendly ones. I closed my mind so as not to invite any unwelcome visitations. Instead, I surveyed the beautifully decorated parlor.

Wooden panels made up the inside walls, with carved cornices at the ceiling. A fireplace framed by six feet of intricately designed white wood rose against another of the walls. In one corner, a bust of two children was displayed on a pedestal, and another corner held a statue of a toga-draped man leaning on a walking stick. Overhead, the decorative ceiling was sectioned into geometric shapes. The room could have been in a museum.

A French style sofa—not vintage—was bordered by William and Mary side tables—definitely antiques. I stroked the veneer reverently. "These are gorgeous."

Laine's eyes were wide as saucers. "Everything is in such good shape. Hardly a scratch."

Faith beamed. "You're familiar with antique furniture, too?"

"That would be Laine's specialty," I said.

"Oh?" Faith said, turning to Laine. "We're considering selling the estate. You might like to look at a few pieces while Darren shows Elle the Staffordshire figurines," she said.

Laine stopped beside the pedestal displaying the sculpture of the children. "The craftsmanship on this is... did someone in the family make this?" she asked, breathless.

"I'm not sure, actually. It dates to the time the sculpture was done, so very likely. The children are Darren's grandmother, Norma, and her brother."

Darren waited patiently beside the parlor door. "Shall we?"

I squeezed Laine's arm. "Have fun." I followed Darren into the hallway. Portraits lined the walls. One showed a man with a thick moustache, his dour wife, and two small children. The children that had posed for the bust? On the opposite wall, single portraits of another man and a woman I assumed to be his wife. "Family?" I asked, pointing to yet another portrait—one of two young men. Beside the painting of the two men, I recognized a portrait of Norma Lombard, based on photos I'd seen in newspapers.

Darren paused, allowing me time to admire the artwork. "Yes. Should we move, I expect the portraits will go to my sister's house, the Tudor next door."

"Who lives in the bungalow beside the parking area?"

"You mean the museum?" He smiled. "My great-grandmother was a collector, much like my great-grandfather who brought home the figurines we're selling. They amassed so many things that they had to build a place to store them. I imagine we'll eventually have to address what to do with those items, as well." He motioned me across the hallway.

Residual energy continued to prickle the hairs on my arms. *I'm just here to look at the figurines.*

I followed Darren into a formal dining room. Display cases built into one wall were filled with the Staffordshire figures. Hundreds of them. The wealthy people I'd encountered had a tendency to jealously guard their collections. If I was going to put in the time and effort to catalogue his pieces, I didn't want him to change his mind. "Are you sure you want to part with the figurines?"

"As I mentioned, my great-grandparents were the collectors." Darren said. "My great-grandfather travelled abroad regularly during World War I. He transported horses to and from France, and later went to England when they started breeding Percherons there. He'd bring home Staffordshire pieces for my grandmother from every trip. My grandmother always said she was delighted at first, and then it became a joke that he filled his pockets with them since they were relatively cheap. After the first couple dozen, she lost interest. When they appreciated in value, she couldn't very well give them away, could she? She used to say she became a collector against her will."

"I'm surprised you wouldn't consider them family heirlooms," I said.

He shrugged. "The kids have all moved away and they don't have the same sense of tradition we grew up with. I hate to sell the old place, but it requires a fair amount of money to maintain, not to mention the taxes. Faith and I have been spending more time in Florida during the winters and decided there's no reason to come north now that my grandmother has passed on."

While Darren unlocked the glass display cabinet, I marveled at the beautiful woodwork. Another fireplace. A built-in sideboard. A coffered ceiling. The curved window overlooked the woods.

Darren retrieved a pair of figurines and transferred them to the crisp white tablecloth on the dining room table. "Oh," I whispered. One piece in particular, a grouping I recognized of two whippets and a King Charles spaniel, was potentially worth over a thousand dollars if it was genuine. I was almost afraid to touch them. I looked for my tote bag, for my gloves.

"You can examine them in here," Darren said. "I expect it may take you a couple of days to assess them."

"I've never seen so many pieces in one place before."

Faith appeared in the doorway. "I suggested we take them when we move, but Darren won't hear of it."

Darren lips drew into a thin line.

A point of contention between them? I wasn't in a position to intervene. I'd earn a handsome fee from whatever items we sold.

Outside, the clouds were growing darker. A flash of lightning lit the pathway through the woods. "Where does the path go?" I asked.

"Oakwood Cemetery," Faith said. "The family tried to annex the property several times over the years, but we haven't been successful. While Darren's setting out the pieces for you, let me show you the porcelain doll we have upstairs. It belonged to Darren's grandmother."

A sense of foreboding hung in the air. I shot one more glance out the window wishing I could leave before the rain started, but I couldn't pass up the opportunity to see a vintage doll. "I'd love to see it." We stood to make a nice commission if they allowed us to consign more of their antiques, not to mention the furniture Laine was assessing.

I followed Faith to the end of the hall. Beside the conservatory, judging by the greenery inside the glass doors, a curved oak staircase held a bronze angel light fixture on the newel post. A grandfather clock chimed the half hour. Everything gleamed, erasing Laine's assessment the house was no longer a showplace.

A stained-glass window decorated the first landing, and a prism of colors shone from the stained-glass skylight overhead. We continued to the second-floor hallway, which consisted of four doors, two of which were closed. I glanced over my shoulder to a rear hallway. Servants' quarters?

Faith opened the first door on our right. The stale air rushed toward me like Florida humidity. For a moment, I struggled to breathe. Every instinct told me to leave Horned Owl Hollow, while the energy in the room invited me in.

"This room belonged to Darren's grandmother," Faith said, a note of reverence in her voice. "She lived to be a hundred and one, God rest her soul. Her death was the impetus we needed to finally make some changes around this place." She remained in the doorway. "The doll's in the rocker."

I took a tentative step inside. Hardwood floors. A Persian rug in front of the fireplace. Two upholstered rocking chairs. A gilt-edged mirror over the mantel. Tall windows overlooking the terrace. Pastel-colored floral wallpaper. A transom over the door. A spindle bed covered with a white-eyelet comforter. A pedestal sink in the corner of the room.

"I was sorry to hear of Mrs. Lombard's death." I turned a circle, taking everything in. "Did she die at home?"

Faith wrung her hands, still in the doorway. "Yes. She didn't want to go to the hospital. She had a litany of illnesses, largely due to her advanced age, but she was determined to hang on as long as she could."

Energy often remained behind when people died, especially when someone didn't want to die. Was the energy I sensed Norma?

Yes.

The word, which gave me goosebumps, was little more than a whisper carried on the rising wind blowing through the trees outside the windows.

I crouched beside the perfectly preserved doll in the rocking chair, hesitant to pick it up. My gloves were downstairs, in my tote bag. I didn't want to risk damaging the embroidered dress or the porcelain head. From the corner of my eye, I caught movement. The other chair rocked on its own, sending my nerves skittering. I rose to my full height, backed away, and glanced at Faith—still standing in the hallway.

"Must be a breeze," Faith whispered.

There was no breeze. The windows were closed.

The house belongs to Martin. Help him find his way home.

The message came through clearly, sending a fresh wave of shivers all through my body.

Who the heck is Martin?

I didn't understand why the dead used me to pass on their messages. Those messages often weren't well received.

Faith took a step back, her face pale. "We should probably get back to the figurines."

I hurried to join her in the hall and she pulled the door closed once more.

Small talk would chase the willies away. "Darren mentioned you were snowbirds," I said. "Who takes care of things while you're away?"

"Darren's sister."

"Why sell the house?" I asked. "Would Darren's sister want it?"

She chuckled. "She won't even come inside after dark." Faith's eyes widened as if she realized she'd given away a secret, and quickly added, "The lighting isn't good when the sun goes down."

More like Darren's sister didn't want to run across the ghost. Was Faith waiting for me to mention the rocking chair? The spirit seemed benign, but if it wasn't, better to find out now, considering I was certain Faith had taken me to the room to see more than the porcelain doll. "What does Darren's grandmother think about you selling the house?"

Faith covered her mouth with her hands. "I think you misunderstood. Darren's grandmother passed."

We stopped at the bottom of the staircase. She held my gaze but didn't say anything more.

No. I didn't want to know about her ghost. Better not to press the issue. I peeked into the parlor on the way by. Laine was busy taking notes, crouched beside one of the tables, oblivious to the residual energy.

Faith turned on the overhead light in the dining room as daylight continued to fade with the oncoming storm.

I was here to do a job.

"What did you think of the doll?" Darren asked. "You know that was the last one my grandmother had. Her brother used to tease her by throwing her dolls out the window. Needless to say, the dolls didn't survive the fall to the terrace."

"I'd be interested to take a closer look another time," I said.

Darren seemed surprised. "A closer look?"

"I didn't have my gloves on."

Faith cleared her throat and left the room. Darren watched her go before he looked at me once more. If he was expecting me to tell him about the spirit in his grandmother's room, he'd be waiting a long time.

"Faith sometimes gets uneasy in that room," he said. "I'm sorry if she hurried you."

I weighed my options, trying to decide if I should pass along the message I'd received. "This might be none of my business, but do you mind telling me who Martin is?"

"Oh, did she show you his room, too?"

The other closed door on the second floor?

He continued to move the figurines to the table. "Without overcomplicating the family tree, Martin Foster was my grandmother's uncle. My great-great-grandfather built this house, and the boys were raised here." He stopped to stare at the ceiling as he rubbed his chin. "I think I've said that right. Too many generations to keep track of sometimes. I know keeping a room for him seems silly, but my grandmother insisted."

"Did he visit often?"

Darren stopped, glanced out the window, where clouds continued to churn. "He was in the Navy in the first World War, but he never made it home. Lost at sea. There's a grave marker for him in the old cemetery next door. My grandmother wanted to annex the property, but the city refused. Can't imagine what the problem was, considering there's a newer cemetery in town."

"Was Martin's ship attacked?" I asked.

"It was lost in the Bermuda Triangle," he said. "They figure a storm swamped it. Disappeared without a trace. My grandmother insisted he would find his way home one day. It's been," he stopped and cocked one eye as he looked toward the ceiling, "more than a hundred years ago now. I can't imagine he'd still be around to come home even if he'd survived. Franklin Roosevelt declared the crew dead a few months after the ship disappeared."

"I'm sorry for your loss. Losses."

Thunder rumbled outside. The storm was closing in fast. Lightning flashed nonstop. I stepped to the window, fascinated by nature's fury. The ceiling light flickered and went out.

"The power's out," Faith called from the hallway.

Darren crossed to the mantle and retrieved matches, which he used to light the candlesticks on the table. "I expect the storm will pass quickly considering how fast it blew up."

Rain pelted the windows, blurring the view, but something solid moved outside. Or someone. I turned to Darren, who was occupied with the figurines.

"There's someone out there," I said. "Should we do something? They could get hurt."

He stepped to the window beside me. "I don't see anyone."

I pointed. "There. By the path."

He stiffened. The color drained from his face. Another crack of thunder was followed by a blinding flash of lightening.

What I can only describe as a horizontal tornado formed between the house and the path, pushing me back a step. The house groaned against gusts of wind.

"We should go somewhere safe." Laine wrung her hands in the doorway, her voice breathy. "Do you have a basement?"

We rushed into the hall as someone pounded on the front door. A man was visible through the glass outer doors, a sailor judging by his uniform.

Faith crumpled to the floor.

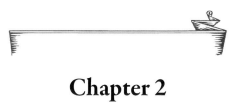

Chapter 2

I checked the dining room window for the tornado's position. It was gone, and the house quieted, indicating the wind had died down.

"Oh, for heaven's sake," Darren muttered. He knelt to the floor beside Faith while the sailor waited at the door.

A loud crack sounded from somewhere outside as rain continued to pelt the windows. The thunder faded into the distance, although lightning continued its strobe effect in the dark hallway.

"We can't leave him out there in this weather," Laine said. "Aren't you going to open the door?"

Faith's eyes fluttered open. "Don't let him in," she whispered.

"Why on earth not? It isn't as if he's a vampire. And don't tell me you believe in vampires now." Darren looked to me. "Will you see what he wants?"

Before I could walk down the hall, the outer door opened on its own.

Faith's voice trembled. "That's why not."

"Oh, for heaven's sake," Darren said again. He rose, marched down the hallway and stopped at the vestibule door.

"Please, come in out of the rain. How can I help you?" he asked the sailor.

The sailor stepped inside, took off his cap and crumpled it between his hands. "Do I know you?"

"Shouldn't I be asking you that question?" Darren asked.

While the rest of us huddled in the hallway, the sailor sized-up Darren. He cleared his throat. "I'm Martin Foster. I'd like to speak to my brother Clifford."

Martin Foster, as in Martin with the bedroom upstairs? No. He couldn't be. The man before us was much too young to be Norma's uncle, and he most certainly wasn't a ghost.

The flashes of lightning became more intermittent. One last splash of windswept rain pelted the window with a distant peal of thunder.

Faith pushed herself up from the floor. "You can't be Martin Foster."

"I'm sure my brother will assure you that is, indeed, my name."

"I don't know what kind of prank you're playing, but Clifford Foster died when I was a baby," Darren said. "And his brother Martin died over a hundred years ago."

The sailor's eyes widened. "A hundred years?" He raised his chin. "I am most assuredly not dead. Is this some sort of joke?"

"Show him the headstone," Faith said softly.

A rush of wind slammed the front door closed, and the portieres at the library entrance flapped. The rain-soaked sailor took the two steps up from the vestibule into the hall.

"Pardon me, but you're trespassing," Darren said.

The sailor stopped beside the portrait of two young men. "It would seem you are the ones trespassing. As you can see by the painting, I belong here. Now. Where is Clifford Foster?"

Faith fanned a hand in front of her face.

Darren glanced at the painting and blood suffused his face. "That's a portrait of my great-grandfather and my great-uncle. I don't know what game you're playing..."

A voice whispered from everywhere and nowhere. "This is Martin's house."

Faith grabbed at Darren's hand. "Did you hear that?"

Laine sidled up beside me, withholding a question if I was any judge of her expressions. She shook her head, indicating she hadn't heard anything.

Darren pulled away from Faith. "This isn't the time for your *sensitivity*."

"I heard a woman's voice saying this is Martin's house," I said, as much for Laine's benefit as everyone else's.

"As did I," Martin said. "If Clifford is dead, this house is mine, as the woman says."

"What woman?" Darren asked.

"Your grandmother," I replied.

Darren pointed to the front door. "The storm is letting up. I think you should go."

Faith turned to me. "You have to tell him I'm not crazy. He thinks I imagine these things."

Me? I didn't see an alternative.

"There goes our commission." Laine's smile was resigned. "No. I didn't hear the grandmother," she said, "but I know you well enough to believe you did. Give him his grain of salt."

When spirits spoke to me, I always told the receiving party to take what I was about to tell them with a grain of salt. Generally, I had some sort of validation for what I parlayed. I had no such proof this time.

Laine nodded at the portrait of the brothers on the wall. "Hard to argue with an exact likeness."

"He can't be Martin Foster," Darren said. "Even if the man wasn't lost at sea, he'd be a hundred-twenty-something now. You can't tell me this man is a ghost."

"I'm no ghost." Martin patted his chest and pulled his dog tags from under his shirt.

"How do you explain the way the doors blew open?" Faith asked.

"The storm," Darren said. "Tornadoes generate a fair amount of wind."

"That was no ordinary tornado, and you know it," Faith argued.

"Further reason to believe the atmospheric pressure impacted the doors." He turned to me. "I suppose you believe in ghosts, too?"

Tornado. Atmospheric pressure. Had he said Martin was lost in the Bermuda Triangle? I'd heard legends about wormholes and vortices in that part of the ocean. Was this man living proof wormholes existed? Had he traveled through time and space?

I took a step toward Martin, who stared at the scraps of metal in his hand. "May I see?"

He didn't take the tags off, but turned one so I could see. The etching was crude, but it bore the name Martin Foster, USN and two dates. The back side had an etched fingerprint.

My mind spun with possibilities. "Suppose this man is Martin's great-grandson, similar to you being his brother's great-grandson—assuming I've got the lineage correct. Wouldn't you be happy to meet lost family?"

Darren huffed. "Let me see that."

Before he could take the dog tag, Martin tucked them back inside his shirt.

"Any charlatan could have had a dog tag made," Darren said.

"When Clifford died, the house and everything in it were left in trust to Martin. Norma was named as executor," Faith said softly. "In the event Martin made it home."

"Wasn't he already dead by then?" Laine asked. "Surely his inheritance was passed down to his descendants?"

"Martin had no descendants." Darren narrowed his eyes. "Although I will admit there is a family resemblance."

A gross understatement. The man claiming to be Martin Foster was identical to the man in the portrait.

"Norma refused to change the trust beneficiary," Faith said.

"Something I have been working to rectify," Darren added.

A door opened at the other end of the hallway, near the conservatory. Another man walked toward us, dressed in dusty jeans and a sage green shirt. I guessed him to be a little older than me, mid-thirties, maybe forty. He addressed Darren. "Tree came down. It's blocking the driveway. Missed this lady's car by no more than a foot."

My car? I took one step toward the parlor to look out the doors.

"Who are *you*?" Martin asked the new addition to the party.

"Robert Chance." He squinted, glanced at the portrait, then at Martin with a look of surprise. "Seems you found your way home."

"Chance is our caretaker," Faith said.

Chance. Not Robert. This man worked for them. I stopped in my tracks, curious to know why the caretaker believed the sailor's story.

"You talk as if you were expecting him," I said to Chance.

He shot a glance at Darren. "His grandmother always said he'd come home."

The hairs on the back of my neck stood up.

"My grandmother was suffering from dementia. Martin Foster is dead," Darren said. "There's a headstone in the cemetery."

"A headstone, but not a grave." Chance gave Darren a half bow. "Seems as if the storm's blowing out. I'll see to chopping up that tree." He marched out through the conservatory.

"If there is a headstone inscribed with my name, I'd like to see it," Martin said.

Darren glanced out the window, where shafts of sunlight broke through the retreating clouds. "No time like the present."

"Do you mind if I tag along?" I asked.

Darren shot me an annoyed glance. "You might as well. It seems you're stranded for the moment."

Chapter 3

"**I**s it *safe* to go outside?" Faith asked, hanging back as Darren and Martin headed for the door.

"Grab an umbrella if you're afraid of getting wet," Darren shot back.

"But the storm. It rolled in so suddenly..."

"And seems to have blown itself out." Darren stomped to the vestibule and waved Martin through the outer doors. "After you."

Laine and I exchanged glances. She lowered her voice beside me. "If you think I'm missing out on this adventure, you'd better think again. Any inside information you'd like to share?"

I put a hand beside my mouth and whispered, "Darren's grandmother told me the house belongs to Martin."

We walked a step behind, out of earshot. "A ghost said this?"

"As near as I can tell."

Laine sighed. "Then we've wasted a trip. Darren won't be able to sell what isn't his."

"Apparently so, but how often do you get to meet a one-hundred-twenty-something year-old man who was lost in the Bermuda Triangle?"

Laine cocked an eyebrow at me. "Really, Elle?"

I shrugged. "Stranger things have happened."

The five of us paraded across the wet lawn toward the path. On the opposite side of the house, the caretaker started a chainsaw, making further conversation difficult.

The mulch-covered path was relatively dry beneath the canopy of trees, although fat raindrops randomly pelted us as we wound our way through the woods. Martin seemed to know the way, walking two paces ahead of Darren. The cemetery came into view on our left. The mulch thinned, giving way to mud puddles as we neared a church parking lot on our right.

Martin stopped, staring at the blacktop pavement. He took hesitant steps toward a car parked in the lot, his mouth hanging open. Darren continued past the Oakwood Cemetery sign, onto gravel paths that ran between the stones.

I touched Martin's shoulder, as much to comfort him as to assure myself he was flesh and blood. "A lot has changed in a hundred years."

"It would seem so," he said.

I cocked my head toward the cemetery and walked alongside him.

He stopped at each headstone, reading the years aloud. "This can't be right."

"Welcome to the twenty-first century," I replied.

Darren stopped several rows deep, near an iron fence along the backside of the cemetery. Arms folded, he waited for Martin.

"I'm quite concerned," Martin whispered to me. "Am I truly dead?"

"You seem to be alive to me," I replied.

We arrived at the stone, engraved in memory of Martin Foster, Lost with USS *Cyclops*, 1918.

Martin stared at the marker.

"Do you still contend to be Martin Foster?" Darren asked.

"I do not contend. It is a bottom fact," Martin replied.

"You're awfully well preserved for a man who was lost at sea more than a hundred years ago."

"I don't understand." Martin glanced at me. "Why would he tell such a thumper?"

"A thumper?" I repeated.

"A clever lie." He waved around the graveyard. "All these stones with dates in the future. And the lot behind the church wasn't paved last time I was here. That automobile? I've never seen anything like it."

"How did you come to be at my house?" Darren asked. "In the middle of a thunderstorm, with a felled tree blocking the driveway?"

Martin stared at him. "I'm not certain. I only know I was grateful to have found my way home."

Darren scoffed.

"What's the last thing you remember before the storm?" I asked.

"I was on the *Cyclops*. A storm blew up quite suddenly, and the captain was concerned because one of the engines had a cracked cylinder." He glanced at the sky, at the clouds retreating against the brilliant blue background. "I saw what looked like a tornado, tipped to one side, and the ship being pulled into it." Martin's eyes reflected fear. "Things flying everywhere. Seamen swept overboard."

"And you want us to believe you survived when no one else did?" Darren asked.

Martin checked his appearance—the bell-bottom pants, the belled sleeves of his shirt. "I am here. Did no one else survive the day?"

"The ship and all aboard were lost at sea," Darren said. "Without a trace."

Martin touched the top of the headstone. "I don't understand."

"It's quite simple," Darren said. "The real Martin Foster died that day, along with the crew aboard the *Cyclops*."

Martin shook his head. "No."

"You must admit his resemblance to your great-uncle is uncanny," I said to Darren. "He could be a relative."

"According to this headstone, my great-uncle was twenty-three when he died. He wasn't married."

"I was engaged," Martin said. "What's become of Alice?"

"I'm not familiar with anyone named Alice," Darren said.

"Alice Mansfield," Martin went on. "She and I were to be married upon my return home."

"Mansfield?" Darren glanced across the cemetery, then walked three rows over.

Martin gripped my hand knowing, as I did, what Darren meant to show him. We stopped beside the stone.

The wide marker covered two graves, with the name Pugh engraved in the center. On one side, Alice Mansfield. Born 1896. Died 1967. On the other, Wayne Charles, born 1895. Died 1971.

Martin's voice was hoarse. "She married Wayne Pugh?" He crouched beside the stone and traced the year of her death.

"He might still have fathered a child," I said, "even if he wasn't married."

"No." Color splotched Martin's cheeks. "Alice and I are yet engaged. We never..."

Darren wore a self-satisfied smile that annoyed the life out of me.

"Assuming, as you might," I said to Darren, "this man was injured in the storm—on your property— you might bear liability for any injuries. If he isn't Martin Foster, he couldn't know your family history."

"Family history?" Darren sputtered. "I don't know anything about an engagement to Alice Pugh."

Faith tugged Darren's arm. "If he is related to Martin, Horned Owl Hollow would pass to him. At the very least, he should have a DNA test to rule out the possibility. You can't deny the resemblance. We can't turn him out."

Martin straightened. "Of my own home?"

"That remains to be seen," Darren said. "How did you come to be here? Today?"

Martin paled. "I can't say."

"Can't? Or won't?"

Martin turned to me, his voice strained. "A moment ago, I was aboard the *Cyclops*. The rain. The wind. The waves. The water spout, or tornado, or whatever it was. I struggled for breath, blinded by the heavy rain. The next thing I knew I fell to the ground. Here. There." He nodded past me, to the path we'd walked moments earlier.

Wasn't that the definition of a wormhole? Being sucked in and transported somewhere, sometime, else? First thing I was going to do when I had my computer was Google the possibilities, extreme though they might be.

Martin retraced his steps at a brisk pace. The Lombards, Laine and I followed until he came to a stop not far from the dining room window where I'd seen the odd funnel cloud.

Martin pointed at the ground. "One minute I was on the *Cyclops*, the next, I was here. What day is it?"

"The fourth of March," Laine told him.

"How can that be?" He walked in circles. "It is the same day? But I'm here rather than in the Atlantic."

"March 4, 2022," Faith told him.

"Certainly, you're joking." Martin paled. "One hundred and four years later?"

"What proof can you possibly provide that you are the man you say you are?" Darren asked.

"There's the fingerprint on his dog tags," I pointed out.

"Which we have nothing to compare to," Darren said.

"The Navy would have his prints on file somewhere, wouldn't they?" Faith said. "I seem to remember Norma requesting a copy."

"If she had them, I think I would know about it," Darren argued.

"She knew he'd come back," Faith whispered. "She kept the room for him all these years. Wouldn't let anyone touch it other than to clean it."

"My room," Martin echoed.

"Don't get excited," Darren said.

"But I can prove who I am if my room remains unchanged." Martin raised his chin as if in triumph. "My clothes. My belongings. I can give you a full inventory of what I left behind."

Chapter 4

L aine and I followed the Lombards into the house—where else could we go?

Darren stopped inside the door and motioned us past the portieres and into the library. "You wait here. Faith will keep you company until you can call an Uber."

Confirmation he no longer wanted to do business with me. "If your caretaker is cutting up the fallen tree, wouldn't it be better to wait? I'd rather not leave my car."

"That will likely take the better part of the day," Darren said.

No doubt. A mature oak. The fact it had fallen away from the house was a miracle unto itself.

Faith made an impatient grunt before she turned to Darren. "None of this is their doing." She waved an arm toward me and Laine. "Don't take your irritation out on them."

"Can we be sure of that?" he asked. "This man didn't arrive until after they did."

Accusations? "Are you going to blame the storm on me, too?" I asked. Lashing out wasn't the best way to win over a client. He lifted an eyebrow and I clamped my mouth shut.

Darren pointed at me. "You. Wait here." He spun around and signaled Martin to lead the way. "Let's see if you even know where you're going." They disappeared up the staircase at the opposite end of the hall.

Faith wrung her hands. Her eyes betrayed fear, or panic, or something I didn't want to label—something akin to unhinged. "He looks exactly the way he did in the portrait. He hasn't aged a day."

Laine leaned closer to me, her voice low. "You ever watch Quantum Leap? Except that guy always went backward in time, and he jumped into other peoples' bodies."

Other peoples' bodies. Assumed someone else's identity. "Do you mind if I check my computer?" I asked Faith.

She waved a hand my direction, giving me permission. I went to the dining room to retrieve my tote bag and my computer.

"What are you thinking?" Laine asked when I returned.

"Bermuda Triangle. Wormholes." I looked up the definition of a wormhole, a storm that could transport something or someone across space and time. *Outer* space, but were wormholes limited to black holes? The possibilities seemed too fantastic to be real, but I couldn't shake the idea the tornado we'd seen might have been a wormhole that had sucked Martin Foster up in the Bermuda Triangle and spit him out here—more than a hundred years later. Hadn't he mentioned he'd seen the same type of storm on the other end?

Laine's mouth hung open as she read over my shoulder. "You don't really think...?"

I closed my laptop. "Unless and until the Navy can provide his fingerprints, seems as if a DNA test to prove he's related to Darren would be the best proof," I said. "Either he is Martin Foster, or he isn't. The chances they have something of his from a hundred years ago to test DNA against are slim, even if the DNA hasn't degraded."

"If we can get Darren to agree to a test... although we might not need to." Faith grinned. "Norma signed up on one of those genealogy sites. I helped her. We sent them a sample of her DNA, as if she knew we'd need biological proof."

A door creaked upstairs, followed by footsteps overhead.

"They're in Martin's room," Faith whispered.

The tenor of the men's voices was audible, but not their words.

The hairs on my arm rose, a sign the energy in the house had shifted. I stepped into the hallway as the sensation of spiders walked across my skin. A transparent old woman motioned me to follow her up the staircase, a woman who closely resembled the portrait of Norma Lombard based on the portrait in the hall. She turned her back to me, floating up the stairs.

Faith clutched my arm with a sudden intake of breath. "Do you see her?"

More notably, Faith did, although family tended to be more sympathetic to the energy of their relatives. I nodded.

"She wants us to follow her."

"Wait," Laine said. "Are you saying there's a ghost?"

I turned to Faith. "It's your house. I can't follow her. Your husband made it clear he doesn't trust me." I rubbed my tingling arms. "I think she wants *you* to follow her."

"But I don't see her anymore." Faith sighed. "Oh, this is ridiculous. I don't care if he does think I'm delusional. I know what I saw, and Norma wants us to follow her. We have to go, don't you think?"

Scraping wood echoed from overhead, followed by Darren's voice. "You don't know what you're talking about."

Faith pursed her lips. "Come on. He might think he can pretend none of this is happening, but that isn't going to make it go away."

She tugged me down the hall and up the staircase. We stopped on the landing, the second floor coming into view. Darren appeared in the bedroom door across the hall from his grandmother's room. He stared at Norma's door as it opened on its own.

"I told you to stay downstairs," he barked at Faith.

Faith pointed at the door. "She summoned us to follow her."

Darren crossed the hall and reached for the doorknob to his grandmother's room. The door slammed shut before he got there and he jumped back.

Faith crossed her arms. "Has he proven he's Martin Foster?"

Darren shot a glare at Faith. "He knew which room to go to. That doesn't prove he's Martin."

Martin walked out of the bedroom beaming. He held a book in one hand, and a raggedy looking stuffed animal in the other. "Still there. The furniture I brought home from China seems to be missing, though." He cast a suspicious eye on Darren. "Might you know what's become of it?"

Darren snorted. "I don't know what you're talking about."

Faith smiled at Martin. "Do you have a place to stay?"

Martin's expression turned to confusion. "What do you mean? This is my home. Why would I stay elsewhere?"

Faith addressed her husband. "What do you intend to do? It's clear this man is related. Are you planning to turn him out?"

"I'm not convinced he *is* related," Darren argued.

"A simple DNA test would prove it," she said. "They can do one at the hospital and have results in a week or less. Have I mentioned Norma sent a DNA sample to one of those genealogy sites? Of course, that test would take considerably longer."

Darren huffed. "He can stay. A week. Only as long as it takes to prove whether he is or is not related to Martin Foster."

"I don't understand," Martin said. "What is a DNA test?"

"In simple terms, it's a test to match a sample of your skin, or your blood, or your saliva against Darren's. Or Norma's, it would seem," I replied. "There are certain markers that are unique to families."

Martin blinked several times. "They can do that?"

While we stood in the second-floor hallway, the door to Norma's room opened slowly once more. A sigh seemed to echo through the hallway, along with a decrease in the energy I'd sensed upon her appearance.

As we all stood staring at the open room, Darren Lombard rounded on me once more. "As I said before, Miss Barclay, you're free to go. We won't be selling anything until this matter is settled."

I pulled out a business card and handed it to the man claiming to be Martin. "If you need anything, please feel free to contact me."

Chapter 5

Laine and I walked past the branches blocking the driveway. My car had come within inches of being flattened by the tree that had come down in the storm.

An Uber picked us up on the street and took us to *Whimsical Collectibles*. We didn't have business hours on Tuesdays, and generally spent the day putting out newly acquired merchandise. I was glad not to have to face customers after our unusual visit to Horned Owl Hollow. Once we walked inside, we both sat in the small office and stared at each other.

"Did you see the stuff in that house?" Laine asked. "They have furniture dating to the 1880s, and did you see the craftsmanship? One of a kind. Shame we won't be able to sell any of it."

"The Staffordshire collection alone is worth at least five figures, possibly six." A commission I'd lost. The curiosity wouldn't let go, though. I booted up my computer to check for information on Martin Foster. Or Clifford Foster. Or both. I wanted to know more about the family who'd lived in that house.

"Here it is," I said more to myself than my sister. I looked up and she raised her eyebrows, inviting me to continue. "Darren told me they raised Percherons back in the day. That's where they made their money. France needed the horses during World War I, so they sent them back."

Laine leaned over her knees. "You don't believe that man, that Martin Foster was magically transported a hundred years into the future, do you?"

"There are more things in heaven and earth, Horatio," I quoted.

"Which brings me to their ghost," she said. "Did you actually see Darren's grandmother? I thought ghosts only came out at night."

"I don't think there are rules to that sort of thing. I imagine the ghost hunter shows that spend the night at places expecting manifestations think they're easier to see at night. How many manifestations have they captured on those shows?"

Laine frowned.

I continued my search for information, including an article about the USS *Cyclops*. "The ship Martin Foster was assigned to was heading for Baltimore with metallic ore to make munitions for the war when it disappeared."

"Elle."

I looked up.

"We've been uninvited to their house. Why are you still looking into all of this?"

"You aren't fascinated to have met a man who claims to be over a hundred years old? A man who looks to be twenty-three?"

Laine crossed her arms. "I prefer to think he's a descendant."

I closed my browser. "I suppose there's no point pursuing any of this. As you say, we lost the commission. It's none of my business."

Laine pulled out her phone and started scrolling. "I'll check the company email account and see if there's another estate sale we might want to look at."

We exchanged glances when someone knocked on the locked front door. Business hours were posted. The store was open four days a week, and this wasn't one of those days. "I'll go."

I left the office and found a man shading his eyes as he tried to see inside. I knew the moment he saw me—he stepped back. I pointed to the sign in the window. "We're closed today, unless you've made an appointment," I said through the glass. "We'll be open Thursday."

"I just have a quick question," he said.

I sized him up, close to Laine's age—late twenties, early thirties. Button-down shirt tucked into jeans. Well groomed. Chestnut hair, animated brown eyes. Handsome, and he knew it based on the smile he flashed me.

"I'm only in town for the day," he said. "Someone said you might have Staffordshire figurines."

I did, and if today had gone the way it had been planned, I would have had a lot more. Coincidence?

"Laine, I'm opening the door," I called over my shoulder.

She stood in the office doorway at the ready, phone in hand.

I turned the lock and opened the door. "I do have Staffordshire figurines," I told him. "A set of cats, and a set of King Charles blue spaniels."

"We also carry a nice collection of Hummels, Limoges, and Lladró," Laine added. "Among others."

Far from threatening, the man's eyes lit up. "May I see them?"

I glanced at Laine, who shrugged.

"They're in a case in the next room." I led him into the shop.

"Are they original?" he asked.

"The Staffordshire? Yes. I had some copies for a while, but they sold quickly."

"No doubt. They're less expensive." He stepped to the locked case and put a hand to the glass. Fingerprints, in case he turned out to be a bad guy. A thief wouldn't be that careless.

"I'd like to buy them," he said.

"You're a collector?" I asked.

"Yes. Any chance you'll be getting more?"

I didn't believe in coincidences. Would he be interested in the Lombard collection? A collection that wasn't mine to sell, and yet...

"I know another collector," I said. "He was going to sell, but his plans may have changed. If you want to leave me your name, I can let you know."

He assessed me. "I'm particularly interested in a grouping that includes whippets and spaniels. It's quite rare."

Yes, I knew the one—and Darren Lombard had one in his collection. Again, it wasn't mine to sell. "I'll check with the collector, and if he's agreeable, I can put you in touch."

The man pulled out his wallet and handed me a business card. I glanced at his name, Gavin Reeves, and passed the card to Laine.

"Let me get the keys to the cabinet," I said.

He followed me to the sales counter, and smiled at Laine as if he'd found lost treasure. "I don't often find what I'm looking for. I'll have to thank my friend for sending me over, and I'm grateful you were here to let me in."

Laine's voice had become softer, sweeter. "You said you're only here for the day? Where are you from?" Full-on flirt mode.

"Iowa. Quad Cities. I work for a family that sends me in search of acquisitions."

"You work for a family?" Laine repeated. "Like you curate a collection?"

"Well, that, too," he said, smiling. He reached across the sales counter and shook her hand. "Gavin Reeves. Majordomo."

"Wait a minute," she said, clinging to his hand. "Majordomo? As in you're an actual butler?"

"Technically, a butler's duties are to serve—wine in particular and also food. My duties go beyond that. I manage the household. Pay the bills. Hire the staff. The family I work for owns several residences around the world, and they are only in-residence in Iowa part of the year."

Laine's mouth dropped open. "Staff..." she repeated.

I set his figurines on the counter. "Something our clients from this morning might benefit from." If the Lombards had a majordomo, they wouldn't have to worry about who was taking care of things when they headed for warmer climates. Not that I was bitter about losing the commission. I adjusted my attitude. "And by acquisitions, you mean the family you work for sends you off to find collectibles?"

Mr. Reeves gave a head bow. "They do."

"Ooh!" Laine squealed. "Who do you work for?"

"My job involves discretion," he said.

"In other words," I said, "none of your business, Laine." I turned to Mr. Reeves. "Would you like us to ship these for you so you don't have to carry them?"

"No, I'm driving. As long as you wrap them, I should be good."

"How does one become a majordomo?" Laine asked, eyes glued to Mr. Reeves.

His lips curled into a wry smile. "I majored in finance in school, with a minor in art history. I did a year abroad, where I became friends with another art history student during a course at the Louvre. When my friend told me about the position, it seemed the perfect way to blend my interests, assuming my employers treated me well."

"And do they treat you well?" Laine asked.

"Once we got past the original period of adjustment, yes, they treat me very well. Not to mention I get free run of their beautiful home while they're away."

Laine giggled. "I'm getting visions of wild, high school parties."

"Not that you have any experience with those," I added.

"No parties," Mr. Reeves said. "But my family occasionally comes for a visit."

"Family?" Laine asked, her rising voice betraying her attempt at subtlety.

"My parents. My sister." His smile turned flirty. "I'm not married, if that's what you're asking."

Laine bowed her head, hair covering her flaming cheeks.

I stepped into the awkward void and gave Mr. Reeves his total.

He pulled out a credit card. "You'll let me know about the collection you mentioned?" he asked.

"I will."

"Thank you, again, for accommodating me."

"I'm glad we happened to be here." I walked him to the door and locked it behind him.

Laine bounced on her toes. "We have to get that collection, if only for the chance to find out more about *him*."

I laughed. "Next thing I know, you're going to want to move to Iowa. Who's going to help me run the business if you leave?" I teased.

"Can I help it that man revs my engines?" She heaved a dramatic sigh.

"Well, you can cool your jets. The Lombards aren't likely to invite us back anytime soon."

"No, you're wrong. They still have your car," she pointed out. "You can schmooze them into selling."

"Not until they figure out who Martin Foster is. If he is the legal heir, they won't be selling anything."

Chapter 6

"You want to come in for popcorn and a movie?" I asked Laine as she dropped me off at home.

"Not tonight," she said. "If I don't do my laundry, I won't have anything to wear tomorrow."

I hugged Laine goodbye, fighting the urge to keep my sister safe and out of the clutches of a handsome gigolo. Or my own selfish need to keep her close after our father had threatened to separate us all those years ago. I had no reason to believe Gavin Reeves was bad news, aside from the fact he was a man.

My sister was a grown woman. She could make her own decisions. That didn't stop me from wishing she might move into my cozy cottage with me.

I walked through the kitchen door. I loved this house. Yes, it was small, but there was room for both of us—spinster sisters.

She wasn't ready to give up on men quite yet, as evidenced by her interest in the majordomo.

I set my tote bag on the kitchen table in the corner, opened the refrigerator and took out a bottle of water. My gaze wandered to the pass-through window over the sink to the printers' drawer hanging on the wall in my living room. Each compartment displayed miniature collectibles, from coffee mugs to woodland animals to tiny beverage cans, another thing Laine chided me for. Junk, she called it. Not valuable. No, the pieces weren't valuable, but they made me happy. As much as I loved Laine, we definitely had different tastes.

Including in men. Hopefully she was better at reading them than I was.

I walked into the living room and set my water bottle on the coffee table, opened the front door and collected my mail from the mailbox. I closed the door and leafed through the envelopes in my hand.

The room seemed to tilt. I reached for the back of the sofa for balance and set the mail on the table. Vertigo generally signaled the onset of a vision. *Why me?* I lost my balance and landed on the sofa.

Eyes closed, I found myself in the parlor at the Lombards, the room where a woman sketched two small children—a boy and a girl, children who sat obediently beside the terrace doors. A man I recognized from a portrait in the Lombards' main hall oversaw the process, and each time the children started to squirm, he hissed through his teeth to get them to behave.

"Why am I seeing this?" I asked.

As expected, my dream narrator stood just out of sight. "He needs an advocate."

"He, who? All the people in this room are long gone, are they not?"

The artist set her sketchbook on the table. "I have what I need to begin."

The man smiled and reached into his pockets. He crouched before his children and extended closed hands. "Which will you choose?" He raised one eyebrow toward his daughter. "Ladies

39

first." The little girl chose the hand corresponding to the lifted eyebrow, as if it was a secret signal. The man turned his hand over and opened his palm to reveal the rare Staffordshire grouping. He offered the other palm to the little boy—chocolate—which the little boy scooped up quickly before he ran from the room.

Was this man Clifford Foster? And the little girl, Norma Lombard?

The little girl curtsied. "Thank you, Daddy."

"Oh, I know you're getting tired of these old things," her father said, "but one day they'll help you to remember me."

"But why would I need to remember you?" she asked.

"We never know how much time we have." He glanced out the windows.

"Are you thinking about Uncle Martin again?" the little girl asked.

Her father picked her up and twirled her in the air. "Such an insightful child. He'll come home again one day. I'm quite certain."

"I'll show him my figurines when he does," she said. "Do you think he'll like them?"

The narrator intervened, whispering in my ear. "Those figurines should go to him."

Him who? And yet, I knew.

I opened my eyes and turned, trying to see the narrator's face, but as always, no one was there.

A shadow darkened the recliner in the corner, the figure of a man. Goosebumps rose on my arms and fear gave me the equivalent of brain freeze.

"Who are you?" I choked out.

He didn't speak.

On those occasions spirits manifested themselves, I'd yet to hear one speak. "What do you want of me?" I asked.

He leaned forward, and I recognized him as the father I'd seen in my dream, the man in the painting in the Lombards' hallway. Clifford Foster? As the realization struck me, he nodded, then sent an exaggerated glance toward my printers' box, hanging on the wall. He returned his empty gaze to me, then back to the printers' box. What did he want me to see?

The figurine he'd given to the little girl seemed to hover in front of the box, surrounded by light—a figurine I'd seen at the Lombards. The most valuable one in their collection, to my knowledge.

"They won't let me near the collection," I whispered to the ghost. "And they certainly won't believe me if I tell them I saw you."

The spirit closed his eyes, blinked, and closed his eyes again. He wanted to show me something else. *Resistance is futile.* I closed my eyes and the bust of the children appeared to me—the bust I'd seen in the Lombards' parlor. The pedestal faded until it was transparent, revealing a sheet of paper inside.

"There's something in the pedestal?" I whispered. I opened my eyes and Clifford Foster's thick gray moustache lifted with a smile, right before he disappeared.

I rubbed my arms to smooth out the goosebumps, my heart racing. No matter how many times I had an encounter with spiritual energy, I doubted I'd ever get used to it. I reached for my bottle of water and took a long drink.

My phone rang in the kitchen, and I rushed to fish it out of my tote bag. I checked the display. My mother. I should have known. I sat at the table and answered the call.

"Want to talk about it?" she asked when I answered.

I didn't. Of course, she knew something was going on. My tendency to see ghosts had been inherited from her. "Talk about what?" I asked innocently.

"Don't play games with me," she said. "I feel a cosmic shift. I know when something's going on with you."

Didn't I know it. Growing up, I'd never been able to get away with anything. She might not know the details, but she'd undoubtedly felt the change in energy. I had to assume that, since she'd called, whatever the spirit had showed me was important. "I'm not sure what I can do about it," I said.

Her voice was soothing, inviting. "Tell me what happened."

I shared the events of the day, my commission for the Lombards and the miraculous return of the man lost at sea. Finally, I told her about my vision before I repeated, "I'm sure I've lost the commission. I don't know what I'm supposed to do with what I've seen."

"Your car is still at their house, right?" she asked. "So you'll have another opportunity to speak with the Lombards?"

"Theoretically. Faith Lombard seems to have some level of sensitivity, so she might be sympathetic. As to Darren Lombard, well, the ghost gave me something to validate, but Mr. Lombard is skeptical. He doesn't want to know about the residual energy lingering in his house."

"Someone has to help this Martin Foster if he is who he says he is." She paused. "Do you think he is?"

"Either that, or he's a delusional relative. The resemblance is there. He has a fingerprint on his dog tags, but they'd have to get Naval records from 1918 to match. It sounds as if Norma Lombard already tried to get the records without much success. Faith Lombard suggested a DNA test. I hope they'll pursue that. If he did come through a wormhole with only the shirt on his back, it will be hard for him to prove his identity."

"Surely, there has to be a way to identify him." My mother let out a quiet gasp. "You don't suppose he's in danger, do you? They wouldn't have a reason to make him disappear so he can't inherit?"

"That doesn't seem likely, but I don't suppose we can know for sure. Besides, Laine and I are witnesses." I raised my head and stared at the wall, searching for answers. "If he is Martin Foster, he has nowhere else to go. No job. A man out of time. Lost."

"Oh, dear." My mother went silent. "I'll contact social services to find out what his options are. When you get your car tomorrow morning you can find out more. Let me know what the situation is."

"What if they don't want to tell me?"

"Didn't you say the caretaker would pick you up? I'm willing to bet he'll share what he knows. Do you want me to stop over so we can talk more? I could make you a cup of tea."

I warmed at the offer. My mother, always ready to take care of her babies, no matter how old we got. "No. I'm pretty wiped out. You know how the visions can zap your energy. I'll call you tomorrow."

We ended the call, and I folded my arms on the kitchen table to rest my head.

Next thing I knew, my phone was buzzing again. I opened my eyes to sunlight streaming through the windows. My aching back told me I'd spent the night at the table. I wiped a hand across my face and answered the call.

"Ms. Barclay, this is Robert Chance. Darren Lombard asked me to bring you to your car. When would be a good time?"

I glanced at the clock on the stove—8:30 a.m. What was the etiquette about calling people this early? But I needed my car. "I can be ready in an hour." Did I dare ask him what they'd done about Martin? Would he know? Still half-asleep, my filters hadn't yet taken control of my mouth and my thoughts tumbled out. "Do you know what they did about their visitor? Since he seemed lost, I thought I could provide resources to help. I have contacts with the county."

"They gave him a bed for the night. Told him he could stay until they sort all this out," Chance told me.

Relief swept over me. I gave Chance my address and went about my morning routine so I'd be ready when he arrived.

Forty-five minutes later, I called my mother to let her know what Chance had told me.

"Well, I'm glad of that," she said. "Now you have to find a way to get them to listen to you."

"It's none of my business," I said.

"I think Clifford Foster—and his daughter, it would seem—will have something to say about that."

As if I needed a reminder of my ghostly encounters. "I'll share what the spirits have told me," I said.

"Yes, with your grain of salt. More often than not, people believe us. Especially when we can validate the experience." She sighed. "Good luck, Elle. Stop over later if you need me. I don't have any showings today, so I'll be home doing paperwork."

Showings. If the Lombards were selling Horned Owl Hollow, they might need my mother, too. She specialized in selling stigmatized houses. I'd keep that idea in my back pocket for now.

I pushed back the curtain in my front window as a car pulled into my driveway. "Thanks, Mom. I think my ride is here. Gotta go." I grabbed my purse and locked the door behind me. When I reached the driveway, Chance opened the door to the backseat of the car—a Mercedes. He was dressed in a plaid shirt and jeans this morning, and appeared to be fresh from the shower.

"Do you mind if I sit in front with you?" I asked. "I'm not used to being chauffeured."

Chance smiled. "Suit yourself." He walked around the car and opened the passenger door.

When he got behind the wheel a few moments later, I asked, "How long have you worked for the Lombards?"

"My father was caretaker before me," he said. "I sort of grew up on the property. Left for a while after college, but when my dad had a stroke, I came back to help."

"I'm sure they appreciated having someone they knew and trusted. They must see you as part of the family."

"You could say that. The dowager duchess," he shot me a glance. "Sorry, that's what we called Darren's grandmother. She asked me to promise I'd stay until Martin came home. Not sure how she knew he would. She used to sit on the bench beside the woods for hours carrying on a conversation with nobody. Or somebody we couldn't see. Dotty as the day is long, but a kinder woman I never met."

"Sounds like you miss her."

"I do." He cast another glance my direction. "Then again, she's never far away, is she?"

I turned in my seat to face him. "Are you saying you believe in ghosts, Mr. Chance?"

His cheeks twitched with a smile. "Question is, do you?"

A few minutes later, he steered between the stone pillars that marked the entrance to the estate. A pile of lumber was stacked in the yard. The tree trunk remained intact a few feet from my car. I counted my blessings that the tree hadn't crushed my car.

Chance parked, walked around the Mercedes, and opened my door. When I got out, Martin Foster crossed the lawn toward me. He wore brown canvas trousers and a vest over a white shirt with a long collar. Clothes he'd left behind a hundred years ago?

"Miss Barclay," he said. "I've been told you're trustworthy. Will you help me?"

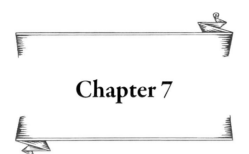

Chapter 7

T rustworthy?

I wasn't sure who might have recommended me to Martin Foster. Darren had made it clear *he* didn't trust me. I stared across the lawn to the mansion, contemplating if I should butt out of whatever was happening here.

I'd been asked, even if a spirit had done the asking. "How can I help?"

Martin's eyes combed over me. "This manner of dress will take some getting used to. Do women not wear dresses anymore?"

I glanced at my jeans and shirt, perfectly normal clothing—unless you were born a century ago. "We do, but not as often as years ago."

"Forgive me if I'm being rude. Won't you come in?"

I hesitated, unsure of my welcome from the rest of his family—assuming they *were* family.

Faith stood on the terrace and raised a hand in greeting. "Please. Join us."

Steeling my resolve, I accepted the invitation. I did have a message to deliver, after all. I wasn't going to get a better opportunity. "Good morning."

As I walked up the stone steps, Martin close behind, Faith poured me a cup of coffee. Darren was absorbed in the Wall Street Journal.

"How do you take it?" she asked, holding the cup.

"Light," I said.

She added a splash from a creamer of hand-painted porcelain, and handed the cup to me. They used the fine china on the terrace?

Darren folded his paper and laid it on the table. "Good morning, Ms. Barclay. I trust you slept well?"

Actually, I had a visit from your great-grandfather. No, he wouldn't appreciate hearing that. "Well enough. And you?" I replied.

"We had an eventful evening," Faith said. "First, we all drove to the hospital to get a DNA test for Martin and Darren." She shot a pointed look at Darren. "Of course, we invited Martin to stay with us. Even if he can't possibly be the real Martin Foster, the family resemblance is unmistakable. We couldn't very well turn him out."

Darren's jaw clenched and his eyes narrowed.

"And then we had a noisy evening," she went on. "The spirits were restless."

"You can only try my patience so far, Faith," Darren said, his voice low.

"Let me rephrase. There were more creaks and groans in this old house than we normally hear."

"At any rate," Darren said, "we agreed that in the event Martin is actually related, we'd offer him the Staffordshire collection as an inheritance. That should provide him with enough money to get the help he needs."

In other words, declare him crazy and screw him out of his house. If I was meant to help Martin, this was my chance. Did that mean I would still get the consignment? "I hope I'm not out of line for asking, but I'm curious," I began, treading lightly. "Clifford Foster." I swallowed hard. "He commissioned the bust in the parlor?"

Darren looked into his cup of coffee. "Why do you ask?"

I weighed how best to ask about the pedestal, but I had to say something. "I know your position on things you can't see, so take what I say with a grain of salt." I drew a steadying breath. "I had a dream last night."

Darren leveled a glare at me.

Faith bounced in her seat. "I had the same one."

"Stop," Darren said. "You don't even know what she's going to say."

Faith pressed her lips together in a coy smile.

"Go on," Darren said.

"The bust is your grandmother and her brother, right? Why didn't her brother inherit the house? In those days, sons usually inherited, didn't they?"

Darren didn't speak for several seconds, as if trying to decide why I was asking. "My grandmother was the oldest living relative at the time. Her brother died in a riding accident when he was sixteen. She outlived them all, even her own children." He took a sip of his coffee. "And damn near us, as well."

Faith sat on the edge of her seat. "I dreamt about the bust, but I didn't know what it meant."

Darren waved his hand to silence her. "Is that all, Ms. Barclay?"

"No. My dream started with the sculptor sketching the children, a woman, and when she finished, Clifford gave your grandmother one of her figurines and her brother a piece of chocolate."

Faith shook her head emphatically. "See?"

"Imagination, derived from seeing the portrait yesterday, as well as the bust." Darren folded his paper and set his hands on the table as if to get up.

I blew out a slow breath. "Well, this is where the grain of salt comes in. Is the pedestal hollow?"

Faith's eyes grew round. "Oh. I didn't see that part."

Darren removed his hands from the tabletop. "Solid oak, to the best of my knowledge."

Not to be daunted, I went on. "It's fairly easy to say I've seen a ghost, but without some form of validation, you have no reason to believe me."

Darren scoffed. "You're saying you have proof?"

"I'm saying when I asked the spirit for a means of validation, he showed me a piece of paper inside the pedestal."

"Well, we can settle the matter fairly quickly, can't we?" Darren brushed his hands together and rose.

I glanced at Martin, who had remained silent this whole time. His expression was tight as he regarded me with something akin to fear. "Are you a witch?" he asked.

I smiled. "No."

"And yet you converse with the dead."

"That has yet to be proved," Darren said. "Would you care to join me, Ms. Barclay?"

I followed him inside, where we stopped before the bust.

"This pedestal was hand-turned—by my great-grandfather, no doubt," Darren said. "I'm quite certain it's solid. No mysterious paper hidden inside."

"May I?" I asked, nodding at the bust.

He gestured toward the sculpture. "Be my guest, understanding that if anything is broken, you will have to compensate us for our losses."

"Of course." I lifted the plaster children and set them gently on the floor. An intricately carved lattice cap ornamented the top of the pedestal. "The craftsmanship is exquisite," I breathed reverently.

My heart pounded with the discovery within my reach. My hands trembling, I lifted the cap off the base to expose the top of the solid pedestal—and the yellowed paper.

Darren blanched. "Your sister could easily have planted that there yesterday."

The door to the terrace slammed shut, followed by a gust of wind that blew through the room. The paper drifted to the floor at Darren's feet.

"Believe what you will. My sister and I have nothing to gain here." I raised my chin, accustomed to the skepticism people showed toward my abilities. "As I said, take it with a grain of salt."

"May I see it?" Martin asked.

Darren stiffened while Martin retrieved the paper.

"What does it say?" Faith asked.

"Bust of Norma and Percy Foster, sold to Clifford Foster this twelfth day of May 1928 for $100. Signed—" he looked at me. "Alice Mansfield Pugh. This is her handwriting."

Chapter 8

D arren's voice dripped with skepticism. "I suppose it's a coincidence the woman Martin claims he was engaged to was hired to make the sculpture of the children?"

"Not at all," Martin said. "Alice is an accomplished artist."

"We can certainly validate its authenticity," I said. "I expect there may be other examples of her work."

"No," Darren said. "*I'll* look into it. Aside from a name on a headstone, I've never heard of this woman before you showed up. For all I know, the two of you concocted this cockamamie story. If Alice Mansfield Pugh was ever engaged to Martin Foster, I'll be the one to track it down. And I'll be the one to determine if she had any artistic talent whatsoever. This is all too convenient for me."

Faith smiled sweetly. "Would you like to borrow my computer? You can Google her. She might have family in the area. Did I mention I subscribe to a genealogy website?"

Darren snatched the receipt from Martin and marched out.

"I'm not certain if I should be grateful or afraid of you," Martin said. "What manner of person are you?"

"Just your average, every day shopkeeper. No need to be grateful or afraid." I glanced to where Darren had made his stormy exit. "We can't be sure Darren will find the information he's looking for. Hundred-year-old records might not be easy to find."

"He'll find them," Faith said. "In the meantime, he's drawn up a contract for you to sell the collection via your eBay store, with the proceeds going into the trust. He's asking a commission of sixty-forty, with you getting forty percent. The collection will remain onsite until each piece is sold. If that's agreeable."

"That would be fine. I should mention I have a collector who might be interested," I told her. "Either way, I'll have to document the pieces. If we can agree to the value, we could forego listing them. Unless Mr. Lombard wants them to go up for auction."

Faith took my hand. "I know he's been rude to you, dear, but you can still call him Darren."

"I'd rather keep things professional," I replied.

"Whatever you want, but will you at least call me Faith?"

I smiled and nodded. "Faith. I haven't come prepared today since I was only expecting to pick up my car. If you'll give me a few minutes to run home for my computer, I can get started right away."

"I'll mention your buyer to Darren and see if he wants to add a clause for that in the contract." She leaned closer. "I don't know if you're aware he was a lawyer before he retired."

That made perfect sense. In his position, I'd probably be leery of someone like me, too. "Understood. He wants to protect his assets."

"Exactly."

Which meant he also wasn't going to let Martin claim his inheritance without a fight. I turned to the man in question. "May I offer you a piece of unsolicited advice?"

He folded his hands behind his back and made a partial bow.

"Don't sign any contracts until you get your DNA test back," I went on.

Martin smiled. "The Navy taught me many things. I'm well versed when it comes to shysters, even if they claim to be my own family."

I laughed. "I expect Mr. Lombard thinks the same thing."

"Which is what I wanted to discuss with you. Apparently, this DNA—" he enunciated each letter "—test he and I took will provide what he referred to as incontrovertible proof."

"Indeed, it will."

Martin shot a glance at Faith, and then at me. "I hope I've not made a false step, but when the doctor at the hospital asked for my phone number to deliver the test results, Darren asked me if I had a cell phone." His face screwed up as if perplexed. "I wasn't quite sure what he meant. When I asked Darren about the house phone, he told me it was no longer in service. I had your business card in my pocket and asked the doctor if he might phone you when the results are ready. I'd rather trust someone other than Darren with the information."

Oh. So much for trying to stay out of their family business. "I understand. I'll be sure to let you know when I hear something. That is, if you don't mind me calling you, Faith?"

"Of course not," she replied.

"And now, if you'll excuse me." I gave them a short wave and let myself out.

I crossed the lawn to the parking area, got into my car, and drove past the stack of logs. The Bluetooth in my car announced a call from Laine. Before I reached the main road, I pulled to one side to answer.

"Where are you?" she asked.

"Picking up my car. Where are you?"

"At your house. I came to tell you I got a call from the county to clean out a house. Neighbors called in a wellness check and the police found the owner dead, an old lady. No known relatives. You want to go with me? We don't have any appointments at the shop today."

I glanced over my shoulder at the mansion I'd left. "The Lombards have decided to go ahead with an eBay shop for their figurines. Since the store is open tomorrow, I should probably work on the appraisal today." After the way Laine had flirted with the collector we'd met, she deserved the chance to date him—if that's what she wanted to do. "Why don't you call Mr. Majordomo and ask him if he wants the whole Staffordshire collection? I should have pictures by tonight."

"I can do that," Laine said. "What about Martin Foster? Odd the way he showed up out of the blue like that. You don't believe he's the real deal, do you?"

"I'm not sure what to think. For now, it's best to keep my opinions to myself. Darren Lombard has made it clear he's suspicious of me." I chuckled. "As if I could make a missing relative materialize out of thin air."

"Do you think the man calling himself Martin was hired to keep the Lombards from selling?" Laine asked.

"One heck of a scam if that's the case." Something Robert Chance had said to me on the drive over flashed in my head like a neon sign. "Do you suppose the caretaker might have a hand in this?"

"He certainly has access, and he knows the family history," Laine said.

"Except that doesn't account for the ghosts."

"Think about it, Elle. A chair that rocks on its own is fairly cliché, don't you think? What if he's staging the ghosts?"

"What about the spirit on the stairs?" I argued.

"I didn't see it, but I have seen some fairly convincing holograms. Is it possible you saw a hologram?"

The one bone of contention I had with my sister. While she didn't treat me like a lunatic, she regularly tried to debunk my encounters with spiritual energy. I had validation for my most recent visit. I recounted what Clifford Foster had passed along and the find in the pedestal.

"Goosebumps," Laine replied. "Unless—power of suggestion? We did spend time looking at that portrait. And the bust."

"Still doesn't explain the receipt in the pedestal."

Laine breathed a sign. "I would have loved to see that pedestal, and the cap. If they want to liquidate, they'll make a fortune with the furniture, alone."

I drove onto the road. "I'm headed home to pick up my laptop. Check in with your new boyfriend and see if he's interested."

Laine laughed. "Not my boyfriend. Besides, if I were to marry him, I'd probably have to move to Iowa or the far reaches of the galaxy. Can't abandon my sister, now, can I?"

I didn't expect her to stay with me forever, but I warmed at her loyalty. After our father left us, she'd become very protective of me—as I had become protective of her. She'd gone all in with me at the antiques store after she'd graduated college—eight years ago. "You are entitled to a life, you know," I told her. "I love working with you and all, but sometimes I worry about you. I don't think I've seen you go on a second date in quite a while."

"That's because most of the men I've dated aren't worth a second look. As Mom says, I'm content to ride the man train to *Happily* for now and forego the long haul to *Ever After.* You aren't exactly burning up the dating circuit, either," she added. "And you're three years older than me, Madame Spinster."

The man train. The one Mom had said derailed for her when she'd reached *Ever*, souring her on long-term relationships.

Hadn't I been thinking of me and Laine as the spinster sisters just yesterday? "Who am I going to date? The County Coroner?" Most men were put off by my sensitivity to *those who had gone before,* or they wanted me to capitalize on it. It wasn't a gift I'd chosen, and as harmless as most ghosts were, they were counterbalanced by demons. I'd prefer not to see any of them.

"We should go to one of those speed dating things together. What do you think?" she said.

I laughed. "Make you a deal. If Mr. Majordomo fizzles out, I'll go, but only to help *you* find a date."

I arrived home minutes later, where Laine sat on my front stoop. She waved and disconnected the call. "Not all men are like Quint, you know," she said.

Seeing my former fiancé in a far-from-innocent lip-lock with another woman was enough to put me off men for a long time. "I'm a firm believer that if I'm meant to share my life with someone, I'll find him. Right now, I have a job to do."

Chapter 9

Darren Lombard was waiting for me when I returned to Horned Owl Hollow. Before he unlocked the display case, he sat me down at the dining room table to go over our contract.

"Faith also tells me you have a collector who might be interested in buying the whole lot," he said.

No doubt he still suspected my motives. "My sister is contacting him now. However, if you'd prefer the pieces go to auction to ensure the highest price, I can direct the collector to the eBay page for your collection once it goes live."

"If you can provide support for any offer he presents, the lot sale might be an option. I'll need three sources for the valuations."

Of course. To make sure I wasn't trying to rob him. "I can do that." I reached for a pen.

"In the event your collector makes an offer, we can draw up an amendment to the sales agreement."

I nodded. "Understood."

What a difference from my first meeting with the Lombards. Darren was no longer excited to show me his treasures. Could he really believe I'd conjured Martin Foster out of thin air?

A woman walked into the library, her back straight, her nose in the air. Her blonde hair was interspersed with light brown lowlights, and was pulled into a French twist. She wore a sleeveless powder blue shift dress that showed off her trim figure. Her impatient glance at Darren was met with a scowl.

"Ms. Elspeth Barclay, this is my sister, Gloria Jacoby. Gloria is here to assist you."

Assist me? More like watch over me. I smiled sweetly. "It's a pleasure to meet you."

She waved a limp wrist my direction. "Let's get on with it, shall we? How long do you think this will take?"

"Considering the number of pieces, the better part of the day, I should think."

She rolled her eyes and speared Darren with a glare.

"Consider your participation a refresher of what is included in Grandmother's collection," he said.

"Even she didn't care for them," Gloria replied. "It's a wonder she didn't dispose of them before now."

"I'm sure she had her reasons," I said. "Since Mr. Lombard has chosen to leave them here until they're sold, I'll authenticate the pieces and take pictures for now. I can do the valuation when I've finished."

"Then I'll leave you to your task." Darren unlocked the cases, nodded and left the room. Gloria heaved a sigh.

I put on my gloves, moved each piece to the table, and snapped pictures. The figurines generally came in pairs, so I positioned them to show them off as such. Gloria pulled out her cell phone and scrolled through.

"I understand you live in the house next door," I said.

She preened. The Lombards hadn't given me *rich people* vibes, but this woman definitely had them. "My father built the house as a wedding gift for my husband and me. He wanted to keep us all close. As the first-born son, Darren was expected to take over the main house." She shuddered. "You couldn't *make* me live in this monstrosity."

My eyebrows rose in spite of myself. Surely, she'd grown up here. Darren had told me she didn't want the house, but to call this beautiful mansion a monstrosity? Part of me wanted to ask her if she'd met the ghosts—either her grandmother or her great-grandfather—but she wasn't likely to engage in that conversation.

"They don't build houses like this anymore," I said. "The attention to detail. The woodwork. The artistry."

"And that stupid Staffordshire collection." She exhaled a disdainful puff through her nose. "I collect Lladró figurines. They're much more attractive and much more valuable."

The valuable part was true. As to attractive, beauty is in the eye of the beholder, as they say. "I understand the Staffordshire pieces held sentimental value for your grandmother, and they *are* collectibles."

"She didn't care for them, either." Gloria set her phone on the table and looked directly at me for perhaps the first time. "She was saving them as a keepsake for her uncle, a man who has apparently returned from a watery grave. We'll expose the charlatan for who he is, and then we can go on about the business of selling this albatross." Her phone rang, startling us both. She glanced at the display and carried it into the hallway.

I went on photographing the figurines. Gloria's voice was a quiet hum outside the door. While I checked the pictures I'd taken in the digital display, Gloria's voice grew louder.

"I simply have to have that flamenco dancer. What's the point of maintaining an account with you if you won't let me use it?" She went silent for a moment then, in that same annoyed voice, she said, "I don't care if my credit card has been declined."

Her credit card was declined? That might have happened for any number of reasons, and not necessarily the first one that came to mind—that Gloria Jacoby was in financial trouble. If she had a Lladró collection, she could certainly sell off pieces to manage her debts—assuming worst-case scenario.

"Hold it for me and I'll pay you in cash," she went on. "And if you're worried about what I owe you, I'm expecting an inheritance that will be more than sufficient to close my account with you."

An inheritance. From the sale of the house? The Staffordshire collection?

A minute later, she stormed into the dining room while I staged the next pair of spaniels.

Gloria continued to scroll through her phone, occasionally tapping buttons in a manner that suggested she might be texting—angrily.

Around noon, Faith walked in with a tray of Subway sandwiches. "I brought lunch. Ham, turkey and veggie. I wasn't sure which you'd prefer." She set the tray on the dining table.

"Finally," Gloria huffed as she snatched a veggie sandwich.

"Thank you," I said. "Do you mind if I take mine outside? I'd love to get some fresh air."

"Of course. Why don't we sit on the terrace?" Faith said.

"As long as I'm not intruding on anyone."

"I'll wait here," Gloria said. "Don't be too long. We have work to do."

As in, I had work to do. She hadn't done anything as far as I could tell. I nodded, selected a turkey sandwich and a can of Coke and crossed the hall to access the terrace via the parlor. While I juggled my food to open the door, I overheard a man outside.

"Yes, I know it's damn inconvenient, but we're so close. If you can hold on a little longer, the payoff will be worth it. She isn't worth a penny today, but after this place sells, I can claim my share in the divorce settlement. We've waited this long. What's one more month?"

Darren? I waited an extra minute, afraid to tip my hand after accidentally eavesdropping on a private conversation.

Darren reached around from behind me and opened the door. Who was outside?

"Thank you," I said as I stepped onto the stone terrace.

The man I'd overheard was seated at the table. He rose and tucked his phone into his pants pocket, flashing me a thousand-watt smile.

"Blair Jacoby, this is Elspeth Barclay." Darren turned to me. "Blair is Gloria's husband."

I blinked several times. I'd guessed Gloria to be in her sixties. Blair might be fifty, if that. Distinguished gray at his temples. Trim. Attractive in a movie star kind of way. "Pleasure to meet you," I said.

He pulled out a chair at the table, relieved me of my sandwich and can of Coke and set them on the table, then

63

clasped one of my hands between both of his. "The pleasure's all mine."

I fought the urge to wipe my hand when he let go.

"Ms. Barclay is here to help with the sale of the Staffordshire pieces," Darren told him.

A different look of speculation shone in Blair's eyes, the kind I related to people seeing dollar signs when I told them what their keepsake was worth. "I'm sure they're included in the sale of the estate?" Blair said to Darren.

"The proceeds will be deposited into the trust," Darren said, which garnered him a barely concealed scowl.

"Of course," Blair replied. "Do you mind if I sit with you while you eat, Ms. Barclay? I was waiting for my lovely wife. I'm sure she'll be along shortly."

"I believe she's eating in the dining room," I told him.

"Much too stuffy inside," he said. "I'm surprised she hasn't come out, too."

"I've asked her to keep an eye on the collection while the cases are unlocked," Darren told him.

Faith breezed out with a sandwich and a can of lemonade. "Such a lovely day." She hesitated. "Blair. What brings you to the main house today?"

"My wife, of course." His smile became strained. "I'll go get her since everyone else seems to be enjoying the terrace."

Darren cut him off. "I'll get her."

And why am I here? I unwrapped my sandwich and popped the top of my can. Something settled on my shoulder. I reached up to sweep it off and stopped when my own hand grew uncomfortably cold. *Probably the breeze.* A ghostly sigh tickled my ear. My breath caught and I fought the urge to run away.

Martin Foster walked out, studying the wrapped sandwich in his hand. "You're here because of your expertise," he said to me.

Did he know what I'd been thinking? "Yes, I am."

"But that isn't what you were referring to, is it?"

Faith set her sandwich down. "What do you mean?"

Blair shook Martin's hand. "I don't believe we've met. You must be the long-lost sailor."

Martin spared him a cursory glance, then sat beside me. "I have no idea how a niece I never met knew I'd find my way home, but I'm grateful she's preserved my legacy."

I wasn't sure of the terms of the trust, but after one hundred years, I doubted his legacy was as intact as he hoped, at least legally.

"Are you disappointed Alice wasn't here waiting for you?" I asked him.

Blair scoffed. "You speak to him as if he really is Martin Foster."

Martin ignored Blair. "Under the circumstances, I'm glad she was able to move on without me." He unwrapped his sandwich and took a bite. "I find myself with a decided lack of contemporaries. You might be the only person who believes I am who I say."

"I've encountered enough other unbelievable things to consider the possibility. I'll reserve judgment, not that it's mine to give. I'm just here to do a job."

Faith nodded in agreement, while Blair looked from one to the other of us.

"No," Martin said. "It's more than you doing a job." He lowered his voice. "Norma Lombard may have crossed the veil, but she hasn't left this place."

Blair sputtered, but quieted when Faith fixed him with a glare.

"Right," Blair said. "Hey, are there more of those sandwiches?"

"I didn't know you'd be joining us," Faith said sweetly.

Martin offered his half-eaten sandwich. "Would you like to share mine?"

For a man caught out of time, I sensed a wicked wit.

The smile slipped from Blair's face. "Maybe I'll head home. Tell Gloria I was here, will you?"

He crossed the yard—I think they referred to the grassy expanse as a park in homes like this—and Darren returned to the terrace.

I ate in uncomfortable silence, and when I finished, I turned to Darren. "Have you discovered anything about Alice?"

His face reflected his suspicions once more. "I have an appointment to meet with one of her descendants today, as a matter of fact." He checked his watch. "In about an hour."

"I find the whole story fascinating," I said. "Regardless of whether or not this man is Martin Foster."

Martin glanced my direction and I shrugged. He had to know how far-fetched the truth seemed.

"Might I be allowed to accompany you?" Martin asked Darren.

"I don't suppose it matters. If you wish."

I bit my lower lip to keep from inviting myself, too. I was dying to know the rest of the story.

I had my own methods of finding out.

Chapter 10

Faith and Gloria had taken to playing gin rummy while I examined and photographed the figurines. When I finished, Darren and Martin hadn't returned. I'd been hoping to hear about their expedition to meet Alice's relatives, but no such luck.

While I packed my laptop, Faith laid her cards on the table. "Gin."

Gloria groaned. "Again?"

Perfect time to make my escape. "You can tell Mr. Lombard I'll email him a preview of the catalog with high/low prices and let him know if my buyer is interested in any or all of the collection," I said.

"I do wish you'd call him Darren," Faith said. "I don't suppose we can blame him if he chooses not to acknowledge the ghosts in the house. People either believe in spirits or they don't."

"You're not going to go on about Norma's ghost again, are you?" In spite of Gloria's whining, she cast a glance around the room as if searching out the spirit in question.

Faith folded her arms and turned toward Gloria. "Then why won't you sleep another night in this house?"

Time to get out of here. I shouldered my tote bag. "Thank you for the opportunity to work with you. I hope we can find a buyer for your collection."

"Truthfully, I'd rather wait until this business with Martin—or whoever he is—is settled," Faith replied. "There's the matter of succession, of who is the rightful owner."

Gloria sniffed. "You can't possibly believe that imposter is the rightful heir to Horned Owl Hollow."

"The property was meant to be left to Martin," Faith said. "Even if the estate passed in trust to Norma, and then to Darren, Martin is still named as the beneficiary."

"Yes, yes, I know," Gloria sputtered. "But Martin was declared dead in 1918, a detail Darren assured me he has been addressing so that we might dispose of the estate."

I felt guilty lingering, listening to their conversation, but I couldn't bring myself to leave. They probably would have forgotten I was there, except I had to ask. "If you don't want the mansion, wouldn't one of your children be interested?"

Gloria looked startled a moment, then quickly veiled her expression. "My children are scattered across the country living their own lives. They don't want to be saddled with this money pit. As for me..."

Faith tittered. "As for you, you're afraid of another encounter with Norma."

Gloria's tight expression revealed the truth in that statement. Once more, she surveyed the dark corners. I resisted the urge to join Faith in teasing Gloria. I was an outsider. A shopkeeper.

"I'll be on my way," I said, heading toward the hallway.

The hairs on my arms rose with an increase in the energy in the room. Once again, I sensed a presence behind me, but I refused to look. I picked up my pace, walking away from the staircase toward the front door, but when I grabbed the doorknob, it wouldn't turn.

The energy was closer now. I closed my eyes.

"What in heaven's name...?" Gloria whispered, right before I caught sight of her running toward the parlor.

Faith spoke in hushed tones. "She knows you."

"She who?" I turned and found my answer. Faith wrapped her arms around herself as if to ward off a chill. Between us, Norma Lombard wavered, translucent. The source of the cold.

Voices carried from outside, the terrace if I had to guess.

"Now settle down, Gloria, and tell me what happened." Darren's voice.

Her answer was mostly incoherent, but a minute later, Martin walked into the hallway.

Help him. The message from the spirit was more a thought than a whisper, and then she was gone.

From the looks of him, Martin had heard the voice, too. "What is this sorcery?" he asked quietly.

I blinked as warmth returned to my fingers. I wasn't going to be the one to acknowledge what had happened. "How did your appointment go?"

Faith broke into fits of nervous laughter. Martin glanced between us, clearly not sure what to think.

Darren stormed into the hallway and shot me an annoyed glance. "Gloria says you've finished. You'll send me your price list?"

Right. Nothing to see here. "It might take me a few days to get the three different sources you've requested, but yes. And I've asked my sister to contact the collector, so hopefully by then we'll know if he has any interest." I tried the doorknob once more and this time it turned. "I'll be in touch."

"I would speak with you," Martin said quietly.

I hesitated, unsure what the rest of his family would think. "Why don't you walk me to my car?"

He followed me out. When we reached the parking area, he stared at my car. "I'm still quite amazed by these automobiles."

"You didn't want to talk to me about my car," I said.

He studied me a moment before he asked, "What did I witness back there?"

Then he saw the apparition. Most people preferred not to acknowledge a manifestation, let alone the existence of energy that lingered after death. "What do you really want to know?"

"Why," he said. "How."

I considered for a moment. Was he asking for confirmation of what he'd seen or support for his claim to the estate? "Assuming you are who you say you are, my best guess is Norma Lombard, who would be your recently-deceased niece, believes you need my help. She is exerting a great deal of energy to make sure I know that."

"You doubt I am Martin Foster?"

I released a sigh. "I have no reason to doubt your story." Aside from the fact that made him over a hundred years old. From the conversations I'd overheard, the Lombards—and Jacobys—stood to lose from his re-appearance. Plenty of motives for murder.

Murder? They were his family. They wouldn't hurt him, would they?

I'd heard stories of other crimes based solely on an inheritance, and this one was worth quite a bit.

I didn't know how I could help him. "You still have my business card?" I asked. "If you need anything, contact me. The card has my phone number and the address of my antiques shop. I choose to believe you aren't in any danger, but these people have a lot to lose once you prove you are who you say."

He pulled my card from his watch pocket and studied it. "I know this street, although I'm not familiar with how telephones work these days, apparently. Everything is quite different. I don't know how any of this came to be, but I remain guarded. Thank you for your kindness." With that, he turned and walked to the house.

Chapter 11

Along the drive home, my mind raced with all the possibilities that might explain Martin Foster's unexpected return. What happened to the other crew members on the USS *Cyclops*? Wouldn't they all have been sucked into the wormhole together? Or would they have been spit out one by one as the wormhole lost strength?

Science had never been my strong suit.

Shaking my head, I parked in my garage, gathered my tote bag and walked into my house. I unpacked my computer on the kitchen countertop and powered it up. Where to start? Wormholes? The USS *Cyclops*? And then there was Alice Pugh. She would probably net me the most results, considering I subscribed to a couple different ancestry sites, but Martin was more interesting to me at the moment.

I searched the *Cyclops* and found information on its final voyage. Interestingly, other ships in its class also disappeared in the Bermuda Triangle, but the results all showed logical explanations for how Martin's ship had disappeared without a trace, along with the usual conspiracy theories.

As I scrolled, a medical article stood out. "Patient exhibits psychosis in addition to Werner Syndrome diagnosis—claims to be a Naval officer from the USS *Cyclops*."

Werner Syndrome? I clicked on the article. Werner Syndrome was defined as premature aging, a dramatic, rapid appearance of features associated with normal aging. Was the man another of the crew members drawn into the wormhole? I combed the article for the patient's name, then looked for a manifest of the crew members aboard the USS *Cyclops*, and found a match. How many other crew members had survived? I could spend all night searching the names on the manifest, but the possibility even one other sailor had come through supported Martin's story.

I looked for an article showing when and where the other survivor might have exited the wormhole, then chuckled at how ready I was to believe the wormhole concept.

I was rewarded with a story from a year ago. *Local Man Who Claimed to Return from the Bermuda Triangle Dies*. I scanned the article for the highlights. USS *Cyclops*. Werner Syndrome. He reappeared during a particularly violent storm at the home he'd left when he'd enlisted—just like Martin. As if the wormhole had the intelligence to know where to drop him off. The article showed a picture of the man from a hundred years ago, a picture of him when he first returned, and a picture of him shortly before he died. The first two pictures looked almost identical. In the third, he looked as if he'd aged a hundred years in a matter of months.

Would Martin's age catch up with him?

Martin's engagement to Alice Pugh might be one more validation our sailor was who he said he was—especially since the Lombards didn't seem to know that detail.

I started a new search for Alice Pugh. Wikipedia returned a sparse article acknowledging her artistry and achievements.

The images showed a variety of family sculptures, which seemed to be her specialty. The bust at Horned Owl Hollow wasn't among the images. The listing didn't show much of her personal life, so I moved on to a genealogy site.

Alice Mansfield Pugh. Married to Wayne Pugh. Five children. When did she have time to sculpt? Three of her children died before reaching adulthood. The other two children, contemporaries of Darren's grandmother, went on to marry and have families. They'd almost certainly be dead by now, too. Those two children had gone on to have three children each. Nothing about Alice's engagement to a sailor lost at sea. I tugged a notebook beside my computer and made a note of names, following the branches several generations in case longevity wasn't a family trait. Would any of them know anything about Alice and Martin's engagement?

The kitchen door opened and Laine stuck her head in. "Anybody home?"

"Just us chickens," I replied, a joke handed down from our grandmother.

Laine waltzed in and leaned over my shoulder. "Tracking provenance on something? What are we looking at?"

"Alice Pugh. Martin Foster's fiancée from before he disappeared."

She pulled up a chair at the table. "He can't possibly be Martin Foster after all these years. I mean, seriously. The guy doesn't look a day over twenty-five. The real Martin Foster ought to be a doddering old man."

"I bookmarked something on another survivor of the *Cyclops*, someone who showed up a year or so ago with the same story. After he returned, he aged very quickly, as if time caught up with him, and he died."

Laine rubbed her arms. "Goosebumps."

"Right? But that still doesn't prove anything. If we can prove Martin was engaged to Alice, something the rest of the family didn't seem to know, I might be sold that he's the real deal." I closed my search. "What did you find out from your majordomo?"

A smile spread across my sister's face, one that warmed my heart—and inspired the familiar panic of what I'd do if she moved away. She was my business partner, but more than that, she was my best friend.

"He said he'd make another trip this way. Stay a week this time. His employers are eager to see the collection. I told him you'd send pictures." She giggled. "We talked for more than an hour."

Then I hadn't imagined the spark between them. "More than a quick business call, then."

"He said he'd take me to dinner while he was here and suggested he'd like to spend more time together." She picked up my salt shaker, and casually added, "And I know what you're thinking. Don't worry. I'd never abandon you, Elle."

"How can you know what I'm thinking?"

"You're thinking all men are jerks, like Quint. You're thinking Gavin's too good to be true. You're thinking he's going to break my heart."

All true, but I wasn't about to admit it. "Don't be silly. If this guy turns out to be Prince Charming, who am I to stand in the way of true love?" Just because I hadn't found the man of my dreams—a person I doubted existed—didn't mean Laine should pass on the chance to pursue hers. "Not to mention, if you become Mrs. Majordomo, you might get the opportunity to go with him on his acquisition trips. You could see the world." Another thought that made my heart stutter.

"Mrs. Majordomo," she sputtered. "We haven't even been on a date yet. For the moment, I'm more interested in a trip to *Happily,* if you get my drift."

Right. Like Mom. I'd seen the guy. He was drop-dead gorgeous, and the two of them had seemed to have instant chemistry. Unless he was a player and flirted with all the women he came in contact with. Except Laine had flirted with him first. He also hadn't flirted with *me*, which eliminated the "flirted with all the women" theory—a point in his favor. Caught between wanting to protect my sister in case the guy was a bum and wanting to see her happy, I changed the subject.

"How did the house clean-out go? What'd you end up walking into?"

"Borderline hoarder," Laine said. "Lots of boxes. Lots of paper. The old lady never threw anything away. The furniture wasn't even thrift-store material. I did run across a collection of vinyl records we could sell, though." She wrinkled her nose. "When the County called, they told me the lady died in her bathroom. Hit her head on the sink or something. She'd been decomposing for a week before someone suggested a wellness check. By then, they had to scrape her off the floor. They said her remains were in a body bag in the garage, waiting for the coroner to pick up." She shuddered and pulled a face. "I wasn't going anywhere near the garage."

Under normal circumstances, I might have been the one to have gone to the house. Too often, the deceased's residual energy had something they needed to say. While Laine was blissfully unaware, the dead woman might have shared information with me to pass on. I was only too happy to have missed the opportunity. Between Norma Lombard and her father, I'd seen enough spirits to last a while.

"Do you ever get used to it?" Laine asked.

I met her gaze, trying to figure out what she was asking me. "What do you mean?"

"You know. Your connection to the other side. Dead people."

"No. Not to mention people think I'm unhinged when I pass along messages." A shiver coursed through me. That connection was the reason our father had left, so yeah, it bothered me. He'd accused our mother of 'poisoning me with her bullshit,' as he had said on more than one occasion. He'd wanted to take Laine with him to protect her from our 'delusions,' but our mother had threatened to send all the demons in hell after him if he did.

She watched me, as if waiting for me to grow another head. I reached across the table and took her hand. "It doesn't get any easier, I can tell you that, and it scares me every single time, even knowing spirits can't—or won't—harm me." At least I didn't think they could. Then again, for every yin, there was a yang. For every lost spirit, I figured there had to be a demon. I'd only seen a demon once, and fortunately for me, he hadn't taken notice of me. I'd gone home after that experience and done a spiritual cleanse, just in case.

Why did I have a feeling the scales were about to tip?

Chapter 12

As curious as I was about Alice's descendants, I reminded myself the Lombards' family business wasn't my concern. I had my own business to attend to.

While I ate breakfast Thursday morning, I called my mother to catch up. I filled her in on my most recent encounters with Norma Lombard.

"She does seem persistent," my mother said. "I understand why you believe the Lombards are none of your business but it appears this spirit has a different opinion. I wouldn't dismiss her so lightly."

"Martin has my business card. I offered to help if he needed anything."

My mother scoffed. "If he *is* from a hundred years ago, he doesn't know *how* to call you. No one has a landline anymore, and you aren't exactly next door. How do you expect him to come to the store?"

"He said he knew the street, assuming he can find a way into town." I hadn't offered him empty platitudes, although if he did need my help, it required effort. *Where there's a will there's a way.* "I'll make sure I check in with him when I go to the house. Faith Lombard would offer her assistance, I'm sure.

Even if he doesn't completely trust her, she'd help him get to me." As if I was the only one in the world who *could* help him.

"Are you certain of that?"

I was, and I reassured my mother. "I have to get going. I have work to do on their collection."

I finished my breakfast and headed to the store, then parked myself at the sales counter to work on the Staffordshire valuations—from three different sources, per my contract with Darren.

I'd made my way through five sets of figurines before Laine arrived to open. "I'm going to inventory the records I collected from the estate yesterday," she said, and disappeared in the back.

A regular customer walked in a moment later, accompanied by an older woman. The customer carried a box that appeared to be full of depression glass and milk glass.

"Hi, Ingrid. What do we have here?" I asked, walking around the counter.

"It's collectible," the woman beside Ingrid said, a tremor in her voice. "Can you sell these things for us?"

Ingrid set the box on the counter and I assessed the pieces. "I'm sure I can," I told her. "This type of thing is always popular."

"My father died a month ago," Ingrid told me, "and my mother is moving into a retirement community. We've been cleaning out the house and deciding which treasures to part with."

"I have more things you might be able to sell," her mother added. "Can I bring them in?"

Ingrid sighed. "Now, Mom, we talked about this. Sentimental value is only valuable to you."

Her mother sniffed her contempt. "Certainly, someone can use them. No sense throwing things away that have plenty of use left in them."

"Nobody wants them," Ingrid said.

Her mother turned imploring eyes on me. "Maybe we should let this woman decide."

"What kinds of things are we talking about?" I asked.

Ingrid's mother raised her chin. "The furniture I have still has plenty of wear left."

Laine appeared, clearly tuned into the conversation. "What kind of furniture?"

Ingrid took her mother's arm. "We've already asked the charities to take it, and they said they couldn't even give it away."

Tears filled the older woman's eyes. "We can't just throw perfectly good things away."

"If you'd like, one of us can stop by after work and take a look," I said. "But if you've contacted the charities, they'd know the value at least as well or better than we do."

"The Business Owners Association meeting is tonight," Laine reminded me.

I hated going to the Business Owners Association meetings. "You can fill me in later, that is, if these ladies want me to check whatever's left at their house."

"Would you?" Ingrid's mother asked.

"I'd be happy to."

We went through the glassware they'd brought in and I wrote out a consignment receipt. They gave me their address and I told them I'd be by around seven.

Laine nudged my shoulder as they walked out. "Sounds like a wasted trip if they've already been turned down. I see what you did there. Anything to avoid going to the meeting tonight, huh?"

I grinned. "Well, when the opportunity presents itself..."

Was she unhappy with me? "You want to get dinner before the meeting?" I asked.

"I'd love that."

My conscience assuaged, I got back to work. By closing time, I'd valued about half of the figurines. Laine swept out of the office as I shut down my laptop. We locked the store and went to the Longhill Public House next door. Manny, the head chef, waved to us from the kitchen when we walked in and came out to greet us.

"What's the special tonight?" Laine asked.

"Meatloaf, with my cheesy potatoes and zucchini," he said. "Can I get you ladies a plate?"

"Sounds good to me," I said. Laine echoed her approval, and the hostess led us to a booth.

"IPA?" Ted, the bartender, called to us.

"I'm going to need one if they expect me to sit quietly at the Business Owners Association meeting," Laine replied.

"Water for me," I said.

A minute later, he brought us our drinks, and within ten minutes, Manny, himself, brought us our dinner.

"Enjoy, ladies," he said, and returned to the kitchen.

Laine dove into her dinner, but I was still uneasy. "You know how much I appreciate you, right?" I asked.

She looked up. Straightened. Set her silverware on the table. "Yes. I know. What's up, Elle?"

I managed a smile. "Can't a girl love on her sister sometimes?"

She returned the smile. "If this is about the stupid ghosts at Horned Owl Hollow, I'm not mad. I get that you're tuned into something I'm not. That doesn't mean I don't love you, or think you're a freak—although you are a freak." She raised her eyebrows to convey her sarcasm before her expression turned somber. "Sometimes I wonder what my life would have been like if I'd have gone with Dad." She left out a soft huff. "But I can't imagine never seeing my sister again. Or my mom. Who would have thought he'd walk away from us and never look back? For the record, I'm glad she didn't let me go."

I was reassured to hear her say that now. She'd said the opposite in a fit of rage more than once while we were growing up, but we'd moved past that as we matured. "I couldn't imagine my life without my annoying little sister," I teased.

"Can't pick your family," she quipped.

"I'd pick you every time," I countered.

"Ditto." She grinned, and changed the topic to the house she'd cleaned out yesterday. According to the County, the woman had no next of kin, which meant the property, other than the record collection Laine had salvaged, would be going to auction.

I hugged Laine goodbye outside the pub around six-thirty. I'd be early for my appointment, but the sooner I finished that business, the sooner I could resume valuing the figurine collection. As much as Norma Lombard seemed to want me to help, I couldn't see how I would be able to. I'd suggested the DNA test, which Darren and Martin had gone ahead with, so I figured I'd done my part.

Ingrid's mother's house was in the old part of town, a well-established neighborhood with mature trees and homes dating to the 1960's. The houses were well-kept, including my destination. I pulled into the driveway, and Ingrid's mother rushed out to greet me.

"Sorry, I'm a little early," I said.

"I'm glad you could come." She escorted me into the house with a hand on my elbow, directing me toward a bedroom.

"Thanks for doing this," Ingrid said, rising from a chair in the living room to follow.

"This set is still in good shape, don't you think?" her mother asked.

The headboard and matching dressers were made from blonde ash. Popular back in the day, but not worth anything now. Likely, this was one of the items the charities had declined. "Unless you know someone personally who's in the market for a free bedroom set, I'm afraid it isn't worth much. I'm sorry."

Ingrid set a hand on her mother's shoulder. "We've already been told, Mom. Now will you let it go?"

"But what about...?" Ingrid's mother showed me pieces in other rooms—outdated furniture for which there was no current market. They'd been well used and well cared-for, but outside of a Hollywood period piece, I couldn't think of anyone who might be interested in buying them. The style had been a fad, but didn't fit into any "classic" categories. All I could do was shake my head.

Then I stopped in the living room. A landscape over the fireplace caught my eye. "Now that might be worth something. Do you know if it's real or a print?" I asked.

Ingrid's mother covered her nose with a tissue. "That painting was a wedding gift from my in-laws. Oh, I miss my husband so much."

I rested my arm across her shoulders to comfort her. "I'm sorry for your loss. If you feel it's something you can part with, you might consult Carson Patterson at the art gallery in town. He can tell you what it's worth and sell it for you."

A familiar hum of energy buzzed through my brain. *Now*? I fought against whatever spirit wanted to be acknowledged. Eyes squeezed closed, my equilibrium wavered. The spirit wouldn't be denied. "Okay," I whispered, and opened my eyes.

A man appeared beside the fireplace, staring at me, a man I could see through. I shivered and rubbed my arms. I would *never* get used to this.

Let them know I'm okay. Tell her not to worry.

The words weren't spoken, more of a thought. Standard fare in my experience.

"They're going to need more to know it's you," I said softly.

"What did you say?" Ingrid asked.

I held up a finger while I watched the vision unfold. A young girl that resembled Ingrid. Another man. Ingrid's mother. *Going fishing with my brother, now. I'll be here when they come home.*

And then he was gone.

Why me? I sighed, shook my head. "This is going to sound odd," I began. "Take what I say with a grain of salt." I drew a deep breath and turned to Ingrid. "Your father wants you to know he's happy. He says not to worry."

She furrowed her brow. "Okay."

I described the man I'd seen, described the other people in the vision, and her mother cried again. I passed along his message about going fishing with his brother until it was their time to come home, and Ingrid started to cry. She nodded. "That's my dad."

I swallowed the lump in my own throat. "I think I should go now."

Her mother took my hands, tears streaming down her face. "Thank you."

Chapter 13

After staying awake half the night, I'd completed my valuations of the Lombard collection. The majordomo was due back in town today, and if he was going to make an offer, I could present it to Darren Lombard, along with my documentation, when I returned to Horned Owl Hollow tomorrow.

Laine was already at the shop when I arrived. While she filled me in on the Business Owners Association meeting, Carson Patterson walked in.

"Hey," he said, tilting one hip. "I wanted to thank you for your referral. I'm going out later today to see the painting you suggested I appraise." He pursed his lips. "Did you hear the owner of my building is selling? They assure me a new owner would have to honor my lease, which I suppose gives me time to figure it all out. Hey. If worse comes to worst, Emilio says I can rent the front of his catering operation for my gallery."

"You have two more years on your lease, though, right?" I asked.

Carson let out an exaggerated sigh. "A lot can happen in two years, no?"

"Yes," Laine said.

"Let me know if the painting proves worthwhile," I said.

Carson leaned toward me and air-kissed in the direction of each of my cheeks. "Ta-ta, ladies. Talk to you later."

Laine giggled as he walked out. "The world needs more people like him. Emilio must really love him to offer him space at his catering company. I need to find me a man like that."

"Maybe not exactly like that. In the meantime, you have your majordomo," I teased, wagging my eyebrows.

Laine waved off my remark. "Stop. I hardly know him."

"Yet." I grinned and nudged her shoulder.

We had a steady stream of looky-loos in addition to actual buyers over the course of the day. I enjoyed chatting with people waxing nostalgic about our inventory. They generally became some of my best customers. Mid-afternoon, I overheard a woman who'd walked in asking Laine about me. Laine raised her hand to get my attention and I excused myself from the conversation I was engaged in.

The woman in question looked to be a few years older than me, golden-brown hair, her features soft but not given to an abundance of wrinkles.

"I'm Elle Barclay. How can I help you?"

"I'm Catherine Payton. I had a pair of interesting visitors yesterday. One of them mentioned your name."

Catherine Payton. Something nudged my memory that I couldn't quite pinpoint. I held up a finger and retrieved my notebook from the sales counter. Alice Pugh's great-granddaughter? My pulse raced. I'd promised to keep my nose out of the Lombard's family business, but circumstances kept pulling me in. "You're related to Alice Pugh."

"Apparently. I have pieces of her art that have been handed down through the generations. Family heirlooms, more than anything else. Or so I'd been told. Are they worth something?"

"I couldn't say. I'm sure *Carson's*, the art gallery three doors down, could give you a better idea."

She took a step toward the door and I was afraid she'd leave.

"As I said, they're family heirlooms, so I'm not likely to part with them." She stopped, her brow furrowed. "Do you know the men who came to see me? The conversation was very odd. They wouldn't explain their connection to Alice, and then the younger man mentioned your name. They aren't scammers, are they? I mean the one guy said he was Darren Lombard, but... Darren Lombard?"

Then she knew about Horned Owl Hollow and its owners. There weren't many locals who didn't. I smiled and invited her to sit with me in the vintage clothing showroom. "Did they tell you about the sculpture she did for their family?"

Catherine's eyes widened. "No. They didn't. They asked if I knew if she'd been engaged to anyone other than the man she married. I'm dying of curiosity now."

How to explain who Martin was when I wasn't convinced myself? Better to keep the strokes broad. "You may be aware Darren Lombard owns a home on the other side of town. The younger man knocked on his door claiming to be a relative. They started looking into the family history and came across a bill of sale from Alice to Mr. Lombard's great-grandfather for a sculpture of his children. There was a suggestion Mr. Lombard's great-uncle was engaged to Alice before he left to fight in World War I."

This was where the story got dicey. I proceeded with caution. "I understand Alice's first fiancé was lost at sea, and that's why they weren't married."

"Oh, how tragic." The woman's brow wrinkled again. "This is all so odd. The younger man asked if I had any family photos. I didn't see the harm in showing him what I could find. He saw a picture of my aunt and teared up. He commented on how much she looked like—and this is a quote—'my Alice.'"

My sympathy for Martin increased. A man lost in time, returning to a different world. What was I supposed to tell Catherine Payton?

"I called my father after the men left to ask what he knew," Catherine went on. "He wasn't aware of the family history that far back. He said Alice lives on through her art. Otherwise, she probably would have been just a name in the family Bible."

The family Bible. Would it have a notation of the engagement?

"I know this is none of my business," I said, "but I'm so curious. Old trinkets and the stories that go with them intrigue me." I waved around the shop. "Obviously. Would your family Bible show if Alice had been engaged to Martin Foster before she married Wayne Pugh?"

Catherine rewarded me with a smile. "I can certainly check. I have to agree. A tragic, years-old love story like that deserves to be unwrapped."

"I hope you'll let me know what you find out."

"Oh, I will," she said as she walked out, waving over her shoulder.

I folded my arms, staring after her. Martin's story got more interesting with every detail I discovered.

"You don't think he really is...?" Laine said again. She shook her head. "I don't think I want to know."

The woman I'd been chatting with previously bought a couple cow parade figurines she'd been debating about, mantle-top pieces that reminded her of her uncle's farm. As she left, a handsome man opened the door for her, letting her pass before he walked in. The majordomo.

Laine grabbed hold of my forearm. Without a doubt, the man was heart-stoppingly handsome, but in my experience, the less attractive men were the more steadfast.

Laine rushed around the counter to greet him. "It's great to see you again. You said you'll be staying a week this time?"

He took her hand and raised it to his lips, which seemed patronizing to me—or I had my own biases about uninvited kisses of any kind.

I put on a smile and greeted him, my hand extended. "Nice to see you again, Mr. Reeves. I've drafted an online store for the Staffordshire pieces if you'd like to take an early look. I'm meeting with the seller again tomorrow."

He shook my hand. "Please, call me Gavin."

"Gavin," I echoed. I returned to the sales counter and navigated to eBay on my laptop. "I've authenticated they are all original pieces and not later copies. They haven't advertised their collection yet, so you would have first dibs, so to speak."

He scrolled through the photos. "Some of these pieces are quite rare. Where did he acquire them?"

"Handed down through the family. Originally *from* Staffordshire, I believe. The relative who bought them got them as gifts for his young daughter. She wasn't quite as impressed, although she held onto them as mementos of her father."

"I see several of these I might be interested in."

Again, I got a vibe from him that put my nerves on edge. "I'll have to consult with the seller, but since he's trying to liquidate his collection, it might be an all or nothing deal."

Gavin shook his head. "No, I don't think my employer would want all of them, but certainly this one," he enlarged one of the photos. "And a few others that are difficult to find. Can you put me in touch with him?"

"I'm brokering the deal on his behalf," I said. "If you aren't interested in all of them, you may have to bid on them like everyone else."

He turned his attention to me. "But you're meeting with him tomorrow?"

"I am."

His sense of excitement came through in his voice, something I was familiar with when I discovered rarities of my own. "Will you let him know I'm interested? I'll be here all week," he said.

"Of course."

"In the meantime, can I take you ladies to dinner?" He slipped an arm around Laine's waist.

Laine stared at him with goo-goo eyes. Whatever my misgivings about him were, she had no such concerns. If he turned out to be shallow and narcissistic, she'd figure it out. I couldn't let my negative experiences influence what might be her train to *Happily,* if not to *Ever After.* "You two go on without me. I have business to take care of."

"It's closing time," Laine pointed out.

"And I'm still adding the valuations to the catalog as part of my contract with the client," I told her.

"Anything I can help with?" Gavin asked.

I shooed them toward the shop door. "This is what I do. I'll see you later."

Gavin escorted Laine out. As much as I worried he might be a player, I envied my sister the attention of a handsome man. How long had it been since a man had looked at me that way?

Not long enough. The last one had left skid marks in his hurry to get away from my particular brand of crazy. The ones who didn't mind the ghost stories—who wrote them off as quirky—tended to be frightened when they came face to face with the reality. My father was a prime example. Being considered crazy was easier than acknowledging unexplained energy.

Darren Lombard seemed willing to put up with Faith's brand of crazy. Then again, their ghost was family. Maybe Faith didn't have prior experience.

When I completed the catalog of Staffordshire figurines, I locked the door, gathered my things and headed out the back way.

When I got to my car, Robert Chance, the Lombards' caretaker, was waiting for me.

"Miss Barclay. I was hoping to have a word with you." He nodded toward the store. "Can we talk inside?"

"I'm closed for the evening." I glanced around the block. The stores in this part of town didn't keep evening hours, and I didn't want to be caught alone. As drawn as I was to Horned Owl Hollow and the spirits that wanted me to help, the flesh-and-blood components made me at least as uncomfortable as the ghosts, if not more so.

"What I have to say won't take long," he went on. "But I didn't want anyone else to overhear. Would you be willing to sit in my car a moment?"

"I would not," I replied. "What's on your mind?"

He surveyed the area, and extended a hand toward a sidewalk bench outside the pub.

I clutched my computer bag to my chest and followed him. When I sat, Chance sat beside me.

"I'll get straight to the point," he said. "I know Darren Lombard hired you to sell the figurines. With recent developments, have you considered they aren't his to sell?"

I had, in fact. Something I'd planned to broach with Darren when I presented the catalog tomorrow. "Yes."

Chance nodded. "Good."

"Not that it's any of my business, but have *you* considered the man who claims to be Martin Foster might also consider selling the estate? If what he claims is true, no matter how far-fetched, he likely doesn't have the means to pay your salary, much less maintain the house."

"Horned Owl Hollow is my home. Has always been my home."

I stared at him, waiting for him to say something more, but he didn't. My brain raced to keep up. "Are you saying you wouldn't ask for a salary in exchange for being allowed to stay on? What if the decision isn't his to make? Certainly, you were making other plans when you learned Mr. Lombard wanted to sell."

"Yes, I was."

The thought struck me with such force that I jumped to my feet. "Are you responsible for the man who showed up claiming to be Martin Foster?"

A slow smile creased Chance's face. "I couldn't find such a convincing doppelganger, even if I'd dreamed up such a scheme. No. Norma always said he'd come home, and now he has."

And people called me crazy. Something was definitely off about this man. Then again, I felt that way about most men, and had been told the same about myself on more than one occasion. I stopped from expanding on a snap judgment.

"Do you have somewhere else to go if he sells?" I asked.

"As I said, Horned Owl Hollow is my home, even if I don't own it. I'd prefer to remain there." He studied his hands. "Before you sell any of the contents, I'm asking you to make sure you're dealing with the rightful owner."

Provenance. How often had I had to confirm the items people brought to me were theirs to sell? "I understand."

"As for what my plans are—I'd prefer not to share those yet." Chance flashed me a mysterious smile, did a half-bow, and walked away.

I wasn't sure what to think. He'd said he'd gone to college when he'd picked me up the other day. If he had a degree, why take a job as a caretaker to a small estate? Family loyalty or not, something didn't fit.

Chapter 14

When I arrived at Horned Owl Hollow the next morning, the energy around the old mansion pulled me in like a tractor beam.

"I can't make them believe me," I said under my breath to whatever spirits lingered. I had no sway over the Lombards. The fact Darren Lombard still wanted me to sell his collection amazed me after I'd all but confirmed his home was haunted. Then again, Faith apparently had experience with the spirits, too.

As I walked up the steps, the front door opened. Nobody was there to greet me. No way I was walking into their house unchaperoned when they already were suspicious of me. I remained on the porch. "Hello?" I called out.

Darren appeared from the parlor on the left side of the hallway, looking slightly miffed.

"The door was open," I said. "I didn't want to come in without announcing myself."

He extended an arm toward the library on the right. "You're right on time. Shall we get down to business?"

I walked up the two vestibule steps and into the library. Darren sat behind the desk and waved me to the chair opposite.

"I've created an eBay store for the figurines, but it isn't live yet," I began. And it wouldn't be until I could be sure who the owner was. If Martin was the rightful heir, he might prefer to hold onto the collection.

"What about the collector you told me about?" Darren asked.

"I gave him a preview, but he was only interested in a few of the pieces. I suggested if he didn't want the whole lot of them, he should probably bid on the ones he wanted along with whatever other buyers you might have. If I've misrepresented your interests, he'll be in town all week and I can circle back."

Darren nodded. The half-smile on his face indicated he was pleased with the idea.

"Did you get the email I sent you?" I asked. "I've put together a booklet of the pieces and the three valuations you asked me for."

"I did, and I must say I'm impressed with your work. I appreciate your professionalism."

Was this a good time to drop the bomb? That my professionalism was going to be a problem for him? A breath of air touched my cheek. My body shuddered in response.

I gathered my courage and forged ahead. "In light of recent events, have you reached an answer on who your houseguest is?"

Darren's lips narrowed. He rested his arms on the desk and folded his hands. "I don't see how that's any concern of yours."

I met his glare head-on. I wasn't about to let him steal someone else's property—lawyer or not. "My concern lies in who actually owns the collection. It's my understanding based on what you and your wife have told me that the house and its contents are in trust for Martin Foster. If that's the case, wouldn't he be the rightful owner? Or his descendants?"

Darren's jaw pulsed. "Martin Foster died a hundred years ago. A dead man can't inherit."

I had to tread lightly. If I told the newspapers the spirits that roamed his house embraced his guest as the rightful owner, Darren Lombard would sue me for a hundred things, not the least of which would include being mentally unfit. "As a lawyer," I began, "I'm sure you'd want to address any claims your guest has."

"That matter will be dispatched expeditiously," he replied.

His *guest* took that moment to walk into the library. Limping. With a black eye.

I gasped and rose from my chair. "What happened to you?"

"An accident." Martin shot an openly accusatory glance at Darren.

Immediately, I remembered the conversations I'd overheard. Darren's sister. His brother-in-law. The family had motives to sell, plans that hinged on the transaction. Was Martin in danger staying here? Time to play my wild card.

"I'd considered running an article in the local paper about your collection," I said. "A human-interest story might attract buyers locally, and I'm sure people would be fascinated by the discovery of a long-lost relative poised to take over so you can retire the way you want to."

A man chuckled in the hallway, launching Darren to his feet. With portieres instead of a solid door, the library didn't offer much in the way of privacy. He gripped the molding on one side of the entranceway, pivoting his head as he checked the hallway. Whoever had been eavesdropping had clearly vanished, because when Darren turned, I was in his crosshairs once again.

"Is that a threat, Ms. Barclay?" he growled.

I pasted on my best smile. "You did hire me to find a buyer for the collection, didn't you? How can that possibly be misconstrued as a threat?" I turned my attention to Martin, whose lips were trembling as if he held back a smile of his own. "Do you feel threatened, Mr. Foster?" I asked, as much to get him to tell me about his so-called accident as to let Darren Lombard know I didn't trust him, either.

"Not at all, and if I did, life in the Navy teaches you to watch your back," Martin said.

Good to know, even if his response was as veiled as my question. "In order to ensure provenance," I said, addressing Darren, "I will hold off publishing the eBay store I've drafted for the figurines until ownership has been confirmed."

"Not that it's any of your business," Darren said, returning to the desk, "but I've begun updating the trust, something my grandmother should have done years ago. No court in the country would believe this man—" he waved his hands toward Martin "—is the named beneficiary."

While that might be true, if Naval records matched the fingerprint on his dog tags, Darren might have a hard time denying the claim. At the very least, DNA evidence could prove he was family.

"And if you're not interested in the commission, I'll find someone who is," Darren said.

"It seems you've come home in the nick of time," I said to Martin. I tucked my computer into my tote bag. "I strongly recommend you find independent counsel to represent your interests, assuming they are legitimate."

"It should be easy enough to prove," Faith said, walking into the room. "And Darren, you know how often Norma assured us Martin Foster would return." She shot me a warm smile. "My husband's grandmother was keen on genealogy. I think I mentioned she signed up for one of those online places that matches DNA—with my help, of course." She turned to Darren again. "I've sent a sample of Martin's DNA for them to match there, as well. In case there are any problems with the samples you gave to the hospital. They can compare his DNA with Norma's, as well."

Darren stormed out of the library.

Faith patted my arm. "I'm sorry you got drawn into the middle of all this, but Norma can be a tad insistent at times." She sighed. "Apparently, she won't rest until this matter is settled, and I'm afraid she's chosen you to help."

"I don't know what I can do," I said.

Faith's smile broadened. "You're already doing it."

Chapter 15

Chance was waiting beside my car in the Lombards' visitor parking when I left the house.

What had Chance said to me? Darren's grandmother had asked him to stay on until Martin came home. Before I could stop myself, I asked, "Where would you have gone if the Lombards sold the house before Martin showed up?"

His face contorted into a twisted smile, which he covered with his hand. "Not sure you'd believe me if I told you." He nodded toward the house. "Martin says he thinks you're trustworthy, and while I'd like to agree with him, there are certain things I like to keep quiet, you know?"

"Next, you're going to tell me you're an illegitimate heir waiting to stake your claim," I joked.

"No, ma'am. Nothing quite like that. I did hear you suggest you might sic the press on Darren, though, and while that might be a wise move to protect Martin, I'd rather not draw attention to myself."

I might have offered my previous comment as an improbable theory, but now he had my imagination working. "A criminal, hiding from the law? Tell me, Mr. Chance, why would a college-educated man choose to work in a job he was overqualified for?"

"Already told you that," he said.

"You said you came home to help when your father was ill. You left me with the understanding your father passed on."

"And he has."

"What about your mother? Should I assume you'd move in with her?"

When he didn't say anything more, I reached for the door handle. Chance covered my hand with his. A warm, calloused hand that sent a spike of heat through me.

"My mother died when I was in high school. Don't suppose you'd have time for a cup of coffee?" His voice was deep, triggering another dormant response inside me.

My comment had been insensitive. I owed him the courtesy of hearing him out. "I might have."

"Whether I tell you why I'd prefer to remain out of the press or not, you strike me as the kind of person who might Google me. Better if I tell you. If you really want to know."

I nodded, my cheeks on fire. Because he'd called me out? "When would be convenient?"

"I need to make a run to the Farm & Fleet. We could go now, if that works."

"The Farm & Fleet on Highway 23? There's a coffee shop in the outlot."

"I know the one," he said, holding my gaze, deepening the trance I seemed to have fallen into. I was sure he was older than me, but probably only by a couple of years. Well within my dating range.

Dating?

My voice broke. "I'll meet you there."

He nodded once, removed his hand from mine. My hand fell, too, as if I'd forgotten why I was standing beside my car. Chance reached around and opened the door for me. Right. I was leaving. I shot a glance at the mansion, and I swear a face looked down from Norma's window.

Seated at the wheel, I blew out a breath to make sure I could think clearly. No, not a trance, precisely. More a haze, one I'd been careful to avoid since my last disaster of a boyfriend. I was alarmed by the way the Lombards' caretaker affected me. Nothing otherworldly about him, just regular old male sex appeal that had caught me off guard.

As I pulled away, I told my Bluetooth to call Laine. She answered giggling. A reminder she was under the influence of a *different* man's sex appeal.

"You on your way to the store?" she asked.

I heard the tenor of a male voice in the background. The majordomo? Would he try to barter prices with her? Sweet talk her into giving away the merchandise? I had no reason to believe he would do that to her. "I'm stopping for a coffee meeting on the way." Should I tell her who I was meeting? In case Chance was a fugitive? "With the Lombards' caretaker."

"Okay. See you in a bit." Her response indicated she wasn't paying much attention to me, confirmed when she ended the call.

If Chance was going to murder me, I hoped she'd remember.

I didn't *really* believe he was going to murder me. More likely, he wanted to discuss the hauntings at Horned Owl Hollow, something we both seemed to acknowledge. Why else would he want to meet with me privately? To discuss his shady past, or so he'd said. He wanted to tell me himself rather than have me Google him.

Which made me want to Google him.

I stopped outside the coffee shop and pulled out my phone. Robert Chance. Common enough name. Dozens of results returned. Dozens of images. A pickup truck rumbled into the parking lot—the man in question—denying me the time I needed to check my options.

If he wanted to tell me, I should let him do so. I got out of my car, straightened my blouse and raised my chin. I could be Teflon to his influence.

He stepped out of the truck and glanced at the sky. "Nice day. You mind if we sit outside while we talk?"

I laughed. "More of the low profile? Do you want me to go in and buy your coffee for you?" I wagged my eyebrows, entertained by his sense of intrigue.

His cheeks took on a ruddy hue. "Don't think I'm quite that notorious, but I do like my privacy."

Privacy he was willing to share with me. *Teflon,* I reminded myself, but he had piqued my interest. One more reason to keep my boundaries in place.

Five minutes later, we carried our drinks to a table on the patio, sheltered from the sun by an oversized umbrella. When he sat, Chance wrapped both hands around his cup and stared into it. He remained that way for a full minute.

"So, about the press." He raised his gaze to meet mine and that *something* about him sent another shudder of awareness through me. I really had to tamp my unwanted response down.

"When I was in college, I developed a software tool," he went on. "Then my dad got sick and I sold out to come home and take care of him. I don't have any other family, and I wasn't about to abandon him to a facility. The fortunate part for me is I sold my shares for a ton of money. The unfortunate part was that the investors who backed me didn't sell their interests and ended up losing later on. They were of the opinion I screwed them over." He drew a deep breath. "I didn't, you know. Just dumb luck I had to leave when I did."

The words seeped in like cold molasses. Was he telling me he'd made millions? Which reinforced my question, "Then why are you working for someone else if you could be doing what you choose?"

He leaned over the table toward me. "That's the point. I am doing what I choose. Out of the spotlight. Those investors thought I took advantage of them. They wouldn't think twice about suing me for their losses, even without a leg to stand on." He straightened. "I'm perfectly happy living under the radar.

"My father took the job at Horned Owl Hollow because my mother fell in love with the place. The mansion represented a real home to her, something she'd never had after my grandmother had apparently been disowned. My dad was happy to take the job when the Lombards offered it to him. Horned Owl Hollow is the only home I've known."

"Your grandmother was disowned?"

He smiled. "My mother never told me the whole story, only that my grandmother died working in a factory during World War II."

I was still confused about the arrangement. "If Horned Owl Hollow is the only home you've known, does that mean you grew up with Darren and Gloria?"

He waved a hand through the air. "Nah. They were older than me and didn't have time for a caretaker's son."

I could see that. The hired help. "Which brings me back to what you were planning to do when the Lombards sold the estate."

A slow, sexy smile creased his face. "I was planning to buy it. As I've said all along, the estate is the only home I know, and the Lombards be damned."

Had Chance told me he believed in ghosts, or was that a mechanism to lower the house's market value? Had he hired an actor to impersonate Martin Foster as a way to buy the mansion cheap?

Chapter 16

When I got to the store, Laine was seated on a stool behind the sales counter, smiling at her phone while she appeared to be composing a text. She giggled when a moment later her phone announced an incoming text.

"Let me guess," I said. "Mr. Majordomo?"

She shot me a mildly annoyed glance. "His name is Gavin."

Her defense of him proved things had progressed since I'd seen her last. I set my tote bag behind the counter and leaned on the display case. "How did your dinner with Gavin go last night?"

She turned to face me and I swear I saw stars in her eyes.

"We talked for hours," she said, in a swoony voice. "Do you know the people he works for own a *castle* in Iowa? He says it's filled with antique furniture and he invited me to visit."

Warning bells went off in my head. This guy was too good to be true. "You hardly know him. You aren't thinking of going, are you?"

Nothing like a big sister to burst her bubble. I immediately felt guilty when her expression fell. "It isn't like he's taking me captive. He isn't a beast in a fairy tale. He lives in a castle, Elle. There are dozens of rooms for company, like a giant Airbnb, and he has *staff*, so there are other people around all the time."

Staff might overlook a clandestine visitor. I made a mental note to Google Gavin Reeves. Laine wouldn't approve, but I needed to check for my own piece of mind, to be sure there wasn't anything shady about this guy. Make sure he was who he said he was.

"What about you?" Laine asked, going on the offensive. "Coffee with the caretaker? Should I be asking you what's up?" She raised her eyebrows.

Guilt poked me in the chest. I didn't know Robert Chance any better than she knew Gavin Reeves. The difference was that despite the spark I'd felt with the Lombards' caretaker, I had no intention of acting on it.

What right did I have to judge Laine's choices? She was a grown woman. No one was threatening to steal her away from me. Whatever happened between her and Gavin, she could take care of herself.

"Elle?" Laine cocked her head and squinted. "What's going on?"

"I sort of threatened to bring the press down on Darren Lombard to make sure nothing happened to his house guest. Chance suggested that might not be the best tactic."

Laine laughed. "Oh, that's brilliant. That way Darren Lombard can't keep the rightful heir under wraps or deal him dirty. If this guy is the rightful heir."

"I overheard several conversations while I was there about what everyone wants to do with their share of the proceeds from the estate. If Martin Foster can prove he is who he says he is, there might not be a sale, and there definitely wouldn't be proceeds to split."

She leaned on the counter. "The Lombards wouldn't do something... nefarious... would they?" Laine straightened with a look that said another thought had occurred to her. "You don't think this guy really is Martin Foster, do you? He can't be."

It wasn't my job to convince anyone. "He might be a descendant, which would amount to the same thing."

We both looked up when the door opened. Quint Webster walked in, in his police uniform, making my heart stutter. Tall and lean, he took off his cap and ran a hand across his bald head, his mesmerizing hazel eyes landing on me. We'd broken up a year ago, but the betrayal of finding him kissing another woman still stung.

"What can we do for you, Officer Webster?" Laine asked, rescuing me from saying anything stupid.

He gave her a cursory glance before he approached me. "I understand you were at Horned Owl Hollow today."

I crossed my arms. "I was."

He replaced his cap and pulled out his notepad and pencil. "Can I ask why?"

"I'm doing business with Darren Lombard."

"Are you familiar with his collection of Staffordshire figurines?"

Okay. Something wasn't right. My arms fell to my sides. "What's this about, Quint?"

"The collection was stolen. Did you see it when you were there today?"

His tone held a note of accusation, which prompted me to cross my arms once more. "I met with Mr. Lombard in the library today. I didn't go any further into the house, so no, I didn't see it today."

"When was the last time you saw the collection?"

I resisted the urge to scream at him, to ask if he thought I'd stolen it. With a deep breath, I answered his question. "Two days ago, when I was photographing and cataloging."

Quint's expression changed to perplexed. "Photographing and cataloging?"

"Mr. Lombard asked me to sell the collection for him. I did an appraisal and drafted an eBay store."

Quint's eyes swept the room, something I recognized as him thinking more than looking for anything. He must have come to a conclusion, because he met my gaze once more. "And you completed your appraisal?"

"I did. Didn't he share my catalog with you?"

If I knew Quint—and I did—his thoughts would shift to Darren, and a motive to collect from his insurance company, assuming the collection was insured. Would Darren Lombard do something like that?

"I'll need a copy of your work to document the loss," Quint said. "I assume your catalog included the whole collection."

"I can email it to you."

Quint tapped his notepad. "He said you knew someone who was interested in the collection."

Laine rose to her feet, ready to defend her majordomo. "Another collector, who offered to buy it."

My pulse rate kicked up. We hadn't vetted Gavin Reeves. Or at least I hadn't. Was he a thief? "We haven't put the two of them in contact," I said weakly. "The buyer doesn't know who the seller is." Although identifying the Lombards wouldn't be difficult if Gavin wanted to know.

"I'll need his information," Quint said.

Laine looked as if someone had kicked her in the shins. She sent me an imploring look.

"He has to rule him out," I said gently.

Laine reached behind the counter for Gavin's business card, tapped it against her hand, and reluctantly handed it over.

"Oh," Quint said. "He doesn't live in town."

"No, but he's visiting with hopes of seeing the collection," I said.

Laine's rapidly shifting expressions turned to daggers—directed at me.

"Unless he's already acquired it," Quint said. "Do you know where he's staying?"

Laine folded her arms, tears welling in her eyes.

"No. I don't," I replied. Gavin deserved the benefit of the doubt as much as I did. Quint hadn't come in accusing me—well, not directly. Time to throw suspicion back on Darren Lombard. "Did you meet the Lombards' house guest while you were there?"

"House guest?" Quint asked.

"A relative. One who stands to inherit the whole kit and kaboodle." I considered telling Quint about the conversations I'd overheard. About Darren's sister who was in debt, and her husband who was counting on the sale before he filed for divorce.

Once more, my thoughts drifted to Chance, but he wouldn't need to steal the figurines if what he told me was true. Still, with the evidence of a man's perfidy standing in front of me, I knew better than to trust any of them—especially Chance.

For now, I'd keep the family—each of them with their own motives—to myself.

Chapter 17

As Quint walked out the door, Laine grabbed her phone. She pushed a button, put the phone to her ear, and stared at me.

"He isn't answering," she said, her voice low.

"Gavin?" I asked.

She turned away and spoke into the phone. "Hi. It's me. Listen. There seems to be a problem. Call me back." She disconnected the call and bowed her head.

Even she had to admit her inability to reach him right now seemed suspicious, but I wasn't going to be the one to point it out to her. She shook a finger at me. "Don't start."

"I didn't say a word."

"No, you didn't, but I know you. 'What do we know about this guy?' Always suspicious of everybody. Just because you almost married a creep doesn't mean all men are creeps, Elspeth." She stormed into the office.

I didn't bother to follow her—didn't respond. Anything I said now would only add fuel to the fire. I wanted to protect my sister from the cold, cruel world, but I knew she'd check on her new man, the same way she knew I would. If I was wrong, I'd apologize. If either of us uncovered something shady about

Gavin Reeves, I'd wait for her to tell me, no matter what I found out. My eyes stung with unshed tears.

I should have told Quint about the rest of Darren's family, shift suspicion to everyone else.

No. Finding the thief was his job. I had to let him do it.

I sat behind the sales counter and opened my laptop, where the shortcut to my Staffordshire catalog stared at me. So much for my commission. Skipping by that, I opened a browser and Googled Gavin Reeves. Plenty of results, several with pictures. I clicked on a LinkedIn profile that matched the man we'd met.

His profile supported everything he'd told us, including his expertise in collectibles. He had recommendations and references, including from the Louvre. His current employer was shown as private, but the profile had a link to contact them for a reference. Should I?

While my finger hovered over the contact button, I considered how a fraud might post misleading information and references to people who would support his scheme. How could I verify they weren't another level of swindlers put in place to support the scam?

I closed the browser, and then the lid of my laptop. When had I become so cynical? Yes, the Lombards' collection was valuable, but the elaborate scheme I imagined would cost a crook more to set up than they'd get from fencing the stolen figurines. Instead of chasing phantoms, I should be worried Quint would try to pin the burglary on me.

I was getting carried away again. If Quint suspected me, he wouldn't have left so quickly. Judging by his responses, my guess was he was leaning toward Darren Lombard and insurance fraud. At least for now.

I should have told him about Gloria and Blair. And Chance. Breaking glass behind me brought me out of my funk. Laine stood in the office doorway, her face drained of color. At her feet was a broken vase—an expensive vase.

I rushed toward her, reaching for a large shard. "What's wrong?"

"It slipped. I'm sorry. I'll pay for it."

"Laine, accidents happen. You don't have to..." Every hair on my body stood on end. The room seemed to sway. I shook my head to clear it, and turned to find an old woman standing near the door.

"Can I help you?" I asked.

The woman didn't answer. In fact, for a moment, she seemed to waver. *I could see through her.* That's when I recognized her as Norma Lombard.

I turned to Laine, who had gotten a broom and dustpan to sweep up the broken vase. I tried to get her attention, but the words wouldn't come. The antiques store disappeared into a vortex, throwing off my equilibrium. I was sucked into the Lombards' main hallway, floating toward the staircase at the rear of the house. The background seemed to move while I stood still, down the stairs and into the basement. I glided through a couple of rooms that were storage one minute, and... servants' quarters the next.

Servants' quarters?

A sense of nausea came over me—motion sickness. I came to a stop facing a wall in the basement.

"Why am I looking at a wall?" I whispered.

The wall cracked—not a crack, a doorway. Behind the door, darkness. In the light from the room behind me, shelves came into view.

From somewhere far away, a phone rang. I recognized Laine's default ring tone.

The Lombards' basement faded as I seemed to move backward, or the background was moving forward. I flailed for balance, squeezed my eyes shut and gritted my teeth...

...And opened my eyes sitting on the floor in the antiques shop with Laine kneeling beside me.

"What the hell was that?" Laine asked.

I looked for the spirit. No sign of her.

"I think I'm going to throw up," I told my sister.

She disappeared and returned a moment later with a garbage can and a bottle of water. "Here. Drink."

I unscrewed the cap and gratefully gulped the cold water.

"Now," she said. "What just happened?"

I glanced to where the specter had been standing.

"Elspeth!"

"I saw something," I replied.

"I'm calling Mom."

I grabbed her arm. "I'm okay. She wanted me to see something."

"She? So, what? You had a vision, or something?"

I drew a shaky breath. "I guess."

"What did you see?"

In my head, I retraced the path the spirit had taken me. "I never got to see the payoff. Your phone rang and brought me out of it."

"You can thank Gavin, who apparently returned my call. I didn't answer because I was too scared about what was going on with you." She straightened and stared at her phone. "Gavin returned my call. He didn't disappear with the Lombards' figurines. He wouldn't call me back if he'd stolen them."

I pushed to my feet. "I don't think he stole them."

Her shoulders relaxed. "You don't?"

"Did you find his LinkedIn profile?" I asked.

"I was afraid to look." She rose and held out a hand to help me to my feet.

"If he's a crook, he's gone to an awful lot of trouble to set up his con," I told her. "I'm not saying it isn't still possible, but highly improbable, considering the payoff. Unless he has other targets lined up, too."

She dumped the shards from the vase into the wastebasket. "I suppose that's the best endorsement you could give him, considering—" she made air quotes "—how little we know about him."

Her tone indicated she was upset with me again, even though I'd defended Gavin. But that wasn't what normally upset her. At times like this, she blamed me for our father's departure, which he'd said was because of my mother's and my sensitivity to the spirit world.

I stared at the spot where Norma Lombard had appeared. She seemed awfully determined to get my attention. "I need to get back inside Horned Owl Hollow."

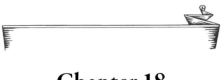

Chapter 18

Laine had another date with Gavin Saturday night. I sat home alone, searching for castles in Iowa. I found a city in the western part of the state that bragged about their castle-like architecture, but Gavin had said he lived in Eastern Iowa. My searches didn't show anything in Eastern Iowa. Then again, he'd said his employers valued discretion. No one wanted trespassers wandering around their private property.

A knock drew me out of my Googling. I sensed my mother—the same connection Laine resented. When I opened the door, my mother stood on the porch with a plate of fresh-baked chocolate chip cookies in her hands.

"Mother." I invited her in, hugged her and lifted the Saran Wrap to swipe a cookie.

She set the plate on the coffee table and dropped onto my sofa. "Now. What's going on?"

I took a bite, as much for an excuse not to talk without giving away any personal information as because I was dying for a taste of the warm, chocolatey goodness. "Are you asking about Horned Owl Hollow?"

My mother raised her eyebrows giving me that "you know what I mean" look. I never could hide anything from her.

"Okay, we had a man stop in the store. Laine seems to have hit it off with him. He's from Iowa, but he's in town on business, and he asked her out." Oh. I should have left that part out. I massaged my forehead, clearly reverting to insecurities about losing my sister.

"A man? From out of state? So what? You think he's going to kidnap her and carry her across state lines?"

I laughed. "You're worse than me. You do know Laine is going to be thirty next month. She's old enough to cross state lines if she chooses."

"And you're thirty-three. Am I ever going to become a grandmother?"

I choked on my bite of cookie. My mother patted me on the back while she laughed. "Well, if the two of you won't get serious about dating, kidnapping a husband for one of you is my only hope."

I retrieved a napkin from the kitchen to wipe my face. "I did get serious about dating. Dating didn't get serious with me."

She squinted at me, looking for a clue to something I wasn't saying, shook a finger at me, then took a deep breath. "Let's stick with Laine for the moment. Tell me about this man."

For the moment? Could she sense the electricity that seemed to have sparked between me and Chance? I didn't want to think too much about that. Better to focus on Laine. "I don't know much, except he seems good enough on the surface. He's handsome, which she's loving. He's polite. Well educated. An appreciation for antiques and collectibles, so they have something in common."

"Tell me what your gut says."

I knew what she was asking. She and I both had an extra sense, the same sense that made us conduits for the residual energy that remained when people passed on. "I'm reserving judgment," I said.

"What aren't you telling me?"

I wasn't ready to tell her about Chance. I hadn't even been aware of him myself until yesterday. I chose to stay off that path and instead told her about my visit from Quint.

"I knew something was off. I tried to balance your chakras for you today." She leaned over her knees. "Did you have another manifestation?"

Again, how did she know? "Yes."

She stared at me, waiting for me to elaborate. Since I didn't know what to do about Norma Lombard's most recent visit, I remained silent.

"Well?" she asked.

Holding out wouldn't solve anything. If anyone knew what I should do, my mother would. "She showed me something in the Lombards' house, but I don't know why. Or what I'm supposed to do about what I saw."

My mom straightened and studied me a moment. "Unfinished business." She held out her arms in surrender. "I don't suppose the Lombards have asked for help finding out what that is."

"No. Darren Lombard thinks I'm a crackpot, at best. Or an opportunist."

"What about Quint? He doesn't believe you stole the collection, does he?"

"My impression was he was focusing on Darren Lombard and the idea of insurance fraud."

"What do you think?"

I chuckled. "There's a house full of suspects, all with a motive to steal those figurines."

"Did you share your list of suspects with Quint?"

I was losing patience. "Why the third degree? Isn't that Quint's job? Figure out who the bad guy is?"

That earned me a reprimand, if not in words, then clearly through her expression.

"I don't know the Lombards. Not really," I said in my defense. "I'm not about to start accusing people of a crime with no evidence."

"Then start with the motive and let Quint find the evidence. Seems to me he could use a leg up. He never could see what was right in front of him." She motioned at me as her example.

"Sometimes what's right in front of him isn't the obvious choice," I said, tongue in cheek.

She shrugged. "His loss."

I loved my mother, and leaned across to hug her—my strongest supporter.

"It wouldn't hurt to tell Quint about the motives." Mom grabbed a cookie, took a bite and shook it at me. "Now tell me more about this new man in Laine's life. You know she never tells me anything."

"Already told you all I know. Not my place to say, even if I knew more."

"Handsome, huh? I suppose that's a good start." She eyed me suspiciously. "And don't think I can't see when you're hiding something from me. There's a certain glow inside of you. One

I haven't seen since you broke things off with Quint. I know better than to believe it's due to him."

I grinned. "Must be my balanced chakras."

She swatted the air in front of her face. "I can wait."

Good. Because even if Robert Chance stirred something inside me, I wasn't sure I was ready to be stirred.

Chapter 19

On my way to *Whimsical Collectibles* on Sunday, I stopped at Carson's gallery. I'd had confirmation of Alice Pugh's artwork from her great-granddaughter, but part of the puzzle was still missing. I walked in and looked for Carson.

He appeared a moment later, munching on a piece of pizza. "Elle, honey. What can I do you for?"

"This might be a long shot," I said, "but are you familiar with a local artist named Alice Pugh?"

"Am I?" he said with enough exaggeration that I knew he was. "There are things of hers all over town, although you'd never know it." He set down his pizza and wiped his hands on a paper towel. He took me by the arm and led me out to the riverwalk behind his shop. "Let me show you."

Old buildings lined the riverwalk, where the city had originally sprung up. Much of the old charm remained, along with improvements that had been made through the years—gardens planted between blocks of pavers, park benches, old-fashioned streetlights overhead. We walked for two blocks before we left the riverwalk and stopped beside the one high-rise building in town. Built in the early 1900s, the stone building had fallen into disrepair. Scaffolding surrounded the perimeter while restoration was being done to keep plaster from falling on passersby. Carson extended his arms to the stone eagles above either side of the entrance.

"Are you telling me she made the eagles?" I asked.

"Have you never read the plaque?" he asked with a note of impatience.

A bronze plaque was embedded in the brickwork on one side of the doors. "Dedicated March 1921," I read.

Carson shook a hand with more emphasis and I stepped closer.

Beneath the dedication, a quote in small script: *May the eagles forever guard those who come and go from this building, with appreciation to Alice Mansfield Pugh.*

I'd lived in Longhill all these years and never noticed the eagles? Granted, when we were kids the only businesses in the tower were a lawyer's office and a realtor. Occupancy had declined as the tower fell into disrepair, until the recent restorations. I'd never had reason to visit the tower.

I stepped back and craned my neck to see the fifteen stories towering above me. Were there eagles on the roof, too?

"Come, come," Carson said. hurrying me along.

We reached the park on the corner, the one with a sculpture of a group of children playing. "Are you serious?" I said half to myself.

"It's right there, honey. Read it for yourself."

A plaque at the base of the statue with a literary quote about children playing in open spaces, dedicated by Alice Mansfield Pugh. "Even if I'd read her name, I don't suppose I would have known who she was," I said.

Carson shrugged. "You know how it is. Nobody pays attention. It's a miracle she even got credit."

I knew that feeling too well. Alice had left her fingerprints on this town. "I think Martin would like to see this. And Alice's great-granddaughter."

"Why all the interest in Alice Mansfield Pugh?" Carson asked.

"She did a piece for the Lombards. At Horned Owl Hollow. They asked me in to assess a figurine collection." I turned to him. "That place is full of treasures."

"If they're looking to sell any of Alice Pugh's work, give them my name," Carson said. "I'll even split the commission with you."

"I doubt they'd sell it. The sculpture is of family, but I suppose you never know." We retraced our steps beside the river. "Isn't it funny?" I said. "You see these things every day and never pay attention to them. Hiding in plain sight."

"No appreciation for the finer things in life," Carson said. "Not like you and me, who look for the stories that go with them."

I chuckled. "Don't give me too much credit. I missed them, too." I gave him a quick hug. "Thank you for sharing Alice's work with me. I think her family will be interested, too." I left him at the gallery and continued on to *Whimsical Collectibles*.

"About time you got here," Laine greeted me when I walked in. She yawned loudly.

"Took a side trip on my way in. Carson was showing me some things in town I hadn't noticed before."

Laine's eyes were droopy, but she gave me a lazy sort of smile, the kind that made me think she'd had an all-night guest.

"Late night?" I asked.

"You might say that."

"You seem pretty relaxed today."

She giggled. "No, I'm not going to tell you. Not yet."

She didn't need to. Her feelings were written on her face. "You know, you didn't have to come in today," I said. "I can manage. If you want to take advantage of the fact he's in town."

She giggled again. "Oh, I definitely want to take advantage of him, but I don't think I could stay awake long enough at the moment."

Likely because she'd already taken advantage of him, or he of her, all night. At least one of us was getting lucky.

Which sent my thoughts to Robert Chance.

Since her divorce, my mother had had several casual relationships. I didn't see the appeal. That didn't stop me from being envious of my sister. I might not want a relationship, but I had my share of lonely nights. Did I want to change that?

Chapter 20

I generally spent Monday mornings at home, updating the inventory on the antiques store website.

Laine surprised me by calling before nine o'clock. After yesterday, I figured she'd probably be sleeping in after another late night with her majordomo. I answered, anticipating she might want to go to breakfast.

"Wanted to let you know I'm headed to Iowa for a couple days. Gavin wants to show me his castle—well, not *his* castle, but the one where he lives. I'll be home in time to open the store on Thursday."

My heart hammered. *Are you sure that's a good idea?* The words played in my head, but I didn't speak them out loud. The last thing I wanted to do was alienate my sister, and questioning her choices would start an argument.

"Promise me you'll text me when you get there. And at lunchtime. And when you're heading home."

She laughed. "You're worse than Mom when it comes to being a hovering parent."

I was aware, but Mr. Majordomo was still an unknown quantity in my book. I didn't want anything to happen to my sister. "Have you told Mom you're going out of town with him?"

"You know I haven't. And don't you tell her, either. Or, if you do, tell her it's a work-related thing. I'm going to see antique furniture and collectibles."

"She knows when I'm lying, you know."

Laine laughed. Better than scolding me for worrying about her. "I'll text you every day. Please don't worry about me, Elle. I'll be fine."

She disconnected and I stared at my phone. Laine was a grown woman, I reminded myself for the umpteenth time. Our father wasn't stealing her away. She'd return home. I had to believe that.

My phone rang again.

"Is this Elspeth Barclay?" a man asked.

"Yes."

"This is Doctor Brown at General Hospital. Martin Foster listed this as his contact number."

I rose to my feet. Had something happened to Martin?

"I have his DNA test results and I'd like to go over them. Can you ask him to come to my office at the hospital? I have an open appointment at ten-thirty. Do you think he can make that?"

"I'll contact him right away, and if it's a problem, I'll call you back." I took the doctor's information, disconnected, and called Faith Lombard.

"Can you take Martin to the doctor's office?" I asked. "They have his DNA results."

"They called Darren, too," Faith said. "Why does Martin need to go to the doctor's office? Can't they confirm they're related over the phone, like they did for Darren?"

They'd confirmed the results over the phone? "I don't know. The doctor made a ten-thirty appointment. Do you want me to take him?"

"I can take him," she said. "You know, I'm worried about Martin. He doesn't look well. Do you suppose that's why the doctor wants to see him in person?"

Didn't look well? Was he aging, the way the other lost sailor had? "I couldn't say."

"I can swing by the store and pick you up if you'd like to go along."

"I would like to, but I'm not at the store. I'm at home," I said.

"Then we'll come there. I don't want to upset Darren any more than he is already. Honestly, I've told him his grandmother is lingering in the house, but having you corroborate what I've said seems to have unsettled him even more."

"I'll be ready."

Faith and Martin arrived at ten-o'clock in the same Mercedes Chance had driven last time he'd picked me up.

I climbed into the backseat and Faith started out.

"Do you mind if we hear what the doctor has to say?" she asked Martin.

Martin craned to look over his shoulder at me. "I think I'd prefer that."

His complexion looked gray, the lines in his face deeper than a few days ago. Had I misjudged my first guess at his age?

We checked in at the doctor's office, where we didn't have to wait long. The doctor seemed surprised to see three of us. I made the introductions without disclosing what was at stake with the test results, and he brought an extra guest chair into his office.

He leveled his attention on Martin. "First, the DNA testing confirms you are related to Darren Lombard. The reason I've called you in is that we stumbled on something else during the testing." He glanced at me and Faith. "If you'd prefer, we can talk about that privately."

"You may speak freely," Martin said.

The doctor leaned over his desk. "You have a DNA repair-deficiency disorder which presents as Werner Syndrome. Werner Syndrome is similar to progeria."

Like the article I'd read. Two men, both lost in the Bermuda Triangle, both returning a hundred years later. What were the odds they'd both have the same DNA abnormality?

"Progeria?" Martin repeated.

"Premature aging in children, except Werner Syndrome presents in adults. This is a fairly rare occurrence, and I'd like to do more testing to determine exactly what's going on. In order to treat you properly, I'll need your medical history, as well as your family history. This sort of thing is usually genetic."

Faith's mouth dropped open. She and I exchanged glances.

The other sailor who'd claimed to have survived the disappearance of the *Cyclops* had been diagnosed with Werner Syndrome. The article had also stated they thought the sailor was mentally unbalanced. No doubt, they'd think the same of Martin if he told them his story. "Uh," I began. "Mr. Foster's medical records were lost. And as to his family history..." I shot a glance at Martin. "Well, that's why they did the DNA test. He was..." How to phrase this delicately without sounding like an idiot? "Lost from the family for a while. In fact, they'd given up hopes of finding him. His branch of the family is... gone."

The doctor nodded. "We are a not-for-profit hospital. Considering how rare this condition is, treating him might provide insight into this disease. We have programs that would allow us to absorb the medical expenses."

That didn't sound philanthropic. "Are you saying he'd be your science experiment?" I asked.

"Not at all," the doctor replied. "He could help us understand what's happening. We have programs to treat indigent patients."

"I'll have you know I am not indigent," Martin said.

Right. Back in his day, they probably gave a horse to the doctor in payment of their medical bills. I took Martin's hand—his skin wasn't as smooth as it had been a few days ago. Wrinkles. "Healthcare is quite expensive these days," I said gently. "Considering your lack of documentation, and until your financial situation is settled, you'd have to accept assistance if you want to pursue medical assessment or treatment."

Faith snapped her mouth shut. She seemed to come around, but I gave her a quick shake of the head to keep her from saying anything.

"This DNA disorder," Martin said. "I don't understand..."

"The blood of Werner Syndrome patients exhibits accelerated DNA methylation changes, similar to those observed in normal aging according to a molecular biomarker of aging known as an epigenetic clock," the doctor said.

Faith sighed. "I don't understand a word you just said."

"Essentially, methylation is alterations to your DNA based on a variety of factors, including your diet, which might make you more susceptible to cancer or certain disease. In this case, these alterations are aging you prematurely."

"Or catching up with the time you've been missing," I said quietly.

Martin looked lost and confused. He turned to me. Right. I was the trustworthy one. His compass.

"I think he'll need time to consider what you're telling him before he agrees to additional testing," I told the doctor. "You said the DNA-repair-whatever-it-is was genetic." Or was he aging faster because he'd traveled one hundred years through a wormhole? "Could this methylation be influenced by extreme environmental influences?"

The doctor tilted his head. "Such as?"

I didn't dare provide a science fiction explanation. How the experience hadn't ripped Martin limb from limb was amazing enough, but had it altered him on a molecular level? "Um," again I hesitated.

I was *not* going to tell the doctor Martin was more than a hundred years old, and my theory for this abnormality was time catching up to him. Martin had no evidence to support his story, even if it was true.

"Give us time to research this Werner Syndrome," I said. "And we'll make another appointment after we've had a chance to learn more."

"Yes, that's a good idea," the doctor said. He wrote a list of things for us to research, slid the paper to Martin, and handed us a printed copy of Martin's and Darren's DNA results. "I expect you'll have more questions after you've had a chance to review the literature. Make an appointment when you're ready to talk, and I'll make sure you get right in. A copy of the DNA test results, as well as the medical aspects we've discovered, will also be on your online portal."

"Online portal?" Martin asked.

"I'll help you," I said.

Faith rose from her seat and extended a hand. "Thank you, doctor."

"Please contact me with your questions," the doctor said once more.

"Of course." She headed for the door, and Martin and I hurried to catch up.

"I don't understand any of this," Martin said while we walked to the car.

He sat in the back seat with me, and I gave him a quick overview of the modern-day healthcare system while Faith drove us home. Then I told him about a movie I'd seen that might help—*The Portrait of Dorian Gray*. Hollywood to the rescue. I didn't know how accurate the portrayal would be, but it should give him broad strokes, at least.

"A movie?" he asked. "At the theater?"

For a moment, I'd forgotten how 'out of time' he was. "We can watch movies anytime we want now. Most movies are available to buy or rent or watch on demand."

"You have a theater in the house?" Martin asked Faith.

"You can watch them on the television," she answered.

He wiped at his face with his hands. When he spoke, his voice was hollow. "What you're telling me is I'm growing older at an accelerated rate?"

I nodded. "My guess is time won't be denied. You've come a hundred years into the future and the powers that be intend to make up for lost time."

"I'm going to age one hundred years?"

I took his hands again. "I'm not a doctor or a scientist. If we tell the doctor you were propelled a hundred years into the future through a wormhole, he isn't likely to believe you. The same way Darren doesn't believe it. What happened to you is quite fantastic. I could well be wrong, and this syndrome the doctor wants to test for might provide different answers." I told him about the article I'd read and offered to look for it again so he could read it, as well.

He shook his head. "No, I think you said it well when you suggested he wanted to use me as a science experiment." He squeezed his eyes closed. "I'm more inclined to believe your hypothesis. As strange as everything around me seems, I cannot deny the truths my eyes show me. This is not the same world I left behind." He sputtered. "I'm not entirely sure I haven't died and this is some sort of afterlife I'm being forced to navigate."

"That would make us dead, too," Faith said. "And I assure you, we are very much alive. I find the fact of your existence exhilarating. Much more exciting than ghosts wandering the mansion."

Speaking of which, she'd driven us to Horned Owl Hollow rather than dropping me at home. "Did you forget about me?" I asked her.

She startled for a moment, then smiled. "I think you should come in. Darren won't be able to deny the DNA report, and there is now a record of a relative he can't expunge."

Did someone want to *expunge* him? "How did you get your black eye?" I asked Martin once more.

He stiffened. "Clumsy."

I didn't believe him. Shivers reminded me of the vision I'd had in the store yesterday. What was in the basement of Horned Owl Hollow?

"I don't think we should tell Darren about Martin's illness," I told Faith.

"No, I agree," Faith said. "But he does need to know about the familial match."

"You said he already got his results," I said. "Seems as if he already knows."

Faith invited me inside and called for Darren. My eyes were glued to the staircase at the end of the hallway. I had to find a reason to visit the basement, to see the crack in the wall and find out what was in the hidden room.

"If you'll excuse me," Martin said. "I need a moment to myself." He headed up the staircase.

"Where has he gotten to?" Faith said, leaving me in the hallway alone.

Now or never. I rushed downstairs.

Stone walls. Concrete floor. Storage. Not a turn-of-the-century kitchen. I followed the path my dream had taken, past a dumbwaiter that was likely out of service. Past another door that might have been the ice chest when this room had been a kitchen. Into another small room that opened to the other side of the basement.

The wall.

My heart pounded as I reached toward the hidden door, but I needn't have bothered. The door opened before I could touch it. I glanced over my shoulder, expecting someone to have followed me, someone to be looking for me when I wasn't where they'd left me. The basement was dead-quiet. The hairs on my arms stood straight up.

"What am I supposed to see?" I asked no one in particular.

I took a step into the hidden room. The shelves along the walls held vintage appliances. Irons and curling rods and bread pans. A step deeper into the room, a spark of light glinted off porcelain.

The Staffordshire collection.

No. I wasn't going to be accused of stealing the figurines. I reached for my phone, dialed Quint—and got his voicemail.

"Quint. I found the stolen figurines. They're here. In the mansion. Listen. Someone here doesn't want the rightful owner to inherit them. Talk to Darren's sister. She's in financial trouble. And her husband. He's planning to file for divorce as soon as she inherits her share of the estate." What about Chance? Where did he fit into the picture. "And there's..." My phone clicked. I checked the screen. Dead.

As I turned, the door slammed shut, closing me into total darkness.

Chapter 21

The hidden room closed in around me. I extended my hands to blindly probe for the door, or a wall, or... something.

If I called for help, would the Lombards find me? Along with their stolen Staffordshire collection. Which made me look guilty.

I found what I hoped was the door handle. I tugged. Pushed. Jiggled. Which way had the door opened? I slapped flat palms against the door and grunted my frustration. Flashes of panic sparked in my head.

"Elle?"

The muffled voice encouraged me. I slapped at the wall again. The door gave way beneath my hands and I stumbled into the arms of Robert Chance.

"What are you doing here? How did you...?" He looked over my shoulder into the room. Surely, he saw the collection. Was he the one who put it there?

As much as I enjoyed drawing on his strength, I regained my composure and pushed away.

"We should probably talk," he said.

My trust issues kicked in. I crossed my arms, struggling for what bravado I could muster.

"Let's start with how you got locked in the Prohibition room," he said.

"You wouldn't believe me if I told you."

He lifted one eyebrow. "You don't give me enough credit. How did you get into the house? I would have expected Darren to deny you entrance."

"I came with Faith."

He nodded. "That explains why I didn't see your car. And you're down here because...?"

How much did he know? "You saw what was in that room, and you didn't seem surprised. Something you want to tell me?"

He glanced over my shoulder once more.

Time to go on the offensive. "I've already called the police." He didn't need to know the call had dropped.

"That's unfortunate." His tone of voice sent another shiver of dread across my skin.

Would Chance kill me? Lock me in again? "How did you know I was in there?" I asked. "Are you the one who stole the collection?"

"I heard noise coming from inside the room." He glanced at the ceiling and wiped a hand across his mouth. "I suppose I'll have to trust you."

Wasn't this where the killer confessed, right before he killed the person he told?

"Over the past several weeks, even before Martin's unexpected arrival, things have gone missing." He reached inside the room and shined a flashlight across the shelves. "This room was used to store booze during Prohibition. To my knowledge, the room was mostly forgotten after they moved the kitchen upstairs. I'm not sure the family remembers it's here. How did you know...?"

Would he believe me if I told him about my vision? Did I care if he thought I was a nutcase? Right now, I was only interested in getting out of here. "Norma showed it to me."

Chance nodded. He believed me?

"The collection should be safe here, especially if I put a lock on the door," he said. "I suspect someone in the family is trying to raise cash, cash they won't get if Martin inherits. At least that's my take. If he is the rightful heir, the collection belongs to him."

Another emotion settled on me. Relief? The fact he wanted to keep the collection safe made him one of the good guys. "The DNA test confirms Martin is family. Do you know how he got his black eye?"

Chance frowned. "He insists it was an accident. He won't leave. This is *his* house."

I took hold of Chance's arm—a solid, well-muscled arm. My breath caught in my throat and I let go just as quickly, surprised at how much this man affected me. "Will that stop someone from trying to force him out, one way or another?"

"What do you suggest?" Chance asked, his voice a tad lower.

"If he's the rightful heir, can he turn the rest of them out?"

"He'd have to prove his identity, and he doesn't have any documentation unless we can match the fingerprint on his dog tags to the Navy's records. Darren was ready to sell. He wants to move. There's the off-chance he'll honor the trust document and walk away."

"I doubt that. I overheard a few things I probably shouldn't have. Too many people have too much riding on their share of the inheritance."

As Chance brushed a strand of hair off my face, heat raced through my body. *Really?*

"I want to help him," Chance said. "Do you trust me?"

Now *that* was the million-dollar question. My trust levels were pretty much depleted. As much as I wanted to, for more reasons than helping Martin, could I trust Robert Chance? "How do I know you didn't hire someone to impersonate Martin Foster?"

"The same way I know you didn't," he countered. "Didn't you say the DNA test confirms he's family?"

I went hands on hips. "I have no reason to hire an imposter, even if I knew the family's financial situation."

"Not even to acquire the Staffordshire collection?"

I scoffed. "Let's be serious. It's a nice collection, and the commission would be a respectable amount of money, but it isn't going to make me a millionaire."

We stared each other down a long moment.

"Realistically, the pieces are still on the property. Technically, that means they're not stolen," he said. "For the time being, I think it best not to mention what we've found. Not until we can prove Martin is who he says he is."

"How do you propose to find proof?" Martin's disease might kill him before he could inherit. On the other hand, if Martin exhibited signs of rapid aging, he might look the part sooner rather than later.

"Norma Lombard was convinced Martin would return. She spent years communicating with the Navy, asking for his

records so he could be identified. She ran into a lot of red tape."
He tilted his head. "I'm not family, so I can't request a copy of
the prints, and Darren doesn't seem inclined to do so. Which
brings me to what you plan to tell the police, since you've said
you called them."

Heat flushed into my face. "I did call them." In spite of my
misgivings, Chance seemed to be on Martin's side. "But the call
dropped before I could tell them where the collection is."

"You can't very well tell them you were mistaken. What are
you going to say?"

Quint could be a bulldog when he wanted to be, especially
on the job. If I tried to tell him I was wrong, he'd see right
through the lie. I guess that meant I trusted Chance—at least
a little. "Nothing? That, according to your theory, they're still
on the property, so technically, they haven't been stolen?" I
shrugged. "I can avoid the person I told. Until we can get the
records from the Navy to prove Martin's identity."

Chance ran a hand through his hair. "It's still an uphill
battle. They'll take one look at him and laugh in his face."

"Maybe. Maybe not."

He narrowed his eyes at me. "Care to explain?"

I trusted him *a little*. Not enough to explain how Martin
was aging at an accelerated rate.

Footsteps sounded on the main staircase. Chance grabbed
my hand, tugged me into the secret room, and pulled the door
closed. I gasped, and he covered my mouth.

While I was attracted to Chance, I was determined not to
acknowledge it. I pushed him away and he quietly shushed me.
"This might be our chance to catch the thief," he whispered.

He turned off the flashlight in his hand.

A faraway voice called my name. I didn't like being locked in, and I wasn't going to miss a chance to escape a second time, unless...

"How will we get out of here?" I whispered.

He clicked the flashlight on for half a second, highlighting the door handle. He turned the beam off and we were in total darkness once more, making me more aware of him.

The voice calling me grew closer—Faith. She'd trusted me, and I'd betrayed that trust by wandering off in her house on my own. Standing in the hidden room beside the stolen goods—or relocated goods, going by Chance's logic—I would look guilty. Again, I chose to trust Chance.

"I can't imagine where she could have gone," Faith said.

"Perhaps she's decided to go home on her own," Martin replied.

"Without saying anything?" Faith said something more, but her voice grew faint. They were leaving.

"Elle." Chance's breath tickled my ear.

Get a hold of yourself, woman.

I drew a deep breath and fumbled for the door. "I have to get out of here."

He turned on the flashlight, pressed his ear to the door, then nodded. "I hear them going upstairs."

I straightened my clothes. How was I going to leave the house without being noticed?

Chance put his hand on the door handle, but didn't open it. "I'll keep Martin safe until we get everything sorted out."

"What do you propose?" I asked, my voice too breathy. I cleared my throat.

"We have two options. We can get his Naval records and prove he is who he says he is, or I can go ahead with my plan to buy Horned Owl Hollow from Darren."

Before I could argue, he held up a hand to stop me.

"It's Martin's home. I wouldn't throw him out."

"Which isn't the same as family. What if he becomes incapacitated? That's a big commitment." One that wasn't lost on me. I hadn't met many men who were big on commitment.

Chance studied me a moment longer. "I've already lived that life. I know what's involved. In the meantime, if I buy the estate, he can remain in his own home." He let go of the handle and moved toward me. I stepped back.

"I've heard the rest of the family's plans for the money, as well," he said. "The longer they're put off, the more desperate they're likely to become. I don't see Darren as the type to have given Martin a black eye, or Blair for that matter, but someone took a swing at him."

"A hired thug? What do we do?" I said the words before the implication—that we were in this plan together—sunk in.

Chance smiled at me, hearing clearly what I hadn't meant to say. "Step one is what you plan to do about the collection. I won't stop you from telling the police where it is, but I will ask you to wait until we've figured out what the best option is for Martin."

"Quint is going to hound me until I tell him. I won't be able to avoid him forever."

"Quint? The policeman you told?"

I nodded.

"Unless you went off the grid for a few days. Can you take time off work? I know a place you can stay where no one would look for you." His eyes darkened. "Except me."

Chapter 22

My cell phone rang, startling me. Hadn't it been dead minutes earlier? I stared at the display—my mother—and answered.

"I think you need time off from work," she said. My eyes widened. Leave it to my mother to sense something was going on.

"Why?" I asked.

"Quint stopped by my office looking for you. He asked if I had any idea where you'd gone. Honey, there's a ripple in the air. What's going on? Do you want to tell me?"

"No." My thoughts scrambled. "And I can't take time off. Laine isn't here to run the store for me."

"Where is she?"

Oops. Laine had asked me not to tell her. "She went to check out some antique furniture. In Iowa."

"There's a spirit hovering near you. I can sense it from here."

I glanced around, searching for signs of Norma. "Yes. I'm aware."

"Are you safe?"

I glanced at Chance. "From the spirit? Yes, I think so. She's asked for my help." Safe from Chance? I wasn't so sure. "I called Quint about a case he's working. I'll circle back to him."

"Be careful, honey."

I disconnected the call.

Chance blocked my way to the door, or at least that's how it felt. The room wasn't big, after all. "What are you going to tell him? Quint?" he asked.

Good question. "I'll relay what you told me about things going missing around the house. Would you be willing to talk to him?"

Chance didn't answer, no doubt assessing how much he trusted me, as well.

"I won't tell him where the collection is," I went on. "Only that it's in the house in a safe place until the questions about Martin's inheritance are resolved."

"Isn't that obstruction, or something?"

Probably, but Quint might let me get away with it. At least in the short term. I could justify not telling him by assuring him that since the collection was still on the property, it hadn't been stolen, the same way Chance had. "He and I have history," I said. "I'm not going to go into hiding, especially since I have a store to run. For Martin's sake, I suggest you tell the police what you've witnessed since Martin's arrival."

"And by the police, you mean Quint? The man you have history with?"

Was he asking about my history with Quint?

Chance had left his job to come home and take care of his father, take on his father's job. A family commitment. He wanted to protect the collection from a thief in the house, or so he said. I still couldn't be sure he wasn't that thief, and yet everything I was learning about him painted him as a caring, trustworthy person. He could have left me locked in the—what had he called it? The Prohibition room? Could have taken advantage of me, and yet he'd shown me the way out, even if he was blocking it. I moved toward the door to prove my theory and he stepped to one side.

I exited the room. "I was engaged to Quint."

"Was," he repeated.

"Turns out he wasn't husband material, so we ended things."

Chance stared at me, probably waiting for me to elaborate. Trusting him with more information was farther than I was willing to go—for now.

"Faith will be wondering where I got to," I said. "Why don't you check to see where everyone is so they don't think I'm running around the house robbing them blind?"

Chance grinned. "I can do that. Tell them you had to use the powder room."

I nodded.

He took my hand and led me to the servants' staircase, put a finger to his lips, and crept upstairs ahead of me. When we reached the main hall, he pointed out the powder room. Again, I nodded. He pressed a kiss to my lips, startling me once more, grinned, and disappeared through the conservatory.

"Oh, there you are!" Faith exclaimed.

I shot a glance at the powder room and a look of understanding crossed her face. "I should have known," she said. "Darren's in the library." She leaned closer and lowered her voice. "I haven't told him about Martin's health."

Faith led me to the library where Darren sat with Gloria and Blair.

Darren's expression was tight. "Faith tells me you have our guest's test results."

"I do."

"How do I know the two of you haven't tampered with the results?" he asked.

A baseless accusation. Did he expect me to confess to a crime I hadn't committed? "It's my understanding you have a similar report."

Faith handed him Martin's printout from the doctor. "Martin is family."

"That's not acceptable," Darren said.

I laughed. "Not sure you have any control over the matter."

"Does that mean we can't sell the house?" Gloria asked.

"We can contest any claims he might make," Darren said. "Or we can give him a share of the proceeds."

Blair rose from his seat and stormed out.

Gloria stared after her husband, then rose to her feet and waved her arms around her head. "This Martin person waltzes into our home out of nowhere and we're supposed to hand everything over?"

"That's not going to happen." Darren scowled at me. "You can go now. You've delivered your information."

"I trust nothing untoward will happen to Martin," I said. "No more accidents? No sudden illnesses?" Even though I knew of his declining health.

"Are you accusing me of something?" Darren asked.

"No. But I *am* reminding you that the number of people who know he's here, who know who he is, is expanding."

Darren's face grew ruddy and Faith touched my arm. "I'll take you home, dear," she said to me.

We walked into the main hall, where Chance leaned against the wall, arms and ankles crossed.

"I'll keep an eye on Martin," he said.

Faith smiled. "I know you will."

My trust issues kicked up once more. Chance had something to gain in all of this, too. Keeping an eye on Martin didn't necessarily guarantee his safety.

Chapter 23

A fter Faith dropped me off at home, I hurried inside.

I had a text from Laine. Martin Foster might not be my personal responsibility, but Laine was—or at least more so than Martin. Her trip to Iowa with the majordomo left me decidedly uncomfortable. Instead of shooting off a text reply, I phoned her.

"Elle, you should see this place," she breathed.

I closed my eyes and exhaled with relief that she was safe. At least for the time being. I made myself a cup of tea and sat at my kitchen table while she described the medieval feel of the castle, despite the modern décor, and what she described as the "museum room." Collections kept under lock and key and security systems she couldn't begin to explain.

Her voice shifted into something on the edge of annoyance. "By the way. Mom was looking for you. Did she find you?"

"Yes."

"I thought you agreed not to tell her where I was."

"I didn't tell her about Gavin, only that you were on an antiques expedition in Iowa."

Laine sighed heavily. "What's going on at home?"

I proceeded to tell her how I'd gotten locked in the Prohibition room at Horned Owl Hollow and how Chance had rescued me. I didn't tell her about the electricity that seemed to exist between me and the Lombards' caretaker. Until I knew what to do with that, I was keeping that to myself. Instead, I told her about Martin's DNA results.

"I read an article recently about the astronauts who'd spent time on the Space Station," she said. "It said their DNA was altered by their time in space. If Martin actually did pass through some sort of space-time wormhole, do you suppose that could be the reason for his broken DNA, or whatever it is the doctor said was screwed up?"

"I was wondering the same thing, but I have no idea who to ask, or even how to bring it up. Can you imagine me asking a physicist if traveling through a wormhole could alter DNA? They'd either laugh at me or want to use Martin as a science experiment."

Someone knocked on my door, a visitor I likely didn't want to see. "I think Quint's here," I whispered as I crouched beside the counter, out of sight.

"What are you going to tell him?"

That was the question of the day. Did I even want to answer the door?

"Open the door, Elle. I can see you," Quint called.

"How can he see you?" Laine asked.

"I'm in the kitchen. He's looking through the window in the door. Are you okay?" I asked her one more time.

"Stop worrying about me," she said. "I'm a big girl, and there are other people here besides me and Gavin."

I'd told Chance I could handle Quint. It was time to find out. "I'd better talk to Quint. Call me later."

Laine laughed. "You know I will. I need to make sure *you're* okay."

I disconnected the call and opened the door.

Quint had one hand high on the door frame, an annoyed gleam in his eye. "Want to tell me why you hung up on me? And where the stolen goods are?"

I glanced at the phone in my hand, the one with thirty-two percent battery life remaining. "My phone lost signal."

"You going to invite me in?"

Not a chance. Inviting him in was one thing I'd sworn never to do again after I'd seen him with another woman. I stepped onto the porch and crossed my arms.

"What? You don't trust me now?" he asked.

I laughed. "That's on you, buddy. No reason for you to come inside."

His jaw clenched while he straightened. "What about the stolen collection?"

I quailed. Time to test how far I could stretch the legal definition of stolen. "It's still at the mansion, so technically, it's not actually stolen, is it?"

"Does the owner know where it is? Because if he doesn't, it's stolen."

I twisted my lips, unable to squirm out of this. Might as well tell him what else Chance had told me, about the other things that had gone missing, things that might also be hidden somewhere in the mansion. I filled him in on Martin's unexpected arrival, and how the family had motives to cheat him out of his inheritance.

Quint's posture relaxed, giving me his full attention, The way he gave people one hundred percent of his focus was one of the things that had attracted me to him in the first place. Now, it made me uncomfortable.

"How did you get involved with them, again?" he asked.

I went over the invitation to sell the collection, then the contract after Martin had arrived.

"Let me get this straight. Darren Lombard was preparing to sell the mansion, and figured he'd unload the figurines?"

I nodded.

"Then this guy shows up on his doorstep saying he's the rightful owner of all of it?"

Again, I nodded. "Apparently, the house and its contents were put in trust for Martin Foster."

"The guy who went missing a hundred years ago."

"Right."

Quint shimmied his shoulders. "This guy isn't a ghost, is he? I know how you can be."

I tensed. My extra abilities often made others uncomfortable, and I could hardly blame them for doubting me, but pointing to my sensitivity as a defect was unkind, at best. "He isn't a ghost." I managed a sarcastic smile and added, "Although the mansion is haunted, and the energy that remains is concerned about the line of succession."

Quint rolled his eyes. "I knew it. What stake, exactly, does a ghost have in who owns the place?"

"Martin Foster is the rightful heir. You want proof he is who he says he is? You can track down his fingerprints with the Navy. Wouldn't they be in AFIS or something?"

"From a hundred years ago? I doubt it. Didn't you say this guy died in 1918?" Quint huffed. "Where is the collection, so I can close this case?"

"I can't tell you."

"Elle..."

I shook my head. "Not until the legalities are cleared up. You still need to investigate Gloria and Blair Jacoby, and I wouldn't put it past Darren and Faith to be putting things aside. They all had plans for the proceeds of the sale." What about Chance? Was the Prohibition room a temporary hiding place, until Chance could sell the figurines? "And the caretaker," I added, albeit more quietly.

"The caretaker," Quint repeated. "What does he stand to lose in all of this, other than his job?"

A mantle of guilt lay on my shoulders. If Chance had told me the truth about his past, Quint would find out, and Chance could still buy the mansion. Would Chance be angry at me for outing him?

Chapter 24

Tablet in hand, I spent my Tuesday morning walking through *Whimsical Collectibles* for items that hadn't sold. Out with the old. I collected those items that had reached their contract expiration date and carried them to the front counter to contact the owners for final disposition.

I didn't bother to turn the shop lights on. The plate glass windows allowed plenty of natural lighting. The dark store—and the business hours sign—didn't stop Gloria Jacoby from knocking on the door.

I was beginning to wish I'd never met the Lombard family.

"I'm sorry, the store is closed today," I called through the glass.

"If I could have a moment of your time," she replied.

Against my better judgment, I let her in.

She pointed at the hours posted in the window. "How do you make any money when you're closed three days a week?"

"It's fairly common in the industry," I said. "How can I help you today?"

The way she surveyed the store made me want to throw my arms around everything to hide it from her. Was she the one stealing items out of Horned Owl Hollow? Selling them to support her Lladró collection?

"I have my own collection, you know," she said. "Lladró figurines."

"So you've told me."

She shot me a questioning look which I surmised was to see if I was being sarcastic. "Once Darren made me aware of your business, I was curious to see if you might have anything I might be interested in."

Pieces she couldn't afford to buy. "You should come back when the store is open," I said.

She sniffed. "From what I see, you deal in nostalgia more than collectibles."

I didn't need to be rude to her, and I did have a business to run. "I do have a couple Lladró figurines if you're interested in buying one."

A glint of interest sparked in her eyes. "I might be. How do you acquire your inventory? Do you sell on consignment?"

I folded my arms. Was she looking for an outlet? "I do. Fifty-fifty split on anything that sells, price based on recent sales of similar items."

She gasped. "That's robbery!"

"Anyone who wants a better deal can cut out the middleman. Sell themselves."

Gloria held my gaze a moment. "I imagine a middleman provides a certain level of anonymity. You don't tell people who your clients are, do you?"

Interesting. What did she have to hide? "I'm not in the habit of sharing who my clientele are, no, although many of them are regulars and send customers to me."

"So, if I had something to sell, you could sell it for me? Discreetly?"

Her Lladró collection? Or did she want to sell the family treasures? I had to tread lightly. "Yes, as long as there isn't an issue of provenance."

"You mean I'd have to prove I own the piece I want to sell."

"Exactly."

Again, she studied me. "How does one go about consigning items? Not that I would need to do that."

Based on the phone call I'd overheard, she definitely needed to, but doing so was likely beneath her dignity. I explained the intake process, the valuation process, and gave her a tour of the shop. When we reached the cabinet of higher-priced collectibles, she fingered the glass, a look of longing on her face.

"You have customers who buy these all this?" Gloria asked.

I swallowed the sarcastic retort that I wouldn't be in business if I didn't and forced a smile. "I do."

"Are there other stores in town like yours?"

Stores with proprietors who wouldn't know she was selling things that might not belong to her? Assuming she was squirreling away the contents of the mansion—provenance questionable. "My inventory is more eclectic than some. There's a bazaar store on the edge of town with multiple vendors, each with a booth selling their specialty," I told her. "I'm not aware of them doing anything on consignment, however. They purchase their inventory outright."

She shot me a sideways glance. "I see." Her gaze flashed toward the door. "How would I go about selling items on my own?"

There was no way I was giving this woman information on how to cheat her relatives, if that's what she had in mind.

"That depends on what you're trying to sell." If she was talking about her Lladró figurines, I guessed from her phone call she was buying them from a collector or a dedicated site, one which would also buy them back. Then again, Gloria was the type of woman with an image to uphold. Selling pieces from her collection might not be good optics.

"You certainly have a variety of items in your store," she said again.

"I do."

She breathed in, paused, breathed in again. Pursed her lips. "As you know, Darren was preparing to sell Horned Owl Hollow. My husband and I were also considering relocating. No point staying on family property if there's no family left, now, is there?"

I didn't respond.

"I guess what I'm saying is that we have several items we wouldn't want to move when we go." Her gaze returned to me. Checking to see if I believed her story?

Did I?

"If you don't want the business, I can stop by the bazaar and touch base with them," she went on.

That would make her their problem, except I'd promised to help Martin. Well, I hadn't promised, but the energy at Horned Owl Hollow had asked for my help, and I was inclined to offer it where I could. "I'd be happy to help," I said. And hold onto the purloined items until they could be rightfully claimed.

"Well, if I were to use you, we might have to negotiate your terms."

"I can give you the same deal I'm giving Darren. Sixty-forty," I said. "But I have to make a living, too."

She smiled as if she was pleased with herself. "I'll consider it. I suppose I should be off." She extended a limp wrist my direction—did she expect me to kiss her hand or shake it? I did neither.

"Stop by anytime when we're open."

I locked the door behind her and drew a cleansing breath. Across the street, my mother bustled toward the store. I waited for her to reach the door, unlocked it and let her in.

She opened her palm, and displayed three crystals.

"Oh, this must be bad if you're bringing me crystals." I reached behind her to lock the door once more.

"I don't know what's going on, but I do sense you need protection," she said. "I know you don't put much credence in crystals, but they can't hurt, right?"

I scooped up the crystals, put them in my pocket, and hugged my mother. "They can't hurt."

"Do you know where the negative energy is coming from?" she whispered.

I hesitated, not wanting to draw her into whatever was going on with the Lombards, but I needed all the help I could get. I tugged her into the backroom.

Chapter 25

A car was in my driveway when I got home. I parked on the street and approached my visitor.

Robert Chance rolled down the car's window. "Do you want me to move my vehicle?"

"Eventually, yes. Is there something you need?"

He cocked an eyebrow. "I wanted to talk to you away from the mansion."

I glanced at my house. "Have you been waiting for me all day?"

He shook his head. "Took a chance you'd be home after regular business hours. I saw Gloria at the store this morning and decided it might be better to meet with you at your home."

A passenger leaned forward. Martin Foster. "And I concurred."

"You know I didn't have business hours today."

He raised an eyebrow. "What *would have been* business hours, then."

Did I want to invite these guys in? Having Chance inside my house felt too intimate, but I was in too deep. I had to help Martin. My inner voice suggested I find a neutral location, but we'd likely have more privacy here. "Might as well come in." I swept an arm toward my house.

Both men followed me to the door. I told them to have a seat in the living room while I carried my tote to the kitchen counter. How much of a hostess did I need to be to two unexpected visitors? My mother's voice resonated in my head. *Manners are important.*

"Can I get you something to drink?" I asked through the pass-through window.

"Don't suppose you have a bottle of bourbon stashed somewhere," Chance said. "Then again, I'm driving. Coffee would do, if you have it."

"For me, as well," Martin echoed.

I made two cups of coffee and carried their mugs to the living room. "Milk? Sugar?"

"Not for me," Chance said.

"I prefer it black, thank you," Martin said.

I stared at Martin as I handed him his mug. The skin of his face was no longer smooth and tight with the blush of youth. He'd developed tiny lines around his eyes.

Martin took the cup from me, holding my gaze.

"I think it would be wiser to keep him away from Darren and Faith until we can resolve things," Chance said. "He doesn't look well."

I raised my eyebrows, silently asking Martin if he'd mentioned his genetic anomaly to Chance. He gave me a slight shake of his head.

I wiped my hands on my jeans and took a seat.

"I also wanted to talk to you about..." Chance's complexion darkened. He glanced at Martin. "Yesterday."

The fact I'd found the figurines? Or the fact he'd kissed me?

"The floor's all yours," I said.

Chance took a sip of his coffee. "I mentioned my thoughts to Martin. About buying the mansion from Darren turnkey and sharing the house until he could re-establish his identity."

Martin scowled, staring into his mug.

"And what do you think of that idea?" I asked Martin.

He set his mug on the coffee table. "I don't understand all that has happened. One thing I am certain of—Horned Owl Hollow is not the same place I left when I joined the Navy. So many things have changed." He met my gaze. "I didn't want to believe the doctor when he told me about my illness, or whatever this is, but it's hard to question my own eyes. If I'm not long for this world, I'd rather see someone who loves my home take it over."

Then he *was* going to tell Chance.

"You do bring to mind the *Picture of Dorian Gray*," I said. "As if a hundred years of lost time is rushing to catch up with you."

Martin's eyebrows rose. "Dorian Gray, indeed."

"Something I should know?" Chance asked.

"You may be able to explain better," Martin said to me. "If you wouldn't mind."

"You want Chance to know?"

He gave me a short nod, and I tried to explain about the Werner Syndrome diagnosis, or at least as much as I understood.

"Did the doctor give any indication how rapidly his condition would progress?" Chance asked.

"No. It seems to be a fairly rare disease."

Chance huffed. "I'm sorry. This is all just so..."

"Unprecedented," I suggested.

"To say the least." Chance held my gaze. "I'm still not certain someone in the house isn't poisoning him to get him out of the way. That was the first thing I thought when I saw the change in him this morning."

"Do you think they're capable?" I shook my head. "I agree he's pale, but his appearance seems to match what the doctor said would happen. I'd hate to think..." My thoughts raced. "Do you know who's been hiding things at the mansion?"

"I've mentioned the missing items to Darren, but all he says is 'I'll look into it.'" He leaned forward. "I don't suppose Gloria was trying to sell anything when she stopped by your store today?"

"She kept her questions vague. I wasn't sure if she wanted to sell her private collection or something else. Have you told Darren you want to buy the mansion?" I asked.

"Not yet. I'm trying to figure out the legalities, along with everyone else."

Martin cleared his throat. "Do you have a toilet I might use?"

"Of course." I pointed at the staircase. "At the first landing."

He rose from the sofa. "Inside?"

"Yes."

Martin chuckled. "When I left, not everyone had indoor toilets." He walked up the first flight of stairs, found the bathroom door, and muttered once more. "Amazing."

Chance scooted to the edge of the sofa, his voice low. "Have you told anyone where the collection is?"

"Only that it's in the house."

"To your former fiancé."

I shifted uncomfortably. "I also mentioned *someone* had told me other things were going missing."

"You didn't tell him where the collection was? Or who told you about the other items?"

Again, I wondered how much I could trust Chance. "I didn't, but I told him the family all have reasons to sell the mansion, or to sell its assets."

He sat back. "Including me."

"Including you."

"If I offended you when I kissed you..."

Heat warmed my cheeks. "No. More startled than offended."

"Why? You're a beautiful woman, and I sense this attraction isn't entirely one-sided."

"No, but this," I pointed between him and me, "isn't going to happen."

"Because of the situation with the Lombards?"

"For starters, maybe. I also have a healthy level of skepticism where men are concerned."

He relaxed. "You don't believe me?"

"I have other issues to move past before I'm willing to consider how important believing you is."

Martin returned to his seat and picked up his coffee. He took a sip and closed his eyes. "Some things have improved in the time I've been gone."

"I don't suppose Martin could stay with you for a few days," Chance said.

I sputtered. "Me? No. That's one step too far. I'm sorry. Norma asked me to help him, but..."

"But you don't trust men in general, and strangers who've traveled a hundred years through time even less?" Chance suggested.

My face heated. "Darren already thinks I'm responsible for Martin's sudden appearance. If Martin were to stay with me, that would add to the implication that I knew him previously or that I have something to gain."

Chance warmed his hands around his coffee mug. "I hadn't considered that. Any suggestions?"

"A motel, maybe?" I said with a note of sarcasm.

"Even if I footed the bill for him, Darren has the means to track him, or his known associates."

Which, for the moment, included me, Chance and Faith.

"I have a thought," Martin said.

The front door opened and my mother walked in. "Elspeth..." She stopped short. "Oh."

Leave it to her to make a well-timed entrance. "Mother, this is Robert Chance and Martin Foster."

Both men stood to shake her hand. She held each one a moment longer than was customary, assessing them.

Martin looked at the crystal my mother had pressed into his hand. "What is this?"

Chapter 26

M y mother patted Martin's arm. "Consider the crystal a good luck charm. Nothing more."

"It is warm to the touch, and it appears to... glow," he said with more than a little skepticism.

"Of course, it's warm. I was holding it. Body heat."

Martin raised an eyebrow. "And the glow?"

She waved off the question. "Reflection. What have I missed?" She glanced from me to Chance. "You could cut the tension in this room with a knife."

Both men remained silent.

"We were discussing where Martin could stay until things get sorted out," I said.

Martin scowled. "Horned Owl Hollow is my home, and I'm adamantly against leaving."

"Proving you are who you say you are may take time—time I'm not sure you have," Chance said.

Martin sunk into the sofa, sending a suspicious look to my mother. "Can we trust this woman?"

"As much as you can trust me," I said.

How could I ask a stranger to trust me when I had my own issues on full display? I shot a glance at Chance, which my mother didn't miss.

"That, right there," she said quietly.

"What are you talking about, Mother?"

She leaned close, her voice low. "Tension."

I pressed my lips closed, my cheeks on fire.

Martin turned to Chance. "All things considered, I'm not opposed to you buying my home with the proviso of allowing me to live there for the remainder of my natural life, but I will not stay elsewhere in the meantime."

"Even if someone inside the house means you harm?" Chance asked.

Martin furrowed his brow. Stroked his chin. "Is there still the stablemaster's quarters in the carriage house?"

"Stablemaster...?" my mother repeated.

Chance's face lit with what appeared to be an *a-ha* moment. "The apartment in the garage. It hasn't been used in years, and it's a bit of a catch-all, but we can certainly clear it out in short order."

"Now that you have that settled," I said sarcastically.

Chance held up a hand. "You and I still have things to discuss." He turned to my mother. "Would you mind keeping Martin company for a few minutes?"

She smiled like a self-satisfied cat. "Tension," she said to me once more, before she turned to him. "Of course, I don't mind. Take all the time you need."

I rolled my eyes. Chance reached for my hand, but I refused to give it to him.

"Why don't we step outside?" I suggested.

"As you wish," he replied, a gleam in his eye.

I followed him to the front lawn and folded my arms. The sun was low on the horizon, shadowing Chance's features in the retreating light. Yes, I felt the tension my mother so aptly pointed out, but I wasn't about to act on it—at least, not until the matter at Horned Owl Hollow was settled.

"You still don't trust me," Chance said.

"I don't know you."

"And my plan to buy the house? Does that make you trust me more? Or less?"

"I have no opinion on the matter." Which wasn't entirely true. He'd said he wanted to buy the estate before he knew Martin was alive, and the fact that he was willing to give Martin a home—allow Martin to live in his own home—if that were true, was a noble thing to offer. Or a sinister way to take possession of the house. "Why do you care about my opinion, anyway?"

"Call it one man's quest to restore your faith in men."

I laughed. "Good luck with that."

He stared at me, as if trying to read me. "You told me you were engaged to the policeman. Should I assume he did something to shake your confidence in the male population?"

He'd certainly contributed, although I gave my father credit for getting the ball rolling. "I'm not sure that's any of your business." And yet his guess had my heart racing. There was more to Robert Chance than met the eye.

He took my hand in his, sending sparks of awareness through me. I closed my eyes against the sensation, but that enhanced it.

"I'm not him," Chance said.

My voice was hoarse. "Clearly."

"Can I take you to dinner? Then we can figure out how to avoid throwing me into the category with a man who obviously didn't deserve you."

I scoffed. "Comments like that don't win you points. It sounds like a line a mile away. Let's not forget you aren't exactly the person you present yourself to be. A wealthy man working as a caretaker at a mansion? You don't inspire confidence, Robert Chance."

"I choose not to call attention to myself. I'm sorry if that makes me appear less than truthful in your eyes. Even after I buy Horned Owl Hollow, if that is an option, I would likely continue to live in the caretaker's quarters." He held my gaze. "My thoughts were to make it into a museum. Share its history with people. The Percherons bred during World War I, the trinkets Clifford Foster bought for his daughter, the untimely death of his son." He nodded toward my house. "The war hero lost at sea."

"And where will that war hero live?"

"The house is his until he dies. He can take full advantage of the property."

"And if he lives another seventy years?"

Chance took a step closer, his gaze cast downward. I held my ground. "From what you've told me," he said, "that isn't likely to happen. Based on the changes in his appearance after only a few days, I'm thinking his time with us is short."

"How fortunate for you."

He dropped my hands. "I don't see it that way. If he lives another seventy years, I'm content to remain in my position as caretaker—at least as far as the outside world is concerned."

The fact he'd lived that way for so many years already supported his words. "How did you get to be so humble?" I asked.

"Those who flaunt what they have inspire jealousy and envy. I prefer more positive emotions."

I liked Robert Chance. It was hard not to. Against my better judgment, I rocked to my toes and gave him a peck on the cheek. "I believe you."

"Is that a yes to dinner?"

Under normal circumstances, I would have accepted, but the practical side of my nature held back. "When all this is settled."

He kissed my hand. "I'll hold you to that."

Chance walked inside and signaled to Martin it was time to go.

"Hold onto the crystal," my mother told Martin. "We all need a little good luck from time to time."

He gave her one last skeptical look, and then a nod.

As he and Chance drove off, my mother stood beside me. "Are you going to tell me about what's going on between you and this Robert Chance fellow?"

"Nothing to tell."

She sputtered. "You know you can't hide things from me."

I grinned. "I can try."

"Are you sleeping with him yet?"

My cheeks warmed. "Mother! Even if I was, that isn't something I'd talk about with my mother."

"I have no such compunctions."

"Which is why I do." I sent her a meaningful glance.

"Sometimes I wonder whose child you are," she said. "You can't deny your attraction to the man. As I said, you could cut the sexual tension with a knife."

No, I wasn't going to deny the attraction. "I'm not like you. I want more than an excursion to *Happily,* and I'm not ready to dive into a new relationship right now."

She waggled her eyebrows. "Have a little fun and let the relationship figure itself out later."

One of the main reasons I didn't talk about these things with my mother.

"Don't be such a prude," she went on.

"I'm not a prude." I gathered the coffee cups and carried them into the kitchen, my mother close behind. "There are mitigating circumstances," I told her. "Everything about Horned Owl Hollow, of which he is a part, is complicated. I don't want to muddy the waters with a conflict of interest. There's the consignment of the Staffordshire figurines to consider, and the unexpected appearance of Martin Foster, which the owners think I'm responsible for, not to mention the possible thefts happening at the house. For now, it's smarter for me to stay out of it."

"The energy in the house doesn't agree. Norma Lombard won't rest until you've done your part."

I held my arms out at my sides. "Why me?"

My mother patted my arm. "Because you can see her."

"So can Chance."

My mother straightened. "Interesting. He's told you so?"

"Not in so many words, but he's implied he can—or at least he believes she's lingering."

"Huh." She leaned back and crossed her arms, a twinkle in her eye. "Surely you can see what's right in front of you."

"Mother..."

My phone rang before I could finish, a call from Faith Lombard.

"Elle, I need you to come to the house as soon as you can," she said breathlessly.

"I don't think that's such a good idea," I said.

"Please!" Faith said. "There's something going on, and you're much more in tune with what the spirits want than I am. The disturbances are increasing."

My mother leaned on the table. "I think you should go."

"But I don't know what to do," I argued.

"The spirit will tell you," my mother said.

I may not have wanted the ability my mother had passed on to me, but I couldn't deny it, either. "I'll be there shortly," I told Faith.

Chapter 27

The sun had set by the time I arrived outside Horned Owl Hollow armed with the crystals my mother gave me and several words of caution and wisdom. Clouds floated across the moon, casting an eerie shadow over the third story windows.

Suddenly, I wished my mother had come with me. Or Laine.

Laine would be home day after tomorrow, unless she decided to elope with her majordomo—God forbid. Gavin was handsome, but Laine was a good judge of character. She'd be able to see past that. I didn't have to transfer my bad experiences with men onto her.

My experience with Chance hadn't been all bad.

Had he managed to sequester Martin?

As I crossed the park to the house, I had the odd feeling someone or something was watching me. When I reached the front steps, Faith rushed out.

"Oh, thank heaven you're here. Darren thinks someone is playing tricks on him. Gloria says something is holding her down in the chair and Blair, well, Blair is of no use on a good day. Maybe if you speak to the spirits, they'll settle down."

"I don't speak with them," I said.

She ushered me inside. "Then we'll have to have a séance, or get out the Ouija board."

"Bad ideas, both of them," I said. "You run the risk of releasing spirits you don't want hanging around."

She stopped in the hall to face me. "Then how do we know how to put them to rest?"

I reached into my pocket and closed my hand around the crystals my mother had given me. "I'm not sure we can."

She considered my answer for minute, then waved me into the parlor.

Darren paced beside the sculpture of his grandmother and her brother. Gloria sat in an armchair, hands clutching the arms, her eyes wide with terror. Blair stood in the opposite corner with a drink in his hand, beside the statue of the man draped in a toga.

"I don't know what you think *she* can do," Darren growled. "None of this happened before she showed up."

"Before Elle showed up, Norma was content to stay locked in her room," Faith argued. "She came out of her room because she knew she could communicate with Elle."

"Don't be ridiculous, Faith."

Gloria's voice was unnaturally high. "She's not being ridiculous. Why do you think I refuse to sleep in this house?" She looked to me, her eyes shining with unshed tears. "Get me out of this chair!"

I was in over my head. My occasional encounters with the lingering energy of those who had passed on hadn't prepared me for this. I should have asked my mother to come with me. She dealt with stigmatized houses in her job as a realtor, knew how to make those houses livable again.

My mother wasn't here. "You said something about an increase in activity," I said to Faith. "What else happened?"

Blair set his drink on an end table and I felt a momentary cringe for water damage. He crossed the room toward me, grabbed me by the arm and led me into the hall.

I shook free. "Let go of me."

Faith followed, but he sent her a threatening glare. "I want a word with Ms. Barclay alone."

Faith shot me a nervous glance.

"I'll call you if I need you," I told her.

She retreated into the parlor, where I watched her kneel in front of Gloria. Blair yanked me out of view.

"I think this has gone on long enough," he said, his voice low. "It's time for you to end this charade with your 'Martin Foster.'"

I raised my chin, determined not to let him unnerve me. "I'm not responsible for his appearance."

Blair's eyes swept across my face, then lower. An ugly smile curled his lips. Help was only a few feet away. Certainly, he wouldn't do anything to me with people so close.

He took a step closer. "I'm certain we could work something out." His breath smelled of alcohol. "I could make donations to your store that would net you a very nice profit, as long as you stop interfering with the sale of this house."

"Donations? Like the missing figurines?"

He yanked the hair on the back of my head, his face an inch from mine. "Speaking of figures, yours is luscious. I'm sure we could come to an arrangement that would be mutually beneficial."

I shoved him as hard as I could with both hands.

Gloria gasped behind me. I took two steps further away from Blair, wanting as much distance from him as I could get. Apparently, whoever or whatever had been restraining Gloria had released her.

"Now, Gloria," Blair said, "it isn't what you think. She's stirring up more trouble, trying to seduce me so I won't say anything."

"I have eyes," Gloria said. "I can see who's doing the seducing, and it wasn't her."

He held his arms out to her. "How did you get out of the chair? You must have been so frightened."

Chance came out of his apartment at the back of the house. He stopped, glancing from Blair to Gloria and then to me.

Gloria started for the front door. The vestibule doors slammed closed, sending her toward the parlor instead, headed for the terrace doors. The hurricane shutters outside the windows closed simultaneously.

"What's going on?" Darren asked.

Gloria did an about face when the door to the hall slammed shut, closing all of us into the parlor. A rush of air swept through the room, along with a feral growl.

Faith tried to open the door to the hall without any success.

Blair raised a chair and charged toward the terrace doors, but Darren stopped him.

"I suspect even if you break the glass, you still won't be able to breach the shutters, and those windows are expensive. Put the chair down." Darren turned toward me. "What's going on?"

"I told you the activity was increasing," Faith whispered.

"And don't tell me it's a ghost," Darren shouted.

"Something was holding me down until she got here. Until..." Gloria glared at Blair.

"Let's all take a breath, shall we? Relax?" Blair said.

"Relax? Sit down?" Gloria screamed. "Grandmother isn't the only ghost in this house. She wasn't the one holding me down and I'm not interested in encountering the demons in the basement."

Demons in the basement?

Laughter echoed around the room, raising goosebumps on my arms.

Gloria circled in place, staring at the ceiling. "What do you want from us?"

Darren hung his head. Shook it. Massaged it. He didn't look well. In fact, he looked...*out of focus?*

"I'm ashamed to call you my family." The deep voice coming from Darren had a hollow ring—not Darren's voice.

Darren dropped to one knee, still massaging his head. The rest of us kept our distance, staring at him.

Gloria sobbed. "I don't care if I don't get my share of the inheritance. I never want to step foot in this house again."

Blair tried to comfort her, but she shrugged him off. "Don't touch me." Her voice was laced with venom. "Don't think I'm not aware of where you really go when you're off for drinks with the boys. Funny how you're never at the bar with them when I go looking."

"You're overexcited," Blair said. "You don't know what you're saying."

"I know exactly what I'm saying, and I won't put up with it a moment longer."

"Perhaps you might save that discussion for a more private time," Faith suggested. She moved toward Darren and rested a hand on his shoulder. When he looked up, he looked confused but no longer blurry.

The hairs on the back of my neck stood on end. The energy that had locked us in the parlor remained. Angel or demon, it didn't appear to be finished. As a rule, I didn't like to open myself to spirits trying to reach across from the other side, but unless I did, we might be here a while.

I searched the dark corners for a manifestation. Chance hung back, watching from a vantage point away from the family. The crystals in my pocket cut into my hands as I tightened my fists around them. Norma Lombard had asked me to help Martin, but I still didn't know how.

"How can I help you?" I whispered.

I glanced around the room, from Darren and Faith, to Blair, to Gloria. My gaze landed on Chance. Was Martin safe? Assuming a conversational tone, I asked, "Which one of you is the thief?" I turned my attention to Darren. "Chance said he told you about the missing items, but you brushed him off."

"The only person who has been in this house other than family would be you, Ms. Barclay," Darren said, his voice weak. "My family wouldn't need to steal what they already own. Shall I assume you've taken things to sell at your store, or our caretaker?"

Before I could defend myself, Darren grunted and doubled over.

Gloria pointed an accusing finger at Blair. "Have you been removing things from the house?"

He raised both hands, affecting an air of innocence. "Now, Cupcake, why would I do that? If I wanted to pawn anything, we have enough things of our own. Why would I want—no, why would I need to sell anything?"

She folded her arms. "To pay for your divorce."

An ugly expression crossed Blair's face.

"Yes, I know," Gloria said. "The beauty of a trust document is that you can't touch even a penny of my inheritance."

"You owe me," Blair said, his voice low and threatening. He turned and pointed at her. "What about you? Your precious brokerage house called me to ask if I could cover your account there. I told them no. They cut off your credit line. You could be pawning things to pay for your exorbitant spending."

"Gloria?" Darren asked.

Tears streamed down her face. "I haven't taken anything." She turned to Darren. "For all I know, you've been moving things out now that you're no longer assured the sale of this monstrosity. Didn't you tell me you'd signed a contract for a fishing boat in Florida? How are you going to pay for that if this house isn't sold?"

Darren turned to Faith. "You seem awfully sympathetic to my recently returned, long-lost uncle. Tell me you haven't been hiding things for his benefit."

Obviously, someone was lying. Or not, since no one had denied the accusations flying around the room—except maybe Gloria, but could she be believed?

Faith backed away from Darren, a mask of hurt on her face. "Are you still going to tell me I'm imagining things? Even after a spirit spoke through you?"

Darren paled. "What happened?" He grunted again, his shoulders rounded. A shadow hovered over him.

"What have you done with my brother?" The hollow voice, not Darren's, echoed from Darren's throat.

Faith glanced around the room. "Where is Martin? Did one of you hurt him?"

"He's safe," Chance said quietly. "I hope."

Darren rose to his feet, the blurry image distorting his face once more. *"He will have what is his. The thief will not leave this house."*

"Don't look at me," Blair said.

Darren collapsed on the floor, and the shadow retreated through the wall.

Was the thief in this room? Was Chance the thief, following a misguided notion to save Martin's inheritance?

"Wanna buy a house?" Blair asked me. "We'll sell it to you cheap."

I jumped and gasped when the door to the hall blew open.

Chapter 28

Martin stood in the parlor doorway. Hadn't Chance said the apartment was in the carriage house? How had he gotten into the main house?

Gloria apparently wondered the same thing. She raced past him, but came to an abrupt halt.

"How did you get in?" I asked Martin.

"I saw a dog and gave chase," he said. "I followed it through the tunnel until it disappeared." He made an explosion motion with his hands. "Poof."

"There are no dogs on the estate." Chance appeared at my shoulder. "You came in through the tunnel? I thought it was closed off. Locked."

"The door opened on its own." Martin managed a wistful smile. "The tunnel doesn't appear to be well-traversed aside from spiders and mice."

Gloria gasped. "You walked through the tunnel?"

Chance kept his voice low and stepped past Martin into the hall. "The storm doors are closed tight, and the conservatory is blocked by some sort of wavering membrane." He locked his gaze on mine. "There's a door leading outside from my quarters, but I suspect it will also be impassable."

Martin stared at the membrane, blocking both the staircase and the conservatory. "That wasn't there when I came in."

Gloria sobbed.

Darren raised his head, still seated on the parlor floor, his voice strained. "Well, Ms. Barclay? You seem to have an open channel to whatever is holding us hostage. How *do* we get out of here?"

"You're overlooking the fact she's trapped in here with us," Faith said. She studied Martin. "Good heavens. You look awful."

The changes in Martin's appearance were accelerating. While I'd thought he'd aged when he and Chance had visited my house earlier, the wrinkles in his face had deepened even more.

Martin crossed to the parlor fireplace, his back to the room.

I needed to distract them from his transformation. "Your ancestors have unfinished business," I told Darren. "Specifically, Martin."

Darren grunted, as if sapped of strength. "I suppose you expect me to sign over my inheritance to a perfect stranger. Despite what the DNA test shows, I have no intention of entrusting my family's legacy to him."

"Then sell it to me," Chance said.

Darren's attention snapped to Chance. "You couldn't possibly afford to buy Horned Owl Hollow. Or is all this a stunt to lower the value?"

"I'll pay you market value," Chance said. "Turnkey. But I want all the missing items returned."

"How do you know what's missing?" Darren asked.

"I'm the caretaker," Chance replied.

Darren pushed against the floor to stand. "Oh, right. And we all know how much intelligence that requires. Where do you think you're going to come up with the money? Or have you been robbing us blind already?" He flailed for the back of the sofa to steady himself.

"You can sell the house to me, or you can sign it over to Martin," Chance said evenly.

Darren glanced at Martin's back. "My grandmother might have believed Martin Foster would return, but I have no delusion this man actually is Martin Foster. Even if he is a descendant, he looks to be in poor health. A court battle will likely last several months, maybe even years. Will he?"

"Maybe he looks that way because you've been poisoning him," Chance suggested, even though he knew of Martin's DNA anomaly.

"You wouldn't want to be accused of murdering a relative," Faith threw in. "Look at him! A few days ago, he was the picture of health—until he came here to live."

Darren's face turned purple. "Whose side are you on?"

She took his arm. "Yours, of course, but you have to consider how all this appears to the outside world. Not to mention the theft you've already reported to the police."

"I won't be blackmailed, and that includes by my own wife," Darren shouted, and then doubled over from the effort.

"The voice said the thief can't leave the house," Faith said. "It seems we're trapped here until someone confesses."

Darren pulled his phone from his pocket. "Does anyone's cell phone work?"

"Mine's dead," Blair said.

"No bars," Gloria sobbed.

Based on my experience in the Prohibition room, I suspected my phone would be dead, too.

Darren raged at me. "How does this happen?"

"Residual energy." The voice that had spoken through Darren indicated there were more spirits at play than we knew about. "Norma isn't the only spirit determined to make herself known."

Darren speared Chance with a glower. "And if I agree to sell to you, how does that make all this go away? From what you've told me, the ghosts, or whatever's going on here, want our guest to have the house. Not you."

"I've asked him to stay on," Chance said. "The house is plenty big enough for both of us."

Darren turned to each person in turn. "Then I guess the million-dollar question is who would want to steal things from the family?"

"You can't believe I'd take something," Gloria said.

"Exactly what is missing? How do we know you haven't taken it?" Blair asked Darren. He pointed a finger at Chance. "Or your caretaker? You're the ones living in the house. And where does your caretaker come up with enough money to buy the place, hmm?"

The scowl on Chance's face indicated he had no intention of answering Blair's question.

Again, I wondered if Chance's story was true. If he bought the estate, he'd subject himself to the publicity he'd said he wanted to avoid.

I had nothing to lose. "Norma Lombard came to me in a dream," I told the family. "The Staffordshire collection is in the house, but hidden for safekeeping. Maybe the other missing items are in the house, as well."

"And why should I believe you?" Darren asked.

I glanced at Chance again, deciding I had no choice but to trust him at least this far. "Because you've had your own run-in with the spirits. Clifford Foster, I suspect," I said.

"Assuming he's the spirit who spoke through Darren, that means Darren isn't the guilty party, right?" Faith asked.

"That doesn't mean anything," Blair sputtered.

Faith's gaze landed on each of us in turn. "I have a Ouija board."

"No," I said firmly. "We don't want to open that door."

"That door appears to already be open," Blair said. "Besides, it's only a parlor game, right?"

"No," I said sharply. I shivered and glanced around the room for lingering energy. "A Ouija board opens a portal to other spirits who might be more hostile."

"The spirits are already hostile," Gloria whispered. "Grandmother told me there were monsters in the tunnel."

Darren sputtered. "Probably to keep you from playing down there."

"Anyone who wants to get out the Ouija board, raise your hand," Blair said.

Faith, Gloria and Blair all raised their hands. Darren and Chance remained still.

"I cannot condone sorcery in my home," Martin said, remaining in the shadows by the fireplace.

"You can't possibly believe a silly game will give us any answers," Darren said.

"You have a better idea?" Blair asked.

Darren snarled. "Do what you want."

"That's four in favor and three against. The ayes have it," Blair said. "Where is your board, Faith?"

While Darren poured himself a drink at the sideboard bar, I wrapped my arms around myself to ward off the chill, and crossed to the fireplace. "I'm sorry," I whispered to Martin.

He rolled the crystal my mother had given him around in his hand. "Good luck charm, eh?"

I nodded. "Don't lose it. You may need it."

Chapter 29

F aith opened the doors of a credenza cabinet to reveal a variety of board games, including the Ouija board.

She couldn't understand the dangers she might invite into their house. If nothing else, I could give her instructions to limit the risk. "If you're going to do this, you'll need to call one spirit, by name," I told her. "I'd suggest Norma or Clifford. None of this 'is there anybody out there' stuff. And only one person should ask questions."

"I'll ask the questions," Faith said. "We'll call on Norma to tell us who has been hiding things, assuming the other missing items are also still in the house."

"But we heard a man's voice," Blair pointed out, nodding at Darren. "The one who told us the thief couldn't leave the house."

"It was my brother's voice," Martin said. "Clifford." He glanced at me. "All the family I knew is gone. Why wasn't I killed when the storm overtook the *Cyclops*?"

"I can't answer that," I replied.

"We all would have been better off," Blair muttered.

Gloria rounded on him. "That's not funny. You don't have a reason to be here."

"Not like I can go anywhere," Blair said. "Why can't the rest of us leave and your ghost can hold the thief hostage?"

"Caught in the same net," Chance said. "If one of us leaves, all of us can."

"Let's get this over with," Darren said.

Faith scooted her chair toward the center of the room. "Everyone, bring a chair into the circle. The board needs to rest on our knees."

Darren, Gloria and Blair pulled their chairs near Faith's. Chance and I sat on the couch while Martin remained standing.

"What if they summon a hostile spirit?" Martin asked me.

I glanced at Faith. This was her party. "They tell it to leave. If any indication of a hostile entity presents itself, you have to stop immediately. Do you understand?"

She swallowed hard but gave me a nod. "Fingers on the planchette," she said. "We'll begin by drawing figure eights across the board to get the right feel, the right pressure. Follow my lead."

The planchette skated across the board easily. The four of them exchanged glances. As they drew the figure, Faith closed her eyes. "We're looking for Clifford Foster. Are you with us?"

The planchette continued to make eights.

"Clifford, are you the one who was with us earlier? The one who spoke through Darren?"

The planchette slowed and slid to the corner, to the word 'Yes.'

Faith went on. "Do you know who has been taking things from Horned Owl Hollow?"

The planchette moved toward the letters, then slowly to the same corner. Yes.

"Will you tell us who it is?" Faith asked.

"This is ridiculous," Blair muttered.

"Only if you're the guilty party," Gloria said before she shushed him.

The planchette moved across the rows of letters, then seemed to stop—between letters.

"You're moving it," Gloria said to Blair. "Stop. Let him speak."

"I'm not doing anything," Blair grumbled.

"You are. Look. The foot of the planchette nearest you is hardly moving, and the others are practically off the board."

He took his hands off the planchette. "Fine. I'm over this stupid game anyway."

Without his fingers, the planchette moved more quickly, racing across the board until it flew across the room.

"Well," Darren said. "I guess he doesn't feel like telling us."

Faith frowned. "Or the person who stole everything doesn't want us to know."

Darren squeezed his eyes shut and winced. Rounded his shoulders. I moved closer to Darren, watching his face for any recurrence of what we'd already witnessed, any signs of possession. "Darren?"

When he opened his eyes, his face looked blurry again. The spirit was back—Clifford?

A guttural voice came from Darren's throat. "Everything. Everything in this house will go to my brother. Do you understand?"

Gloria screamed, rose from her chair and backed away.

"Martin is here," I said gently.

Darren's clouded gaze moved to Martin. "Keep it safe for him. All of it."

"Do you know where the missing things are?" I asked.

Darren rose from his chair and shuffled toward the hall. He headed toward the staircase, where the wavering membrane blocked the way to the conservatory. Should I stop him? Would the membrane hurt him?

As I reached for Darren to prevent him from coming in contact, the membrane receded. Darren started up the stairs, one hand on the railing, his head tilted as he looked toward the skylight overhead. We all followed.

"Where is he going?" Gloria whispered.

Faith shushed her.

Gloria gave way to a sob. "That's not Darren. What if he means to hurt us?"

"Let's see where he goes," Chance said from the back of the line. He flipped a switch that lit the stairway chandelier.

We climbed past the second floor. Moonlight shone through a window at the end of the third-floor hallway, casting eerie shadows over a settee and two antique chairs. Darren walked past the ballroom on the left, past a door and a wardrobe on the right and opened a door beyond the wardrobe.

Faith walked inside and gasped. "This should be in the library." She stroked a miniature bust of two small children. "And this." Her hand brushed across an intricately carved dragon on the back of a wooden chair, faces on the end of each arm. "And that painting came from the dining room."

"Everything in this house will go to my brother," Clifford's voice repeated.

I had to get Darren to take control before the spirit did any more damage. "Darren Lombard!" I called his name loudly and firmly. "We need you here."

He exhaled loudly, but Clifford's voice answered. "Breath."

"Not your breath," I said. "Darren's breath. Leave him."

A cloud rose over Darren, accompanied by laughter that echoed in the stairwell. Darren dropped to a knee. Faith ran to his side.

"Darren!" She shouted, smoothing his forehead.

He opened his eyes, free of the spirit, and blinked. "No more Ouija board," he said weakly.

"No more Ouija board," she agreed.

Darren massaged his forehead. "I don't feel right."

I took his wrist, checked his pulse. "It seems Clifford Foster sees you as a kindred spirit. He used your energy to speak."

"Yeah, well, I want my energy back," he said.

"That could take a few hours. Maybe even a few days. He touched you twice tonight."

Darren glanced around the storage room. "The missing items."

"Some of them," Chance said.

"The wavy stuff blocking the conservatory is gone," Blair called from below.

Gloria raced down the staircase, followed closely by me and Chance. We arrived in the main hall in time to see Blair open the front vestibule doors, take the two steps down, and open the outer doors. The eastern horizon glowed with shades of violet, rose and gold.

191

"We've been here all night?" Gloria whispered beside me.

"It appears so."

Faith helped Darren down the staircase. "Running away?" she called after Blair.

"Getting outside where I can't be held captive anymore." His gaze shifted to Gloria. "By ghosts or anyone else."

Gloria raised her chin. "No one's stopping you." She turned to Chance, who hung back by the parlor door. "If he wants to buy the house, let him."

Chapter 30

D arren leaned heavily on Faith, her arm around his waist. Her voice wavered. "We need to get out of here before Clifford decides to possess you again."

Darren broke away from her, scowling. "You're talking nonsense. I'm not about to leave this house while someone is trying to rob us."

I glanced at Chance. Had he moved the items we'd found in the third-floor storage room?

"What do we do?" Faith asked me.

I was out of my league. I'd never seen a spirit take possession of someone. "With your permission, I'd like to ask my mother to come over. She's more knowledgeable about this sort of thing." At least I hoped she was.

Faith nodded, and I placed the call.

I walked out through the parlor, into the early morning sunlight on the terrace to wait. Ten minutes later, my mother arrived in the parking area and walked toward the house.

"Oh, no," Gloria said, holding up her hands as if to push my mother back. "I've seen that woman's picture all over town on real estate ads." She turned toward me. "This is some sort of scheme to sell the house."

"My mother *is* a real estate agent," I said, "But that's not why I asked her to come. She knows how to put spirits to rest, or to determine if they want to coexist peacefully in their former home."

"Coexist?" Faith asked.

"Like Norma. This is her home. Sometimes spirits don't want to leave."

"You know what? I don't even care anymore. Sell the house," Gloria said to Darren.

My mother mounted the terrace steps. "What Elle says is true. When a spirit doesn't want to leave, it's energy diminishes over time, generally speaking. The haunting becomes residual. Going through familiar patterns, so to speak."

"Like rocking in the chair," I added. "Visiting places they were most comfortable. They cease to interact."

"I'll assume they're interacting," my mother said.

"Martin's brother spoke through Darren," I told her. "I'm concerned he'll put in another appearance."

"Oh." My mother set her purse on the wrought iron table. "The first order of business should be cleansing the home, then. Smudging."

Darren leaned on the doorframe. "You're going to what, now?"

I made formal introductions. "Darren Lombard, this is my mother, Abigail Barclay."

My mother approached and shook his hand. "Cleanse the house. And you."

"I beg your pardon?" Darren said.

Mom laughed. "By burning sage. At least as a start. It will make you less appealing to..." She turned to me.

"Clifford," I supplied. "His great-grandfather."

"Oh," she said. "That might make things more complicated. Family tends to gravitate toward family. We'll stand a better chance of cleansing if you come outside. In fact—" She glanced over her shoulder, at the park that was their side yard. "—You might want to sit on one of those park benches while you recover your strength."

Faith took his arm and led him toward the terrace.

Darren brushed her away, scowling at her proffered help. "I don't buy into any of this nonsense."

"What's the harm?" my mother asked.

"You might try to hypnotize me, or something. Not that I think you could, but I'd rather not take any chances."

She reached into her purse and pulled out a bundle of sage. "It's as simple as this. I light the sage. You close your eyes. You relax, do your own meditation, and let the sage cleanse your spirit."

"I don't meditate."

"Do that thing you used to do before your court dates," Faith suggested. "Breathing exercises."

Darren's expression indicated he was skeptical.

"Unless you want Clifford to possess you again," she added.

He frowned his displeasure and walked down the terrace steps to the park, taking a seat on a bench, where he crossed his arms with an exaggerated *harumph*.

"Breathe," Faith said.

A hint of a smile creased his face. "I learned the breathing exercises from you, when you had the children."

She knelt before him and took his hands. "Then you know it works."

Mom lit her bundle of sage. She stepped behind Darren and waved it over his head, then traced his body with the smoke. She stopped abruptly, but before I could ask why, I saw what had her attention. Wisps of the smoke took on the image of a man's face staring back at her.

"What does it mean?" I whispered.

"At least one spirit here is not interested in peaceful coexistence." She blew the smoke to disperse the image. "Leave this place. Move on to your final destination."

The face blew away with the wind.

"Tell me everything, Elspeth," my mother said. "What spirits have you identified?"

"Clifford Foster, Martin's brother. I assume his is the face we saw."

"Face?" Darren asked.

Faith held up a hand to quiet him.

"And Norma, Clifford's daughter. She was Darren's grandmother," I told her. "The two spirits seem intent on making sure Martin gets his inheritance."

"We haven't proven this man is Martin Foster," Darren said.

My mother walked around the bench to stand in front of Darren. "You don't want him to have the house." She met my gaze. "And the spirits do. And that accounts for the conflict? For the manifestations?"

"That, and several items in the house have gone missing," I said.

"But we found them," Faith said. "In the storage room."

"Did you find everything?" I asked. "The Staffordshire collection wasn't there." I glanced toward Chance, who leaned on the stone railing of the terrace.

"You said the collection is still in the house," Darren said. "But you haven't told me where."

I raised a finger. "What else is missing?" I called to Chance.

Martin walked down the terrace steps to join us. "I had several Oriental artifacts in my room. When I asked, Darren told me they were in storage."

"The ivory elephant is gone, too," Chance added.

"And you have no idea where they are?" I asked Chance pointedly.

"No."

My mother touched my arm. "I believe him."

I turned toward her, hands on hips. "Just like that?"

Mom nodded, then glanced at each member of the Lombard family. She approached Gloria. "You know something, though."

Gloria gasped and took a step back. "No, I don't."

Mom glanced around the park, at the bungalow to the right—Darren had called it the museum—then at Gloria's Tudor home at the end of the park on the left. "The home. That's yours?" she asked Gloria. "What's in the bungalow?"

Gloria's gaze didn't leave my mother. "It's for storage." She clasped her hands.

"Like storing missing items?"

When Gloria didn't answer, Faith moved to face her. "Gloria?"

She swallowed hard. "I haven't been inside for years, but I saw something. When we were talking to the Ouija board."

"Go on," my mother said.

Gloria's voice cracked. "I saw my grandmother, pointing toward the museum."

"Why don't we have a look," Faith said.

"We'll all go." Darren rose from the bench and produced a ring of keys from his pocket.

Chapter 31

Darren unlocked the door to the museum house. Blair rejoined us, obviously as curious as the rest of us to see inside.

Dust motes floated through a sunbeam. Oblong wooden tables were staged in rows.

A pewter tea service and water pitcher sat on the table closest to me. I glanced around, at porcelain dinnerware with crackled glazing. Rocks and minerals, including some that appeared to be gemstones. Leatherbound books on the shelves that lined the walls. Picture frames with mounted butterflies. Polished seashells. Another table held war relics—shell casings, an old canteen and a soldier's metal helmet—detritus labeled from all over the world. What an odd collection of things.

Shoeprints were visible in the dusty floor leading to a tarp-covered mound in the corner.

"That wasn't here before." Darren pulled back the tarp.

Martin stepped beside him to stroke the top of a black lacquer Chinoiserie cabinet. Beside the cabinet, a Chinoiserie writing desk with a Buddha and an ivory elephant vase on top. "The things I brought back from China. They've held up better than I have."

Faith ran a finger across the desk, which appeared to be relatively dust-free. "How could someone take them out of the house without being noticed?"

"Who else has a key to this place?" my mother asked.

Darren turned to look at the rest of us. "Me. Gloria. Chance."

Chance. My heart dropped. Why did he seem so guilty? And yet my mother said she believed him. I couldn't afford that luxury.

"We might be the ones with the keys, but certainly our keys are accessible to our spouses," Gloria said. She turned on Blair. "Shall I assume you stole my key?"

"Only if you're trying to shift the blame from yourself onto me, Cupcake," he said. "You have more to gain than I do. Aren't you the one who told me your money is inaccessible to me?"

"All the more reason for you to steal heirlooms to make a quick buck," she said.

I was getting impatient with the family drama. I turned to Chance. "Are all the missing items accounted for?"

"Everything I'm aware of, yes," Chance said.

"What about the Staffordshire collection?" Darren asked.

"It's in the house," I replied, not taking my eyes off Chance.

Darren raised his eyebrows. "Where." He wasn't asking, he was demanding to be told.

I turned toward Chance.

"In the Prohibition room in the basement," Chance said.

"And you know this how?" Darren asked. "Shall I assume you put it there?"

Chance held my gaze. "I moved the Staffordshire pieces, but not until after I noticed other things growing legs. I did tell you things were disappearing, Darren. The collection never left the house."

My heart dropped. I'd started to trust Chance. His confession proved my trust had been misplaced.

"Why shouldn't I deduce you moved the other pieces, too?" Darren asked. "You're fired, by the way."

"Why would I point out they were missing if I'd taken them?" Chance asked. "And why didn't you care about everything else?"

"Which doesn't change the fact someone has been moving things out of the house." Darren issued a soft groan. "I suppose since nothing was officially stolen, we can call this whole episode poor judgment." He glared at Blair. "Seems to me you would have been the only one to benefit from selling these things."

"It wasn't me," Blair growled.

"Anyone else care to explain how these things just walked out of the house?" Darren asked.

"And why is everything still here?" I gawked at the treasures all around me. "If someone meant to make a quick buck, they could have sold any number of these things which might have gone unnoticed for... how often do you come into this—what did you call it? The museum?"

"Norma's mother had it built to be a storehouse," Faith said. "She collected things when she accompanied Clifford on his travels. Norma used to talk about all the useless treasures her mother brought home." She blew out a slow breath. "She didn't inherit her parents' love of abandoned objects. That's what she called all this. Her mother's garbage dump."

"Many of these things are extremely rare," I said.

"Now, maybe. Back in the day?" Faith waved a hand across the table. "Stuff. Left behind. War litter."

"What about the tableware? The pewter?"

"My guess is the thief hid everything here until it could be sold," Darren said. "I think we've seen enough. As soon as we get back to the house, I'm arranging to have alarms installed. Security, so no one comes and goes from this building unnoticed."

"Isn't that like shutting the barn door after the horses are gone?" Faith asked.

"The horse," Martin's head swiveled as he scanned the room. "Where is the Percheron carousel horse?"

"I don't know what you're talking about." Darren doubled over and gasped as if he'd been punched in the stomach. Faith knelt beside him.

Darren's voice was strained. "What makes you think there was a carousel horse?"

"I helped my brother unpack it." Martin's hands tightened into fists. "When he was asked to send the real horses back to France, he found the carousel horse as a souvenir. A horse he could keep."

I had a bad feeling about this, and a bad feeling about the source of Darren's recurring discomfort.

"You can track down the sale of an antique carousel horse, can't you Elle?" my mother asked.

"My grandmother sold several things when I was a boy," Darren went on. "Maybe the horse was one of them." He grunted again, as if he'd been dealt a fresh blow. "All right. Stop," he said. "I sold the horse."

"Fascinating," my mother whispered beside me.

"What's happening?" Faith asked.

Darren pushed her away and stumbled out. Faith followed close behind.

"Maybe we need security to protect our belongings from my brother," Gloria said.

Faith scowled at my mother. "You said you'd cleansed him of the spirit. What's happening to him?"

My mother shrugged. "Guilty conscience?"

I touched Martin's hand, which had become dry and papery. The rate at which he aged alarmed me. "I suggest you contact a trust attorney. Sooner, rather than later."

Chance directed us out, and when he'd locked the museum door, he clapped Martin on the back. "I'll call an attorney for you to make sure nothing else disappears."

"If I heard you correctly, you made the figurine collection disappear," Martin replied. "I prefer to find someone on my own, as much to protect myself from my own family as from the people who present themselves as looking out for my best interests."

"I am looking out for your interests," Chance said. "We've talked about this. You don't have the money to hire an attorney, or to pay the taxes on this place."

"Certainly, my interest in this house should amount to something, and until this DNA disorder kills me, I can do with it as I please." Martin stomped across the park to the terrace, walked up the steps and disappeared into the parlor.

"No good deed goes unpunished," Chance said quietly.

"Is it a good deed to hide someone's belongings from them?" I asked.

Chance swung an arm toward the museum. "You've seen the pieces that have been moved. I didn't want him to lose anything else."

"Then you might have called the lawyer you mentioned rather than add more fuel to the fire." I held his gaze a moment. "Did you move the furniture to the storeroom? To the museum?"

His eyes darkened. "I. Did. Not. You heard Darren say he sold off the carousel horse. Doesn't that make him the more likely suspect?"

I didn't know how to respond. Didn't know what to think. While I considered the familiar reminder this was none of my business, Faith shrieked from inside the house.

She ran from the parlor to the terrace, waving frantically. "Please hurry! He needs help!"

Chapter 32

My mother grabbed my arm before I could climb the terrace steps. She leaned close and lowered her voice. "Something's not right."

I stopped. "Care to elaborate?"

"You said Clifford's spirit spoke through Darren."

I nodded.

"How long was Darren under Clifford's influence?"

Chance joined our tete-a-tete. "There were a few minutes before they brought out the Ouija board, then several minutes when the thingamajig flew off the board and he led us upstairs."

"Darren looked to be in pain when we came out to the museum," my mother said. "As if he was fighting someone off." She glanced from me to Chance and back again. "Each time a spirit possesses a body, it grows in strength. Ouija board?"

"I told them it was a bad idea," I said.

"Elle, please," Faith called from the terrace door, a desperate note to her voice.

When my mother, Chance, and I entered the parlor, Darren was pushing himself from the floor. I moved to help him, but again, my mother grabbed my arm. I looked to her for an explanation, but she shook her head. What was that supposed to mean?

Darren crossed the room to a wall and tugged the edge of a painting, which swung open on hinges to reveal a dial combination lock. A minute later, he opened the safe in the wall. He reached inside, hesitated, and to our horror, banged the safe door against his left hand.

"I am in control here," the hollow voice coming from him raged. Darren reached into the safe with his right hand and withdrew a document.

Faith rushed to my side, sobbing. "Elle, what's going on?"

"The spirit is fighting for control of your husband," my mother replied.

"He's hurting himself," Faith cried. "Or he's being forced to hurt himself."

"As a means to make him comply," my mother said.

"Can't we make him stop? He fell flat on his face when we came inside. His feet stopped moving before he did. He didn't do anything to stop the fall."

"What about the cleanse you did?" I asked my mother.

"Clearly, it didn't work." My mother stepped toward Darren. "Clifford Foster, you're not wanted here."

Darren turned to face us, blood running from his nose and lip. The shock sent me a step backward.

"This is my home," the hollow voice declared.

"Your time on this plane has passed," my mother went on.

"So I thought, until greedy relatives attempted to steal my brother's birthright."

Okay, I'd never experienced anything like this before. The spirit was clearly angry, and his ability to inflict harm on Darren scared the bejesus out of me.

"Your brother is here," my mother said, looking for Martin. "He's come home. All will be as it should be."

"Not as long as this sniveling coward exists."

Faith gasped, her hands over her mouth.

"We are here to help Martin," my mother went on.

Darren—or, at least Darren's body—limped our direction. "I will make this poor excuse for a man comply with my wishes. He has fooled you all, but he cannot fool me."

"He has not fooled me." My mother nodded at the document in his hand. "Are these your wishes?"

"They are."

She held out her hand. "We will see that they are honored."

"It's too late," Darren/Clifford said. "Only this weasel can undo the damage he has wrought."

Martin walked through the terrace door. "It is my legacy. I will claim it for myself."

Darren/Clifford laughed. "It's far too late for that, little brother. I will, however, require your help." He extended his hand, streaked with blood, toward the hall.

Martin stepped past him and Darren hobbled in the direction of the front door.

"Where are you going?" Faith shrieked. She turned to my mother. "What are we going to do?"

"This is much worse than I anticipated," my mother said. "We need to go after them."

Faith took Darren's hand, then gasped and released it as if she'd been burned. "You can't go outside bleeding like that. People will see that my husband is being forced to act against his will."

Darren/Clifford stopped. He turned to Faith. "*You* will take us where we need to go." He tilted his head. "*You* will help Martin collect his legacy."

Faith gave a quick nod.

My mother stepped forward. "Mrs. Lombard—Faith—you must know your husband isn't acting of his own volition."

Faith managed a timid smile. "I know. But I'm certain I won't get my husband back until he does the right thing—what Clifford Foster wants him to do." She turned to Darren. "You will leave him once this matter is resolved, won't you?"

"My life has passed. I have no desire to live another, especially not inside this shell of a man."

Faith retrieved a washcloth from the powder room and washed the blood from Darren's face. She stared into his eyes for several minutes—looking for a sign her husband was still in there?

Darren raised the document he held in his good hand. "This is the trust document. Darren Lombard is an attorney. He will do what he must to see that my wishes are honored." Darren's voice emerged, strained. "I have documents to prepare at the law office before we go to City Hall."

Faith drew a shuddery breath. "I'll drive you."

She handed me the washcloth and walked Darren and Martin outside.

My mother turned to Gloria, who hovered on the terrace outside the parlor. "Are there other spirits in the home?"

"You mentioned demons in the basement," I prompted.

Gloria took several backward steps, her eyes as wide as saucers, before she walked swiftly toward the Tudor house.

I frowned, well acquainted with Gloria's fear. "The only other spirit I've encountered is Clifford's daughter. Norma," I told my mother.

A slow smile creased her face. "Excellent. She can help us control her father. Where did you first become aware of her?"

"Her bedroom."

My mother turned to Chance. "May I see it?"

He led us up the stairs and opened the door to Norma Lombard's room.

My mother closed her eyes. "I feel her energy." She turned to me. "She's frightened."

"I am, too," I said. "Is her father a demon?"

"Not a demon, merely an angry spirit. At least that's what I'm hoping for." Mom closed her eyes and took several deep breaths. "Norma Lombard. Will you speak with me?"

Chapter 33

A reminder chirped on my mother's phone. Undeterred, her eyes remained closed. She opened her arms and raised her face toward the ceiling in Norma's bedroom.

"I don't feel her. Norma," I said.

My mother opened her eyes and looked directly at me. "She's fled. You told me she'd manifested for you. Maybe she'll talk to you." She pulled her phone from her pocket to check the notification. "I have a showing in half an hour. I can postpone..."

"No," I said. "Go. As long as Clifford isn't a demon, I think I can manage things until you get back."

"Yes, well, they'll be lucky if Darren isn't arrested. I suspect Faith will keep him in check while they're out." My mother took my hands. "That doesn't mean there aren't demons lurking nearby. Every yin has a yang. For every spirit that manifests, there is a demon waiting for its opportunity."

Not something I wanted to encounter. "Then you'll have to do a cleanse for me before you go."

"Do you have the crystals I gave you?" she asked.

I nodded.

"Show them to me."

I pulled them from my pocket and displayed them in my palm.

Mom smiled and closed my hand around them. "They're still glowing. That's the positive energy of your life force." She glanced around the room. "Is there another place you might find Norma's spirit?"

The Prohibition room.

"You said she sent you to the cellar," Chance said. "We could look there."

"That's what I was thinking."

My mother scanned Norma's room one last time before Chance closed the door behind us. "I'll check in with you after the showing."

Chance and I walked her to the front door.

She hugged me once more. "Be careful," she said, and left.

My skin tingled with awareness as Chance led me down the staircase, to the opposite end of the basement. We were definitely not alone, but the energy was stronger than it had been when I'd encountered Norma. Were there other spirits at play?

Chance paused at the Prohibition room door, head bowed. "What's going to happen to Darren?"

I blinked several times. "He fired you. You'll be lucky if he doesn't have you arrested for stealing the figurines. For that matter, he might press charges against me as an accessory." This was a bad idea. I should leave.

He took my hands. "Trust me?"

I stared into his eyes. My thoughts warred with one another. Hadn't he lied about hiding the Staffordshire collection?

But it was to protect Martin's assets.

He heaved a sigh. "Until we can be sure Norma has moved on, and the demon has left Darren?"

He believed me. And he wasn't running the other direction.

I *should be running the other direction.*

I glanced around in search of whatever was in the basement with us. "We don't know that Clifford is a demon." I sighed, suckered in by the guy one more time. "Once Clifford is satisfied his will is being honored, I expect he'll leave Darren. Most spirits are more interested in moving on to wherever they are destined to go. Martin is Clifford's unfinished business. By the time Faith brings Darren and Martin home, both Clifford and Norma should be free to leave this house."

"Assuming Martin lives long enough to inherit."

I studied Chance, wanting to trust him. "What aren't you telling me?"

"My father taught me to love this place as if it were my own." He bowed his head. "And I do. Clifford and Norma aren't the only spirits who walk Horned Owl Hollow."

"And you know this how?"

His forehead creased with his frown, as if I'd hurt his feelings.

"Who else is here?" I stared at him a moment, not sure if I could believe him. "Why haven't you said anything before now?

"I don't know who they are." Chance opened the hidden Prohibition room door with a tad more force than was necessary.

Had I offended Chance? He hadn't questioned my ability to see the spirits—because he saw them, too?

My mother had sent me to find Norma—who didn't seem to want to be contacted at the moment. I didn't like extending myself to spirits in the best of circumstances. This didn't feel anywhere close to a best-case scenario, but knowing Chance was sensitive to the spirits in the house gave me courage.

"I'm sorry if you thought I didn't believe you," I said.

"Yeah. So am I." Judging by his tone, I didn't hear his words as an apology, but more as regret for trusting me.

With one hand around the crystals in my pocket, I closed my eyes and drew a deep breath. "Norma Lombard. Are you here?"

The only sounds in the basement were the whirring of appliance motors as they cycled on.

"She can't speak, can she?" Chance asked.

"Not on her own, but she can relay a message." I opened my eyes to look at him. "I don't feel her here, either. Do you?"

He shook his head. "Maybe now that Clifford's put in an appearance, she no longer has a reason to be here."

I wasn't so sure. The only thing I did know was her spirit wasn't in the basement, or in the Prohibition room. "Is there another place you've sensed her presence?"

Again, Chance seemed to study me. "Outside? On the bench by the path. That was one of her favorite places." He closed the secret room and we started toward the staircase.

In the laundry room, hinges groaned as a heavy wooden door swung open slowly. I stopped. Cold air seeped from the opening. Static electricity charged the air.

"Chance?" He hadn't stopped. Hadn't seemed to notice. I called to him a second time. "Robert?"

"It's Rob, if you're going to use my first name," he said sharply. As he turned around, his gaze went to the open door.

Orbs of light floated from the dark chamber, bounced an inch away from me before they continued toward Chance. One orb seemed to pass into his chest. The crystals in my pocket grew hot.

"Chance?" I whispered once more. "Rob?"

His eyebrows furrowed and his expression tightened into one of rage. He stomped past me and slammed the door shut. He shook his head as if to clear it and snarled. "I don't feel right. I have to get out of here."

I pushed him toward the stairs. I had the crystals to protect me from invasive spirits. He didn't. I hoped it wasn't too late.

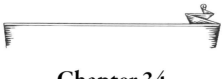

Chapter 34

C hance stormed outside through the conservatory, fists swinging by his side, head bowed. He stopped beside a towering hickory tree and hugged it. I watched with fascination. His body trembled as if he'd been electrocuted.

My heart raced, wanting to help but not sure how. Instinctively, I recited an incantation against demons. Chance's body relaxed while he continued to hug the tree. His head rested against the shaggy bark. When he let go, the anger was gone from his face.

"What happened?" I asked. "Where does the door in the basement lead?"

"It's the tunnel to the carriage house."

"The one Martin used the other night?"

He nodded. "The story goes that's how they smuggled booze into the Prohibition room in the '20s."

I led Chance to the bench beside the path to the cemetery and sat beside him. "Are you okay?"

He nodded. "Something happened in there. I suddenly felt angry. No. Not just angry. More like furious."

"I saw..." I hesitated. Glanced toward the house. "I saw an orb of light fly into you."

Chance took a shaky breath. "Is that what happened to Darren?"

"No. With him, you could see the spirit, like a shadow overlaying him."

He nodded. "Whatever came over me seems to be gone now."

"Are you sure?"

"Yes. I feel more myself again." His brows drew together. "I saw the orbs, too. They bounced off you. Why?"

I took the crystals from my pocket and showed him.

He chuckled. "Force field."

"In a manner of speaking."

Chance took my hands. "Elle, what if the spirit inside Darren isn't Clifford?"

I considered Darren's erratic behavior. The way the spirit had injured Darren to ensure compliance. "I wondered about that myself, but I can't imagine who else it might be." I tilted my head, assessing Chance. "What was that thing you did with the tree?"

He rose and returned to the hickory tree, stroking its bark. "My father taught me there is healing in nature. He wasn't what you might call spiritual, but he respected the earth. And the trees. I have to say, I would have liked to have had one of those crystals, though."

"I'll mention that to my mother."

Hadn't my mother cleansed the house when she'd arrived? "How did the darkness break through?" I said half to myself. We'd have to think carefully before we went back inside the mansion. I understood why Norma Lombard and Clifford Foster might be lingering, but not whatever entity Chance and I had encountered in the basement—unless the house had a history we weren't aware of. The Ouija board might have stirred other spirits—or demons.

"Gloria mentioned demons in the basement. Do you have any idea what she meant?" I asked.

Chance glanced over his shoulder, at the path through the woods. "I don't, but I've always wondered if the proximity to the cemetery might have something to do with the increase in spiritual energy."

"Are Clifford and Norma buried there?"

Chance shook his head. "No. When they couldn't acquire the property, they built a mausoleum in another cemetery down the road."

Another cemetery? A mausoleum? "Now, that's interesting. They have a family mausoleum down the road, but there's a grave marker for Martin at the other end of this path. Why wouldn't he have a spot with the rest of them?"

Chance's eyes widened. "I never thought of that before." He drew a deep breath and rubbed his forehead. "Why don't we pay Gloria a visit? I'd like to know more about her demons."

"No time like the present. Not to mention I'm not eager to go into the mansion again right away. Shall we?" I motioned to the Tudor house on the other side of the mansion's park.

As we approached, Blair stomped down the front porch steps, got into his car, and drove away. Gloria stood at the door, arms folded.

"This might not be the best time," I said quietly.

"Or no better time," Chance replied. "She might need to unload some of her emotional baggage. Focusing on history might take her mind off..." he nodded toward Blair, "that piece of..." His lips pressed closed, not finishing the thought.

Gloria scowled at us, watching our approach. "What do you want?"

"Help," I replied.

"I can't help you." She turned to go inside.

"I disagree," Chance said. "You might be the one person who can. Something in that house frightens you, and I'd like to know what."

She stopped. Dropped her arms and chuckled. "Changed your mind about buying the place, have you?"

"No. But I would like to know what I'm dealing with."

Gloria sashayed across the porch and settled in a swing. "You want to know where the bodies are buried?"

"In a manner of speaking."

As good a place to start as any. "Is there a reason Martin's headstone is in Oakwood, and not in the family mausoleum?" I asked.

Gloria folded her hands and bowed her head. "Funny no one else ever questioned that."

I walked up the steps. "Was there something more going on with the family? Is that why your grandmother was so adamant about holding Martin's inheritance for him?"

Gloria rocked in the porch swing several moments before she spoke again. "He threatened to sell my Lladrós, you know."

"Martin?" I asked.

She chortled. "No. Blair."

Apparently, we'd have to listen to her grievances before we got the family story.

She glanced toward the big house, a faraway look in her eye. "We all have our endowments, you know. Personal income. Blair was never able to touch that, but the house will come out of trust when it sells. Darren was planning to dissolve the old trust now that Grandma's dead. Blair was banking on collecting his share." She glowered. "He isn't going to get a dime."

I debated asking her about her credit line with the Lladró dealer, the credit that had been denied. Better to let her tell the story in her own way.

"But you don't care about my sad story." She went on. "You want to hear about the haunted house."

"Is it haunted?" Chance asked.

"You know it is. Especially after what we all witnessed today."

"Why don't we start with why Martin's grave marker isn't at the mausoleum," I said.

"Because he wasn't dead. At least that's what my grandmother said." She fixed me with a pointed look.

I kept my voice soft so as not to upset Gloria further. "Was the house haunted before your grandmother passed?"

She heaved a sigh. "Even when I was a child I dreaded sleeping there. My grandmother told me she was my guardian angel. Who's going to keep me safe from her?"

I might be reassured by a loving grandmother, but I also didn't grow up with spirits threatening me. "Why did you need a guardian angel?"

Gloria stopped swinging and leaned toward me. "My great-grandfather imported cognac during Prohibition. The story goes that after receiving a shipment one night, the two men who delivered his precious brandy used the tunnel

219

between the carriage house and the main house to hide what they were unloading." She sat back again. "The tunnel caved in and they were buried alive."

I turned to Chance. "The tunnel Martin used last night? The one in the basement? How can that be?"

"They reinforced it after the accident." She shivered. "I've never seen the tunnel, personally. I used to have my own nightmares about being buried alive. My grandmother suggested they might be related to the tunnel, even though the cave-in happened long before I was born. She told me never to go near it, and I was only too happy to comply." Gloria rolled her eyes. "I thought she was looney tunes, but I'll tell you something. I've never had that nightmare sleeping anywhere else. Only in that house. And then when she died—" She stopped. Wrung her hands. Lowered her voice. "The rocking chair in her room rocks by itself."

"Yes, I've seen that," I said. "Which might be reassuring to you if you believe your grandmother is your guardian angel."

Gloria's voice raised to a near hysterical level. "Didn't I just tell you she was looney tunes? I'm not interested in being haunted by the ghosts of dead men or by my guardian angel grandmother, or anyone else. Do you understand?"

Chance raised his hands to calm her. "We understand." He waited a moment until Gloria seemed to have collected herself, and then pressed on. "I know the memories are unpleasant, but can you tell us about the nightmares? About being buried alive?"

I laced my hand with his. Dreams were often the way spirits communicated with the living—something he apparently knew.

"I haven't had a dream for years now. Not since I've moved out of the house." She snagged a fingernail between her teeth. "There were... animals is the only description that comes to mind. Crawling on four legs. Red eyes. Claws. Chasing me. And then a sprinkle of dirt from the roof. A little at first, and then a shower of dirt and rocks. And then I can't breathe." She clawed at her neck, her breathing fast. "I should sell this house, too. Get as far away from Horned Owl Hollow as I can."

Gloria reached for her ringing phone, checked the display and answered. Color drained from her face. "I understand. I'll be there as soon as I can." She rose from the swing and held Chase's gaze. "I need you to drive me to the hospital."

Chapter 35

Gloria shared with me that Darren had collapsed and they'd taken him to the hospital. As curious as I was, I had no reason to accompany her. If he'd collapsed, most likely Clifford's spirit had left Darren.

Chance walked me to my car. "I'll check in with you later."

I nodded and gave his hand a quick squeeze. Chance trotted off to the garage and, a moment later, backed the Mercedes out. I waited while Gloria got into the car and watched them drive off.

Phone in hand, I checked my calendar to see if we had any appointments at the store. Laine wasn't due home until tomorrow, which meant I couldn't push off anything work related on her. I typed a quick text to check in with her, then checked the store's email account.

There was an email from Ingrid, the customer whose father had recently died. *Are you in the store today? Was wondering if I could pop in for a quick second.*

What I really wanted to do was go home and fall into bed after being up all night. The store didn't have business hours on Wednesdays, but for a regular customer, I'd make the effort. I typed a quick reply for an afternoon appointment, time enough to shower and change. With that settled, I got into my car and drove home.

After lunch, I went to the store armed with a travel mug filled with strong coffee, functioning on autopilot. I unpacked my computer and settled on the stool behind the sales counter to see if I could determine who the spirits in the tunnel at Horned Owl Hollow were. The men who had died in the collapse?

Ingrid showed right on time, with a bakery bag in hand. I opened the door, and locked it again behind her.

"Thank you for meeting me," she said. "And for stopping over the other day." She handed me the bag. "Cookies to show my appreciation. I keep telling my mother she has to accept that no one wants her 'perfectly good' things. It helps to have someone else tell her."

I raised the bag. "Thank you. As for the furniture, I'm sure a college student would be happy to have it. That's about the best option I know of if the charities won't take it."

"The reason I wanted to stop by..." She eyed me, wringing her hands. "How did you know about my father?"

I was too tired to try to explain my sensitivity to the spirit world. "I didn't. I can't explain it."

Tears welled in her eyes. "Can you... do you...?" She stopped, blew out a breath. "I would give anything to talk to him again."

"I'm afraid I can't help you."

"But if he spoke to you before, couldn't he do it again?"

The possibility existed, but I preferred to help spirits find their way rather than anchor them to this life. "Attempting to summon him would keep him from moving on." I took

Ingrid's hand. "The message he sent was so you wouldn't worry. He's happy, and he'll be there waiting for you when your time comes."

She nodded and forced a smile. "Laine isn't with you today?"

"No, she took a quick trip."

"Do you need help?" Ingrid glanced around. "Would you like me to set anything out for you?"

I laughed. "Then I'd have to pay you. Besides, the store is closed today."

"I'm volunteering an hour of my time. You went out of your way for me, I'd like to do the same for you."

"When you put it that way..." I walked over to a display cabinet where I'd made room Tuesday. "Since I'm here, I'd planned to put out the carnival glass you brought. I was thinking of displaying it here."

Ingrid's smile brightened. "I'm on it."

I gulped a big slug of coffee from my mug. What had I been planning to do before she'd arrived? My brain struggled beyond basic functions. I worked with Ingrid while she told me about how her mother had come to collect the carnival glass, and her decision to let it go. Downsizing was a common reason for people to part with their collectibles.

When Ingrid left a couple hours later, I went to my computer, redirecting my focus to Horned Owl Hollow. I stared at the screen, trying to clear the fog from my brain. Another customer knocked on the door and I was surprised to see Catherine Payton, the woman related to Alice Mansfield Pugh.

"Hi. I didn't realize the store was closed today," she said. "I hope you don't mind me dropping in like this."

"Come on in." As she walked inside, I told her about the sculptures Carson had shown me around town.

She gasped. "Oh, I forgot about those, but now that you mention it, I remember the one at the park. When my dad told me my great-grandmother made it, I thought he meant the plaque—that she'd funded the playground. I'm so far removed from her that I couldn't quite wrap my head around who she was, you know? As a kid, you tend to overlook those things."

"What brings you by?" I asked.

"Well, I asked my dad what he knew of the family history, about Alice being engaged before she married my great-grandfather. He got out the photo albums and had some interesting stories to tell, but he didn't know anything about Martin Foster. He did say there was a family feud between the Mansfields and the Fosters, although he didn't know what it was about. He suggested I talk to my grandpa."

"Your grandfather? Alice's son?"

"Yes. He lives in the Veterans' home in Ashbury. Henry Pugh."

Some of the sleep-induced fog cleared with the burst of adrenalin. "Would you mind if I tagged along?" I asked. Her grandfather might be more willing to talk to me about family matters if I went with her.

"We could go tomorrow," she said. "If you have time."

Thursday. Laine would be back. I checked my phone for any new texts while I asked, "What time would be best?"

"In my experience, mornings. He's more alert. Will that work for you?"

No texts from Laine. Even if she was delayed, I should still be back in time to open the store by noon. "Tomorrow morning would be perfect."

"Ten o'clock?" Catherine asked. "Would you like me to pick you up on the way?"

"I'll have to open the store. If I go on my own, you can visit with him longer."

She fiddled with her purse, searching inside. "Do you need directions?"

"No, I know where it is." I handed her my phone. "Do you mind giving me your contact information? In case something comes up."

She smiled and closed her purse. "I was thinking the same thing." She took my phone and added her number. I immediately sent her a text to confirm my information. "I've found out things about my family I never even thought to ask," she said. "More of those things you take for granted. I'm curious to hear what stories Grandpa will share."

"Thank you for letting me tag along," I said.

"I'll see you tomorrow." With a parting wave, she walked out.

I was fading fast. Even though it was only four o'clock, I needed to go home and fall into bed. As I gathered my things, Chance darkened the doorway, firing off a fresh round of adrenaline. Why that man appealed to me, I wasn't sure. Overtired, I'd have to keep my guard up.

I walked out and locked the door behind me. "How's Darren?" I asked.

"He's home."

I waited for details, which weren't forthcoming. "Well?"

"Well, what? Why was he in the hospital or what did I find out about where they went?"

"Yes?" I replied. "And are you still fired?"

He grinned. "Good news, first. Martin told me they went from the law office to the courthouse and filed the paperwork allowing him to inherit the estate."

"But Martin doesn't have documentation. How...?"

"As to the documentation issue—and for the record, I did make an inquiry regarding his fingerprints with the Navy," Chance said. "The person I spoke to wasn't sure they still had them. Thanks to Darren, the fingerprints won't be necessary. From what Martin told me, Darren awarded the trust to Martin as beneficiary. Apparently, more than one person challenged Darren's decision, including a judge. Darren—or Clifford, as Darren—told them it was his family and to mind their own business."

I walked slowly toward my car. "So the estate is Martin's?"

"That's my understanding."

"Wow. And Darren?"

Chance stopped walking. "That's a tad more complicated. Faith updated Gloria out of earshot. I did hear her say after everything was settled a shadow passed out of Darren's body and he collapsed. That's why they took him to the hospital."

"Clifford. Leaving his host. Not without some repercussions, it would seem," I said.

"From what we saw at the house before they left, the spirit wasn't treating him gently. The doctor said Darren broke his hand, but other than that, they couldn't find anything wrong with him."

I started walking again. "A spirit exists as energy. Clifford would have had to use Darren's energy when he took possession of his body. In my limited experience, when I've seen a spirit pass through someone, it can take a few minutes or hours to feel normal again. Clifford did more than pass through Darren." I shot a glance at Chance. "You were affected by a spirit in the basement, but not to the same extent."

"I've gotta say, whatever's in that tunnel, I hope it stays there."

My lightbulb moment. I raised a finger in the air. "That's what I wanted to do."

Chance tilted his head. "What?"

I chinned toward the library, two blocks down. "You have time?"

"Probably more time than I'd like. If I go back to the estate, I'm likely to be reminded I've been fired, unless Martin reinstates me, but he wasn't happy with me, either. What're you thinking?" he asked.

"I wanted to check on those men who died in the tunnel."

Pace quickened, we covered the two blocks and walked into the library. I made my way to the study room and sat at one of the library's computers. Chance sat beside me while I navigated to the local newspaper's website.

He hovered over my shoulder. "Archives? When I was a kid, we had to look this stuff up on microfiche."

"It's all digitized now." I typed Horned Owl Hollow into the search bar. "If there's something about the men who died in the tunnel, we can identify them and put their spirits to rest."

"Gloria mentioned Prohibition, so that narrows the timeframe. Start with 1919," Chance suggested.

Nothing showed in 1919, but a timeline on the page showed references in 1922. I updated my search, far too aware of the man at my shoulder.

"Bingo," he whispered, sending chills across my skin.

Neighbors were called to Horned Owl Hollow to clear a tunnel leading from the carriage house to the main house after a cave-in trapped two men Friday night. Clifford Foster told this reporter the tunnel was used for passage between the two buildings in inclement weather. The trapped men, long-time family friends Edwin and Leland Mansfield, died in the collapse.

"Mansfield?" Chance said. "Like Alice Mansfield?"

I reached into my tote bag for the notes I'd made when checking the genealogy site. "She had seven siblings. You don't suppose...?" I opened the notebook and read the names. "Irene, Laurence, Alice, Leland, Edwin, George, Clark, and Florence." I stared at Chance. "The men killed were her brothers."

Chance followed the names in my notebook with his finger. "This is her family tree?"

"Yes."

He stared at the page a long time.

"What is it?" I asked.

He shook his head. "Do you mind if I copy this?"

I tore a page from my notebook and he copied the names.

"Something I missed?" I asked.

"Something I want to look into. Unrelated." He turned my computer to read the article. "It doesn't say anything about smuggling."

"The Fosters were a wealthy family. The paper likely wouldn't want to get on their bad side. Bootleggers tended to be mobsters." I gasped. "The Fosters were mobsters."

"Or trying to outsmart the mob by smuggling liquor through the tunnels."

I gripped Chance's arm. "Clifford made a bunch of trips overseas. He transported Percheron horses. That's a documented fact. He could easily have smuggled the liquor with the other artefacts we've found on the estate. Do you think Martin knows?"

"Martin died before Prohibition was ratified—or at least he was believed to be dead."

"But Alice did the sculpture of Clifford's children." My mind raced with all the unanswered questions. "How come Alice's descendants don't know anything about her engagement to Martin?"

"Was there a notice of their engagement in the paper?"

I did a search on Alice Mansfield around 1918, the year Martin disappeared. Nothing, not even a reference to another year.

Chance looked off into space, the wheels in his mind practically humming with whatever he was thinking. "That's a lot of generations to trace. Family histories can get forgotten."

Smuggling wasn't one of those nuggets people forgot. Everyone knew the history of the Kennedys—or at least historians did. Joseph Kennedy was said to have sold liquor during Prohibition. One of my history teachers had blamed the Kennedy curse on Joe's shady dealings, while another of my teachers insisted Old Joe had been maligned and mistaken for another man with the same name. In either case, the Prohibition stories lived on. "We're talking a couple of well-known local families during a notable period in time."

"Families with skeletons in their closets." Chance chuckled. "Or ghosts."

"Clifford hired her to make the bust of his children," I said again, thinking out loud. "This can't be coincidence. We need to know more about the brothers who died in the tunnel. If they're the spirits we encountered—oh, I'd much rather they were angry spirits than demons—we can find a way to send them to their rest."

"Aren't demons lost souls?" Chance asked. "Gloria said her grandmother appointed herself as a guardian angel. If her brothers were smugglers, would they be angels who weren't allowed into heaven? Wouldn't that make them demons?" He shuddered. "Whatever I felt was pretty malevolent."

"And we're back to mobsters," I said. "The newspaper clearly didn't want to ruffle any feathers."

Chance studied me several moments. "How are we going to verify any of our theories?"

I grinned. "I'm going to visit one of Alice's sons tomorrow."

Chance's face lit up. "Alice's son? I'm coming with you."

Chapter 36

I arrived home around seven p.m. and made myself a sandwich for dinner. After eating, I fell into bed and overslept Thursday morning. When Chance arrived at nine o'clock, I was dressed, but still finishing my breakfast.

Still no word from Laine.

I met him at the door. "Maybe I should drive myself. I'm already putting us behind, and if I have to open the store, I can't stay more than an hour."

"Don't you have help at the store?" he asked.

"My sister should be back today, but I haven't heard from her." I checked my cell phone once more to see if I'd missed a text or a call. Nothing. A fresh wave of concern washed over me. "I should call her." I dialed the number, but it went to voicemail.

"I'll make sure you're back in time," Chance said.

Laine could be in the shower. Or still sleeping after getting home from her trip.

Or being held captive by her majordomo.

I considered rescheduling my visit to Henry Pugh until I could talk to Laine, and then decided I was borrowing trouble. I shook my head to clear my wandering thoughts. "Let's go."

When we arrived at the Veterans' home, a nurse escorted us to the solarium, where a pair of men sat hunched over a chessboard. A woman read a book in a wheelchair beside the windows. Another man sat on a plastic sofa staring at a wall-mounted television, crutches beside him, and yet another woman was situated in a recliner, her lap filled with a knitting project.

Catherine had arrived ahead of us and stood beside a man in a wheelchair. Henry Pugh, or so I assumed, had a thick shock of gray hair, and while his eyes were wizened with age, they held a mischievous sparkle like sunlight on Lake Michigan. He grinned, clearly happy to have visitors.

"How do you do," he said after Catherine introduced us. "My granddaughter is coming to visit me today."

I glanced at Catherine, wondering at this man's level of cognizance.

She sighed. "She's here. It's me, Grandpa. Catherine."

He pulled a pair of glasses from his shirt pocket and took a closer look. "Of course, you are."

I sat on his other side. "Catherine was kind enough to let us join her."

He chuckled. "I always enjoy company. Why you would want to bother with an old man, I can't begin to understand."

Catherine bent to kiss Henry's cheek and squeezed his hand. "How are you doing today, Grandpa?"

"Can't complain. Tell me, what brings you young people here?"

"Elle was asking me about your mother's art," she said. "They found a sculpture she did and they were hoping you

233

might know about a man she was engaged to before your father."

Henry looked at me. "I'm ninety years old, you know. That was a long time ago." He scratched his chin, thoughtful for a moment. "But I remember something. Was it one of those Fosters she was engaged to? The one who died during the war?"

"Yes," I said. "Martin Foster. I understand the two families remained friends, even after he was lost at sea."

Henry nodded. "Friends might be a bit much. Business partners, more like. At least that's the way my mother told it."

"What sort of business?" I prompted.

The old man's eyes twinkled. "Oh, you know the old stories. People were full of get rich quick schemes. Prohibition. The country was headed toward the Great Depression."

Chance settled in beside me. "We understand two of your uncles died in a tunnel at the Fosters' home during the Prohibition era. We'd heard a rumor they were smuggling liquor into the house."

Henry's brow creased. "Well, of course, there were always stories. No one spoke of those things back then. The bootleggers and the smugglers tended to be gangsters. Now what was that other Foster man's name?"

"Clifford?" I suggested.

"Yes, he's the one. Clifford Foster." He repeated Clifford's name in a mocking tone, as if he'd heard it in a negative connotation. "There was quite a to-do when Clifford asked my mother to make a bust of his children. The family talked about that for years. My father told my mother to stay away from that house." He furrowed his brow as if searching for a memory. "The place had some sort of fancy name." He shrugged. "My mother seemed to have a soft spot for those Fosters that the rest of the family couldn't comprehend. It all turned out fine, didn't it? I suspect Clifford Foster was more of an entrepreneur than a gangster." He rocked his head back and forth as if weighing the options. "I suppose my mother's sympathies came from her connection to—what did you say the man's name was? Martin Foster?" He chuckled again. "If she'd married him, he might have been my father, eh? But then I'd have been one of the dreaded Fosters."

Catherine smiled and squeezed his hand once more. "I never knew that story."

Henry leaned back in his chair and wheezed out a deep breath. "History has a way of coloring the truth. Over the years, the family took the position that—what was his name again? The man who owned the place?"

"Clifford," Chance provided.

Henry nodded. "Clifford. That Clifford roped the boys into his schemes without any concern for their safety. Naturally, our family painted Clifford as the villain in their version of the story. Likely because my uncles died at his house. Can't imagine he twisted their arms to be there, if you know what I mean. I expect the Fosters have their own interpretation."

Chance bowed his head and folded his hands. "Do you mind me asking you about Florence?"

Florence? I turned to Chance, wondering who Florence was.

"You would be referring to my aunt?" Henry asked.

Chance nodded.

"She was always full of life. A force of nature, that one."

Chance glanced at me before he pulled out the family tree he'd copied. "This shows she had four children."

Henry nodded slowly.

"I'm particularly interested in her youngest daughter. Bonnie."

Henry's expression darkened. "Can't help you there."

"You don't remember Bonnie?" Catherine prompted.

"Oh, I remember her."

"Then, what?" Catherine asked.

"We don't speak of such things," Henry replied.

"What things?" I asked.

"She was a wild child. Made her own bed, in a manner of speaking."

Catherine tilted her head. "Grandpa?"

He leaned toward Catherine and lowered his voice. "Bonnie had a child."

The three of us exchanged glances before Catherine pointed out Bonnie's brothers and sister also had children.

"They were married. Bonnie didn't have a husband."

Chance straightened.

Not unheard of, but in Henry's day, an unwed mother would have been quite the scandal.

Henry folded his arms and turned his head away from us. "She was disowned."

"Which explains why her part of the family tree stopped so abruptly," Chance said.

Why was he asking about Florence's branch on the family tree? "Do you know something about Bonnie?" I asked.

He folded the paper in his hands and shoved it into his pocket, not meeting my eye. "Bonnie Evans was my grandmother. My mother was the reason she was disowned."

Catherine gasped. "That means you and I are related."

I did the calculations in my head, checking the branches of the family tree. "Third cousins, by my reckoning."

Henry's gaze narrowed while he assessed Chance.

"Oh, Grandpa," Catherine said. "Getting pregnant isn't a crime. She made a mistake. You can't hold this man responsible for questionable decisions from the past."

"Don't know what this world has come to," he grumbled. "No morals anymore."

She laughed. "You're more upset about an unwed mother than about your uncles being mobsters?"

He folded his arms. "Don't know that they were. For all I know, Clifford Foster deceived them. They paid the price for their sins."

"Just like Bonnie was deceived, and paid the price for hers," Catherine pointed out.

I had so many questions. Considering the ties between the families, was it purely coincidental Chance was the caretaker at the same home where his great-uncles had died? Was there a sentient spirit guiding him, either for retribution or to heal a rift between the two families?

Listening to Henry Pugh tell it, there wasn't a rift with the entire family. Alice had done the sculpture of the children, after all. He'd written off the death of Alice's brothers as misadventure. The only member of the family who'd been disowned was the unwed mother—Chance's grandmother.

Chance was related to Alice Pugh.

All the scents I'd ignored when I'd walked into the Veterans' home suddenly became cloying—the piney scent of cleaning solution, bleach, the mild body odor of the people around us. *The energy of those who had passed, lingering nearby.*

"I need to step outside a moment," I said.

"You don't look well," Catherine said. "Are you okay?"

I managed a smile. "Don't worry about me. I just need a breath of fresh air."

"Do you want me to take you home?" Chance asked.

He'd just discovered family he didn't know he had. I couldn't take him away from that. "Take your time. I'll be fine."

On the brick terrace outside the solarium doors, I sat on a semi-circular stone bench beside a memorial wall. I wasn't surprised the brothers had become a folk story, similar to Al Capone or other Prohibition-era miscreants. Henry Pugh was probably the last historian left to remember them. Interesting that Alice had taken a sympathetic view while the rest of her family painted the Fosters as the bad guys.

What were the odds Chance was related to Alice Pugh? In an alternate universe, the man who wanted to buy Horned Owl Hollow might have been related to the man who'd inherited it, if Alice had married Martin the way she was meant to. Now Chance worked for the family, instead—or at least he used to.

Chance was related to the men who'd been killed in the tunnel.

I checked the time on my phone. Eleven o'clock. Still no word from Laine. I hit redial.

"Yes, yes, I'm here," she answered.

I breathed a sigh of relief. "Can you open the store? Will you be okay on your own for a little while?"

She sighed. "You're going to be late? Or not coming in?"

"Late, but if you can manage, there's something I'd like to do before I come in." I grabbed a handful of my hair. "I can fill you in later."

"Yeah, later. I have to talk to you, too." Her tone of voice didn't make it sound like good news.

Had her majordomo shown his true colors?

Chapter 37

Laine's cryptic comment had my nerves jumping. I was anxious to get back to Longhill and the antiques store.

When I walked inside the nursing home once more, Henry Pugh was clasping Chance's hand. Apparently, they'd made peace in spite of Bonnie's unforgiveable sin. Catherine stood by, her eyes welling with unshed tears—the epitome of a family reunion.

I cleared my throat. "I'm afraid I have to go. I can get an Uber home if you want more time together."

"May I visit you again?" Chance asked Henry.

Henry's voice was gruff. "I'd be pleased if you would."

"Thank you for introducing us to your grandfather," I told Catherine.

"I feel like I should be thanking you. This has been quite an eventful morning."

"I never dreamed I had family, especially not in the area," Chance said. "Who woulda thunk it?"

"Indeed," I replied absently.

Chance hugged Catherine. "We'll be in touch."

While Chance and I walked to his car, my thoughts swirled to the spirits in the tunnel at Horned Owl Hollow. We'd seen Clifford's spirit take over Darren first-hand. Spirits had a tendency to gravitate toward family. Was that why the smuggler brothers had gotten into Chance? Would they make another attempt to control him?

The brothers had died helping Clifford—or working for Clifford. How did Alice figure into it? Had she urged her brothers to take part in Clifford's dealings? When Martin had been lost, had she felt cheated? Tried to establish a toehold in Horned Owl Hollow?

I had to get to the store, to Laine, but I also had to expel the angry spirits in the tunnel at Horned Owl Hollow.

"Do you want me to take you to the store?" Chance asked.

The question of the hour. "You said you took Faith and Darren home? And Martin, too?"

"Right."

"Then I think we should go there to check on them." We climbed into his pickup. "Now that we have an idea who we're dealing with, I'd like to put the spirits to rest. At least I hope to." Except I'd bungled the situation when Clifford had possessed Darren. The same sort of thing threatened to happen to Chance if the spirits in the tunnel were related to him. "If we're going back there, I'm going to need my mother's help."

Chance nodded and I placed the call.

"Mom. We need more crystals. When can you come to the mansion?"

"I'm presenting a client offer in an hour. I can swing by after, if that's okay?"

The trip back to Longhill would take almost that long. I recapped what had happened since she'd left, how Darren had collapsed once Clifford had completed his unfinished business, and the additional spirits we'd found in the tunnel. "There's more going on here than we originally knew about."

"I'll be there as soon as I can, honey, but it may be a while yet." She hesitated. "I think you should go on without me. You have your crystals, right?"

"Yes."

When we arrived at Horned Owl Hollow, my first impressions of the manor returned with a startling sense of déjà vu. I glanced at the third-floor windows that seemed to be watching me, and then at the second-floor window over the terrace, where I now knew Norma Lombard's bedroom was located.

As Chance parked in the carriage house—now, the garage—Martin approached.

I jumped out to meet him. "Is everything okay?"

Martin walked slowly, his step not as sure. He'd aged at least fifty years in the ten days since I'd met him.

"You don't look well. Do you want me to call a doctor?" I asked.

His voice was gruff. "I don't want anyone studying the odd man who's traveled through time. The doctor we talked to told me to expect accelerated changes." He sighed. "I'm sorry. I scared myself when I caught sight of my face in a mirror. The changes are somewhat alarming."

"We can go into the house through the tunnel," Chance said.

I shook my head. "Not until we put the men who died there to rest."

"Who died in the tunnel?" Martin asked.

"Leland and Edwin Mansfield." How well had he known the two men—men who had been dead a hundred years?

"Alice's brothers?"

Chance stood beside me. I glanced from him to Martin. "We met with one of Alice's sons. He thinks they were working with Clifford to smuggle liquor."

"Alice had sons?" Martin's brow creased. "Smuggle liquor?"

"Are you familiar with Prohibition?" I asked.

"Yes, but I didn't think they'd actually ratify it."

"It was the law for thirteen years," Chance said.

Martin seemed to take it all in and then chuckled. "Those boys always were rascals. Younger than Alice, and often up to no good. I wouldn't be at all surprised. Clifford traveled abroad often. He could easily have brought home things he shouldn't have. He had a keen sense of business, and I can imagine him filling the demand for ill-gotten goods."

"Like the Staffordshire figurines," I said. "When they were first made, they were commonplace. Over the years, they've become more valuable."

"It all seems so fantastic. Not quite real." Martin sighed. "I don't understand how so much time can have passed. I also don't understand how the dead can walk the earth. Are you quite certain you aren't a witch?"

"Not a witch," I assured him. "Just sensitive to restless energy."

"Why is all this happening now?" Chance asked. "I mean, I get Norma not wanting to leave. She loved the old place, but I wasn't aware of Clifford haunting Horned Owl Hollow until Martin returned."

"I suspect Martin's return prompted a response. Clifford had unfinished business."

"What about the men in the tunnel?" Chance asked. "Where did they come from?"

"Gloria mentioned demons in the tunnel," I pointed out.

"You say the men who died, Alice's brothers, were in cahoots with Clifford?" Martin said.

"That's the assumption," I replied. "Their spirits may have been more benign until Faith got out her Ouija board."

"But what sort of unfinished business would they have?" Chance asked. "Delivering contraband brandy?"

"If they were working for Clifford, his records might hold a clue," Martin said. "My brother was a meticulous recordkeeper."

Chance's eyes lit up. "I think I might know where those records are. You've officially inherited the estate, right? Do I have your permission to show you where they are?" he asked Martin.

Martin nodded.

Chance crossed the yard and entered the house through the conservatory with Martin and me following. I paused beside the main staircase. No unusual energy patterns jumped out at me—not even Norma. "The house is quiet," I whispered.

"Where are Darren and Faith?" Chance asked Martin.

"I believe Faith has taken him to their bedroom. He's still quite weak."

Chance started up the stairs. "Clifford's old desk is in storage, assuming it hasn't been relocated like some of the other furniture. To the best of my knowledge, his estate papers are still in it."

On the third floor, Chance opened the door across from the ballroom. A large cistern dominated the room, with pipes angled from the ceiling to deposit rainwater—the remains of old-time plumbing. In the corner opposite, a rolltop desk sat beside a wood cabinet with glass inset doors.

"His desk," Martin said.

Chance lifted the rolltop to reveal cubbyholes filled with receipts. Martin stroked the top as if he'd found an old friend. He retrieved a ledger from beneath the cubbyholes and paged through it.

"These are dated from the forties," Martin said. "The handwriting changes around 1948. I would assume that would be the time he passed his legacy on?" He glanced at me. "It's still quite alarming to see these dates and know they are in the past and not the future."

"Clifford died in 1968," Chance said. "It stands to reason he retired in the late forties." He opened a drawer to another stack of books and leafed through them. "The dates on these are from the teens and early twenties. Books of account."

Martin took one and traced a finger down the page. "Transactions for the horses." A smile touched his lips. "They were beautiful animals. So strong."

"Any notations for payroll, or unusual entries?" Chance asked.

"I believe unusual transactions would be—what's the phrase? Off the books." Martin flipped a couple of pages. "Payroll for household help. Christmas bonuses. Accounts with the local merchants for food and sundries. What year did you say Alice's brothers died?"

"1922."

Martin flipped a few more pages, stopped, and ran his finger down the columns. "Nothing here. I suspect we're looking for something else. If my brother was involved in illicit activity, as you have suggested, I wouldn't be surprised if there is a second set of books."

Martin met Chance's gaze. Were there more crinkles around Martin's eyes? His face was beginning to resemble Henry Pugh's in age. No. He couldn't age that quickly, could he? In ten days?

Martin reached beneath the center drawer of the desk and rooted around, smiling as he stopped. The bottom of the open drawer popped up, revealing a hidden compartment. "The other books, I presume." He took the top one out and began reading. "Two barrels brandy. One case champagne." His face lit up with a smile. "I believe we've confirmed he was smuggling alcohol." He scanned the pages, journals rather than neat ledgers. "1922." He scanned several pages before he stopped. "It says, *E and L arrived with cargo. Tunnel collapsed upon transferring it to the house.* The next entry has been lined out."

"What's the crossed-out part?" Chance asked.

Martin squinted, holding the book closer, then farther away. "*Payment to E and L for safe delivery.*"

"Crossed out because he didn't pay them?" I asked.

"He likely assumed since they were dead, the money was no longer due." Chance stroked his chin while he studied the cistern.

"The next entry is a week later," Martin said. "*Mansfield demanding compensation for the loss of his sons. Have been advised by my lawyer to put everything into trust. As the Navy has returned no body, will name Martin as beneficiary despite his being declared deceased and lost at sea. All would have gone to Alice had she married him.*" Martin's forehead furrowed. "Did he mean to punish her for marrying Wayne Pugh?"

Chance read over Martin's shoulder. *"Have commissioned Alice to make a sculpture of the children in payment of the debt,"* he read. *"She can choose to settle the matter with Mansfield as she chooses."*

"He paid her commission as settlement of her brothers' unpaid salaries?" I asked. "Instead of paying her for her work?"

"Indeed, it seems she was dealt with poorly by my brother to soothe his conscience," Martin said softly.

"Is that all it says?" I asked.

Martin flipped a page. "Here's another entry. *Alice's husband has claimed payment for the sculpture as a business transaction—with a woman! Now Mansfield wants to extort more money from me for the loss of his sons. Good luck to him getting money from a dead man.'*" He bowed his head. "All to avoid paying the compensation he owed Alice's brothers? Certainly it couldn't have been worth all this fuss."

"Sounds like her father wanted more than what was owed," Chance said.

"He did lose two sons to a bootlegger," I said.

Chance shot me a glare as if I'd taken a radical stance.

"All I'm saying is the man was probably grieving," I added. "Mansfield, that is."

"There are entries detailing the cave-in of the tunnel, finding the two men dead, and reconstructing and reinforcing the tunnel." Martin glanced at Chance and then at me. "He didn't honor his contract with Alice's brothers, and he continued his shady business dealings. My legacy feels like ill-gotten gains, but what am I to do after all these years?"

"Why don't we take these books downstairs. We can sort through Clifford's notes, and maybe something will pop out at us," Chance suggested.

As we started down the staircase, a door opened on the second floor.

Chapter 38

Faith walked out of the master suite at the other end of the second floor. She looked as startled to see us as we were to see her.

"Darren insists on having a drink, although I'm not sure that's best," she said.

Darren's voice carried from inside the room. "I don't care what you think."

I glanced at Norma's bedroom door—still closed. "Do you mind if I check?" I glanced from Martin to Faith. "To see if she's gone."

"By all means," Martin replied.

"Do you want me to go with you?" Chance asked.

"You don't have to. If her spirit is still here, it may be because this is where she wants to be."

The three of them gathered around as I opened the bedroom door and walked inside.

Contacting spirits was never my favorite thing to do. Like before, I was aware of the residual energy. I crossed to the fireplace and glanced at the empty rocker. "Norma Lombard," I whispered. "Are you here?"

The hairs on my arm stood on end as the chair began to rock.

"Martin has claimed his legacy. Your business here is finished." I blew out a slow breath. "As to the rest, we'll figure it out," I said half to myself.

The rocker continued its slow rhythm.

I walked out and pulled the door closed behind me.

"Well?" Chance asked.

"The empty chair rocked. As long as the house stays in the family and her room remains untouched, she's unlikely to create a disturbance." I shrugged. "This is her home, after all."

"Then she's still...?" Faith asked.

I nodded. "In time, her energy will fade until it's little more than a memory. I don't believe she'll bother anyone."

We walked down the stairs together. In the parlor, Faith went to the sideboard bar, made a drink for Darren, and downed one of her own.

"How is Darren?" I asked.

"He's returned to himself," Faith said. "He's quite weak, but the doctor couldn't find anything wrong with him other than his broken hand."

Darren shuffled into the room and took the drink from Faith. "That's because there is nothing wrong with me. I don't know how all of you managed to wrest control of my estate from me." He fixed me with a glare. "Hypnotism. I can't imagine why else I don't remember anything. Faith tells me I've signed everything over to this imposter." He raised his drink Martin's direction. "It won't hold up in court. I wasn't of sound mind."

"I was there," Faith told him. "The spirit who possessed you seemed quite pleased you had the knowledge he lacked to prevent any challenges."

"Spirit." Darren sputtered, then drained his glass.

"You've done quite well in your own right," she said. "Hadn't we already decided we don't need the added burden that comes with the estate? Let it go."

Through the windows in the terrace doors, my mother's car came into view as she drove into the parking area. "My mother's here, and with your permission, I'd like to check the tunnel once more."

Faith chuckled. "You don't need our permission anymore. Martin is the rightful heir and owner."

"The tunnel to the carriage house?" Martin asked. "I walked through it the night you played that infernal game and nothing was amiss."

"I suspect the Ouija board provided a portal for them," I said. "Or Clifford's appearance. Something stirred the energy that resides down there."

"Alice's brothers," Martin said.

Chance bowed his head. "There's something else you may want to know."

Martin met his gaze. "Go on."

"I discovered today I'm related to the Mansfields. Do you remember Florence?"

Martin nodded. "Alice's younger sister."

"Turns out she's my great-grandmother."

My mother knocked on the door.

"May I let her in?" I asked Martin.

He tore his attention from Chance and nodded to me.

"What have I missed?" my mother asked.

As I led her into the parlor, I filled her in on our encounter in the basement, and what we'd discovered about the brothers who'd been buried alive. She reached into her purse and handed a crystal to Chance. "I assume you still have yours?" she asked Martin.

"Good luck charm?" Martin asked.

She grinned. "Yes. Can't do any harm, right?"

She nodded at Darren. "You say the spirit left him after he'd signed off on the trust? Assigned the estate to Martin as beneficiary?"

Faith wrung her hands as she nodded.

"Well, then," my mother said. "One piece of unfinished business has been accomplished. Which brings us to the brothers who were buried alive. Shall we see what they want?" She turned to Chance. "Can you tell me what you were feeling when you encountered the spirit in the basement?"

"Anger. White-hot."

"You say an orb floated into him?" she asked me.

I nodded.

My mother straightened her shoulders and faced Faith and Darren. "As you know, I am a realtor. I specialize in stigmatized houses. I have experience removing the stigma." She addressed Martin. "It appears to me the 'heart' of this house now is that tunnel. The spirits that remain have made a rather dramatic attempt to be noticed. Elle, will you show me the tunnel?"

"I can show you," Martin said.

"Of course," my mother replied. "But I must warn you if what Elspeth and Mr. Chance have discovered is true, the negative energy might well be directed toward you, as Clifford Foster's brother."

"Pffft," Darren sputtered. "Clifford Foster's brother. Poppycock."

Martin scowled at Darren before he replied to my mother. "Perhaps this is why I've been catapulted one hundred years into the future, to put a wrong to rights."

My mother smiled. "That may be. Shall we go, then?"

"I won't have Darren harmed any further," Faith said. "We'll stay here."

"That would be for the best," my mother said. "Your husband has proven to be susceptible to the lingering energy. If we want the negative energy put to rest, we must face it."

"Why should we care?" Darren said. "We're moving out."

Chance held an arm toward the hallway. "Shall we?"

Martin led the way, followed by my mother and me, with Chance bringing up the rear. At the bottom of the staircase, Martin turned toward the laundry room, to the door we now knew led to the tunnel. Before we reached it, the tunnel door blew open with a rush of wind that circled around us.

Chapter 39

My mother grabbed hold of my hand. Her voice was nearly lost in the tempest. "This is going to require both of us."

Chance fell to one knee. I tried to go to him, but my mother held me tight.

"He has a crystal," she said.

"Which doesn't seem to be helping."

She met my gaze. "If the spirit wants to speak, it will need a host."

Did she plan to offer herself? My gut instinct kicked in. "No."

"I know what I'm doing. I'll be okay." She dropped my hand and closed her eyes.

"Tell us what you want," she called out. She convulsed. Grimaced. Gasped. When she opened her eyes again, a shadow overlaid her face. A man spoke through her. "He owes us."

"Are you one of the Mansfields?" Martin asked. "Leland? Edwin?"

My mother turned toward him, her face a mask of rage. "I am Edwin Mansfield." My skin crawled hearing the man's voice coming out of her mouth. "The prodigal son returns. Too late." She pointed at Martin. "Does he mean to punish Alice for moving on instead of waiting for a dead man?"

"As you can see, he isn't dead," I said. "This isn't about Alice, is it?"

"He owes us," the voice repeated.

"I do not fault Alice for marrying someone else," Martin said. "And I do not know what forces have returned me to claim what is rightfully mine."

"Alice bartered her skills to settle your dispute," Chance said. "None of you hold a claim here any longer. It's time to move on."

"She did not barter her skills. Her husband claimed the money as his own," the hollow voice countered. "The debt remains."

A trickle of dirt fell inside the tunnel, followed by a brick falling to the floor.

Martin raised his hands as if to forestall any impending collapse. "I acknowledge my brother refused to pay the Mansfields as he promised. I have now claimed my inheritance. I have the opportunity to pay his debt. With interest." Martin turned to Chance. "This man is *your* relative. I would name him as beneficiary upon my death, if that would be acceptable. Restitution, one hundred years late in coming, but freely given. I promise you this on my soul."

"Martin," Chance said. "I can buy the house. There's no need to make it a bequest."

"It will repay the debt to your mother's family," Martin said. "You have been kind to me. Looking out for me when my own family would reject me. Our families are intertwined, as this spirit will remind us. I was unable to honor my promise to

Alice, and my brother refused to pay her brothers' family what he owed them. If I can make this right, I will." He turned to the spirit inhabiting my mother. "Will that allow you to move on? To find your peace?"

A chill seeped through me, starting at my toes and working its way through my body. I spoke—with another woman's voice.

"Wicked boys, both of you. Did you not agree to the devil's work when Clifford Foster came to you? How was he to pay dead men when the devil took his due? Be gone, both of you."

"He owes us," the spirit inside my mother insisted.

The voice inside me spoke again. "Has he not paid all these years? Have we not suffered all these years, as well? Fate has played a trick on all of us. I will not be used as a pawn any longer."

Martin paled. I looked at him through someone else's eyes. A sense of love and loss softened my heart.

"I do not know how this strange event came to be," the voice inside me said, "but know I never forgot you. I did my duty to my family, and then to the man I married. My heart was always with you, Martin Foster." Unable to control my own thoughts and movements, I approached him and placed a gentle kiss on his lips. A breath of a sigh escaped and warmth filled my body once more.

My muscles cramped and I grew dizzy. Martin reached for me, his hands under my arms to support me. When I looked into his face—the face of an old man now—his eyes were damp.

Martin's voice broke. "Miss Barclay, I cannot abide these visitations any longer. Please, can you make them stop?"

"They're gone," my mother said, kneeling on the ground.

The wind had stopped, although the door to the tunnel remained open.

Martin didn't take his eyes from my face, as if searching for the spirit that had spoken through me—Alice.

"My time grows short," he said. "I have much to do if I am to honor my promise to Mr. Chance." He raised his eyebrows, as if silently asking if I was well enough to stand on my own. I replied with a nod.

I crossed to my mother and crouched beside her. "Are you okay?"

She took my hand and I shared my strength with her.

Martin turned to Chance. "You might have been my nephew had fate not taken a hand and sent me hurtling through time and space. I know I will be leaving Horned Owl Hollow in capable hands, if you will accept it."

"I am willing to pay you," Chance repeated.

"It is something I wish to do, as payment of a debt from my family to yours, and as recognition from a friend to a friend. Please. Stay on, and consider this place your home as much as it is mine until such time as I no longer walk the earth." Martin extended his hand toward Chance. "Do we have a deal?"

Chance swiped at his face with his left hand and shook Martin's hand with his right. "We do."

As I tried to help my mother to her feet, her body went limp.

Chapter 40

"Mom?" I checked her pulse, which was beating much faster than it should be. "Call an ambulance." I looked over my shoulder as Chance pulled out his cell phone and placed the call.

"I'm so dizzy," Mom said softly.

Chance bounded up the stairs.

Martin knelt beside her. "Can I get you something to drink?"

"I could do with a glass of Clifford Foster's French brandy," she joked.

Faith hurried down the stairs. "Not Clifford's, but we do have a lovely cognac." She took my mother's hand. "Chance said he's calling an ambulance for you. You're quite pale. I'm afraid to ask what happened."

My mother labored to breathe. "I believe the spirits are at rest."

Faith looked at me. "She looks the same way Darren did, when the shadow left him. Maybe she just needs rest, like him."

My eyes burned with unshed tears. "I've never seen her like this."

My mother let go of Faith's hand. Her voice was strained. "Paramedics."

"They're on their way," Faith reassured her.

It seemed an eternity before Chance led the paramedics downstairs.

My mother smiled at me. "Don't fret, Elspeth. They'll take good care of me."

Chance eased me away to give the paramedics access to my mother.

"Has this happened before?" the paramedic asked.

I wrapped my arms around myself and shook my head.

They'd barely had a chance to check her when the second paramedic said, "Let's transport."

My breath froze in my chest. "To the hospital? What's wrong with her?"

"She's exhibiting signs of a heart attack," he said.

"I'm coming with you," I sobbed.

"Better if you meet us at the hospital," the second paramedic told me. They eased her onto the gurney and carried her out.

Chance touched my shoulder. "I'll drive you."

"Can I do anything?" Faith asked.

I hugged her. "Other than healing thoughts, no. Thank you."

We followed the paramedics upstairs. I stopped when I saw Darren on the couch in the parlor, his head leaning against the back. They'd taken him to the hospital and he'd been fine. My mother would be fine, too, right?

Darren opened one eye and scowled at us. Gloria sat in another chair, her hands in her lap, her expression guarded.

"Have you cleared out the ghosts, then?" Darren grumbled.

The paramedics wheeled my mother out the front door and into the waiting ambulance. I gathered my wits and stepped into the parlor. "I believe Norma wants to stay."

Gloria rose and took two steps toward the terrace door.

Faith breathed an impatient sigh. "*Norma* hasn't bothered us other than knowing she's still there."

"Overactive imaginations," Darren muttered.

"Says the man suffering from a ghost hangover," Faith shot back.

Darren narrowed his eyes at Faith, then turned to Martin. "If you want this headache of an estate, it's yours. I don't have the inclination to quibble, and I suspect whatever I've done legally will be difficult to undo. As my wife has pointed out, we're better off not paying the capital gains on this place, and we have a home in Florida to go to." He glanced between Chance and Martin. "I've given you shelter this past week. I'm hoping you'll afford us the same courtesy while we prepare for our final move." He turned to Gloria. "Any objections?"

She shook her head. "I've already told you I'm selling my house."

"You are family," Martin said. "I would not throw you out."

Chance took a step toward Gloria. "Do you have a buyer for your place?"

"Why would you care?" she asked, a hint of vinegar in her voice.

"I'd like to keep the properties as a package," he said. "I can turn your house into the caretaker's cottage if I open the main house as a museum."

"That's a great idea," Faith said. "I'm sure people would love to see the antiques and the beautiful craftsmanship that went into building this place."

Gloria gasped. "Caretaker's cottage?"

"Well, my house," Chance said.

"Museum? You're selling to him?" Darren asked Martin.

Through the terrace doors, I watched the paramedics navigate the driveway toward the road. These people had a lot to talk about and I didn't have the time to wait while Chance filled them in. *I needed to go.*

I pulled up my phone and ordered an Uber.

Martin told Darren what we'd learned and the deal he'd struck with Chance.

Darren held his head in his hands, inhaled deeply, and then met Martin's gaze. "You'll need a lawyer to draw up the paperwork. If you'll permit me, I can handle the transaction for you."

"Thank you, but I'll find someone else," Martin said.

Darren heaved a sigh and addressed Gloria. "And you'll need help keeping Blair's hands off your assets now that you've filed for divorce."

"He's agreed to half the proceeds from our house as a settlement." She pursed her lips. "And not a penny more."

Martin faced Chance. "There's still the matter of who moved the furniture from the house. Do I need to guard against a thief? Mr. Chance, you said you moved something—a collection of figurines, if I'm not mistaken?"

"I did," Chance said. "I'll be happy to show you where it is."

"Then we've accounted for all the missing items, haven't we?" Faith asked.

"But not the thief," Martin said.

Darren growled. "I'm not a thief." He closed his eyes again and sighed. "At the time, it was mine to sell." He glowered at Martin. "Until you returned from the dead. I wasn't about to let Blair stake a claim to anything." He chinned toward Gloria. "I knew he was planning to leave my sister. Blair isn't exactly the soul of discretion." He pushed off the sofa, poured another drink and took a healthy sip. "I figured my sister and I could split the proceeds after her divorce was final, assuming that was the course her husband was taking, with no one being the wiser."

"But Chance noticed," I said.

Darren scowled. "Yes. Chance noticed. Once we made the decision to sell, I began moving things. I'd considered offering Blair the proceeds from the Staffordshire collection as incentive to walk away with money in his pocket."

"You might have told me," Faith said.

"Plausible deniability." He downed the last of his drink. "In the event Blair caught on to the other disappearing items. As it stands, the only thing I've sold is that stupid carousel horse."

"The one thing that represented Clifford's fortune," Martin said.

"That might raise a spirit's ire," Faith said.

Darren heaved another sigh and relaxed into the sofa once more. He focused on me. "How can you believe this man is Martin Foster?"

I checked the driveway for my ride, which still hadn't arrived. Truth time. No equivocations, even if it made me sound like a lunatic. "He's a familial DNA match." I met Chance's gaze. "Unless I've drunk the Kool-Aid and someone's—" I raised my eyebrows in case he wanted to make a confession, "—masterminded a swindle of epic proportions."

Chance wore a sardonic smile. "Even if everyone in the world has a doppelganger, the odds of finding one are astronomical."

I wanted to believe him. To trust him. His actions had been altruistic. Was it fair to doubt him just because he was a man? At some point, I'd have to stop blaming all men for what Quint—and my father—had done to me. I swallowed down my doubts and nodded.

A car pulled into the driveway. "I need to get to the hospital." I turned to Chance. "I called an Uber. You have matters to attend to here."

Martin laid a hand on my shoulder. "I am grateful to you. And your mother. My best wishes for her health."

When I looked into Martin's face, instead of the young man who'd knocked on the Lombard's door not quite two weeks ago, he now resembled a man Henry Pugh's age. "Thank you." My heart tugged hard with worry. My mother wasn't the only one whose health was in jeopardy.

Chapter 41

I called Laine on my way to the hospital.

"About damn time," she said when she answered. "When are you coming in?"

"I'm not." I gave her the short version of what had happened to Mom.

"I'm closing the store. I'll meet you at the hospital," she said.

When I walked into the Emergency Room, a nurse told me to have a seat while she checked on my mother. Five minutes later, Laine walked in. I greeted her with a hug.

"You're a sight for sore eyes," I said.

"What's going on? Is Mom okay?"

Tears spilled down my cheeks. "I don't know. They said they'd let us know when we could see her." I went on to share everything that had happened since she'd left for Iowa.

"Holy cow," she said when I'd finished. "So, this Martin Foster guy is the real deal?"

"Real enough to inherit."

She stared at me. "A ghost actually spoke through you?"

I nodded. "And Mom."

She pressed her lips closed, a gesture I recognized as her feeling left out of the private club, as she often put it. Her voice had an edge. "So Mom had a heart attack after she was possessed?"

"I don't know. I think so. Maybe."

Tears fell down Laine's cheeks as she clutched my hands. "Is the same thing going to happen to you next time you go on one of your ghostly tangents? Like when you had that—" she waved her hands in the air "—vision in the store?"

I met her gaze. "I don't know."

The nurse came over. "Miss Barclay? Your mother is alert and awake. They're taking her for an echocardiogram. I'll show you to her room when they bring her back."

I brushed the tears from my face. "Thank you."

She disappeared behind automatic doors once more and I turned to face Laine. "That's good news, right? She's awake?" I drew a shuddery breath. "Let's think happy thoughts. Tell me about your trip."

She sat back and fiddled with her purse strap.

My heart thudded, anticipating her reticence had something to do with Mr. Majordomo. I wasn't sure I could handle more bad news. I fought my frantic musings, ready to console her or send Quint after Gavin if Gavin had done anything to hurt her. "Out with it."

"I'm going to Spain with Gavin next month."

Dumbstruck, I stared at her.

She raised her hands to forestall a response. "I can tell him I can't go if Mom needs me."

I swallowed the lump in my throat. "And if she doesn't need you?"

Laine inclined toward me and took my hands in hers. "The family he works for has asked him to join them there, in Seville, and he invited me to go, too. Spain, Elle. I've always wanted to visit Europe, and he's promised we can fan out from there."

I didn't know what to say. I had visions of a stranger luring her away with candy. Holding her against her will.

"It's still a month away," she went on. "A lot can change in a month's time."

I nodded dumbly. "So, you and him...?" I managed to sputter.

Her cheeks flushed. "I think this might be the real deal, Elle. It all happened so fast. A month together should help us to know better, right?"

Tears rolled down my cheeks. I'd come to depend on Laine. I had visions of all the horrible things that could happen to her—of my father threatening to take her away. That was a long time ago. I had to trust her to know what she was doing.

I was going to lose my sister, and maybe my mother, too. I swallowed a sob.

Fresh tears welled in her eyes, too. "Say something."

I didn't trust myself not to say something unsupportive so I hugged her instead. "Be happy," I whispered.

"You know I wouldn't even consider going with him if I didn't believe he could be the one." She pulled away. "But you guys are more important than anything. If Mom..."

I struggled to find my voice. "Is alert and awake," I finished for her. "I'm sure she'll be happy for you, too." I shook a finger at her. "He'd better take good care of you."

Laine looked over my shoulder and swiped at her face. I turned to find Chance hovering behind me.

"How is she?" he asked.

My face had to be splotchy from all the tears, and I could only imagine what my eyes looked like. I grabbed a tissue from a box on the table beside me and wiped my face. "It doesn't sound as bad as the paramedics made her out to be."

"I'm glad to hear."

"Are you going to introduce me?" Laine asked.

While I made the introductions, Chance produced a bouquet of flowers from behind his back.

"You promised me a dinner date," he said.

More tears threatened, this time as a result of his thoughtful gesture. I accepted the flowers. "So I did."

"This might not be the best time, but I wanted you to know I still want to. Take you to dinner, that is." He brushed a renegade tear from my cheek with his thumb.

"This is where you say yes," Laine answered for me. "Might I suggest tomorrow night?"

"But Mom..."

"You'll still need to eat," she said.

I managed a smile. "It might mean dinner in the hospital cafeteria."

"We can do that," he said. "I'm meeting with a lawyer to finalize the details at the estate. You might be interested in how everything's coming together. But I had to make sure you were okay. And your mom."

I wiped my face and forced a smile. "We'll be fine. I can call you later."

"Promise?"

I nodded.

Chance shot a glance at Laine, then hugged me before he left.

"Looks like you've found someone special, too," Laine said.

I considered making excuses, assuring her no man would be able to get past my armor, but it was no use. He already had, and she knew it. "We'll see."

The nurse approached us again. "If you ladies are ready, I can take you to your mother."

We followed her into the emergency suites just as an orderly wheeled Mom into her room. She looked tiny and frail, attached to a heart monitor and with a cannula in her nose.

Laine rushed to her first. "Mom." She bent to hug her. "Are you okay?"

"I'm well enough," Mom said.

"Did they tell you what's going on?" I asked.

"They think she had a mild heart attack," the nurse said. "They're running a host of tests to see what the damage is."

My chest squeezed with anxiety.

"The prognosis is good, or so they say," Mom added. She turned to Laine. "How did your trip go?"

I nudged Laine, encouraging her to spill her news, a gesture that didn't go unnoticed.

"What's going on?" Mom asked.

Laine looked at me, then at Mom, then at the ceiling. "Oh, all right. I met someone and I'm taking a trip with him."

Mom sighed and smiled. "I'm so happy you've found someone."

"Tell her where you're going," I prompted.

"Now?" Laine shot me a dirty look. "I don't have to go. If Mom needs me..."

"Mom will be fine. Where are you going?" Mom asked.

Laine winced, then said, "To Spain. For a month."

Mom blinked. Drew a deep breath. "That sounds exciting. You must be serious about this man, then."

"She just met the guy," I blurted. My cheeks heated. I hadn't meant to rain on Laine's parade, but someone had to worry about her.

"Sometimes you just know," my mother said. She must have seen the shock on my face, because she quickly added, "I didn't hear her say she was marrying the man, although a vacation together would certainly help them determine how compatible they are.

"I've always worried about you girls, about the way your father left, if that left an imprint. It isn't your fault he left, you know."

"He as much as said it was," I reminded her.

"If he was as worried about Laine as he said he was, he would have made an effort to contact her," Mom pointed out. "Even if what he said was true—that he was leaving us because of my..." she shimmied her shoulders and rolled her eyes. "Oddity? It was an excuse."

Her words struck me. I'd always taken that day at face value, but she had a point. Why hadn't he come back to visit Laine?

Mom reached for my hand. "You know it's true," she said.

Laine folded her hands in her lap, head bowed. "If he was so intent on saving me, he did a lousy job."

Mom managed a laugh. "Because he wasn't trying to save you. I have spent all these years trying to love you both enough to overcome his hateful words, but I always worry I didn't do enough."

"It *was* a hateful thing to say." Laine looked at me. "Singling you out. Or rather, singling me out. I never knew if I should be jealous of your ability to see spirits or grateful I didn't share it." Her smile was conciliatory. "We did okay without him, didn't we? Our childhood wasn't so..." She rolled her eyes. "Strange."

"Don't all families have their own version of strange?" Mom asked. "We weren't all that different." She smoothed her blanket. "So tell me about this man."

Laine gushed about Gavin, about how much they had in common, and about how he lived in a castle, even if he didn't own it.

Which made me think of Chance. Was Horned Owl Hollow his castle? One he would soon own.

Mom glanced between me and Laine. Was she sensing my thoughts? If she was, she kept the conversation focused on Laine and Gavin.

Laine stopped to take a breath. She furrowed her brow. "Are we wearing you out? You should be resting. When are they going to let us know what's going on?"

"I'll be right as rain tomorrow," she said. "Today took a lot out of me, but I'm feeling much better now. I'm in good hands."

Laine turned to me. "Is she okay? You'd know better than me."

"The doctor said I had a mild heart attack," Mom said. "They want to monitor me for a few hours, and the test results will tell them if there's anything to be concerned about."

I'd seen my mother destigmatize houses in the past. She'd always looked tired afterward, but she'd never reacted the way she had today. She had lines in her face. Had they been there before? Or was I looking for them, the way I had looked for the changes in Martin Foster? I'd never thought of my mother as old before. I'd never considered her mortality.

"I'll be fine," she said, as if seeing my concern.

But she wasn't. She'd suffered a heart attack, even if it was mild. "Maybe you should let other people deal with the stigmatized properties from now on," I suggested. "You've done your part."

She sighed. "You might be right. It does wear on one's soul. You did a good job today." She held my gaze. "So did Mr. Chance. There's something there, you know. He seems like someone who might help when you encounter spirits in the future." She wagged her eyebrows. "Among other things."

Laine sputtered and started laughing. "He's asked her to dinner. There's hope for her yet."

I groaned. "Hope for what?"

"That one of you will give me grandchildren!" Mom said.

"Mother!" I complained.

She reached for my hand. "How many people do you know understand your sensitivity? Who accept that it makes you special and not odd?"

I shot a quick glance at Laine.

"Don't look at me," she said. "I'm still in the odd camp."

I laughed. "I suppose that's a point in his favor, then, but I hardly know the man."

"Yet," Laine and my mother said at the same time.

"I'm with her," Laine said. "Promise me you'll give Chance a..." she giggled. "A chance, I guess. Look, I never made any bones about my opinions of Quint. I don't know what you saw in him, but this guy—Elle, this guy seems good for you."

"Quint was a policeman. Like Gordon. Remember him?" I looked at Mom. "I really thought you might marry him."

"I told you girls I wasn't interested in making another trip to *Ever After*. Gordon knew that."

I smiled and held my mother's hand. "But he was one of your longest trips to *Happily*. When he left, he took Laine and me aside and told us if we ever needed anything, he'd be there. All we had to do was ask."

"At which point I asked him for a car," Laine joked.

I scowled at her. "Yes, well, he was one of the only men in my life I trusted. I suppose I projected my feelings for him onto Quint, another policeman." I held up my hands. "Don't worry, I've learned from my mistakes."

No, Chance wasn't like Quint—or my father, as my mother had pointed out. Chance had his own sympathy for earthbound spirits. I'd promised him a dinner date, if for no other reason than I was curious to know how things had turned out at Horned Owl Hollow.

I wanted to spend time with him for more than to fill in the blanks about his new home.

Chapter 42

Laine and I spent Friday at the store, chattering about all the things we needed to do to help Mom when she got home from the hospital tomorrow. We also talked about the impact Laine's trip to Spain would have on the store, but I was determined she should go. At four o'clock, she shooed me in the direction of the salon where she'd made me an appointment.

"I want you to look your best for this guy tonight," she'd said. "Chance deserves a chance." She chuckled at her play on his name—again.

I groaned and rolled my eyes. Still, I had butterflies.

After a fresh haircut and style, I went home, did my make-up and put on a dress. By six-thirty, I was ready for my date—way too early. Not that I was eager.

Chance's pickup steered into my driveway at six-forty-five. Did that mean he was looking forward to our date, too? He walked the front sidewalk and knocked on the door. I closed my eyes and took a breath. It was just a date. He was just a man. Clean slate.

As I opened the door, his gaze swept over me and he smiled. "You look great."

So did he. He'd donned black dress pants and a gray button-down shirt. "You, too."

"How's your mother?"

"She's doing well. She should be going home tomorrow," I said.

"I'm glad to hear. You ready?"

I grabbed my purse and we walked out.

He drove to Chandler's Steakhouse, the kind of restaurant where I expected to find the Lombards. The hostess walked us through the elegant décor to a booth in a room with a fireplace. I opened the menu and nearly choked on the prices. I glanced over the top of my menu to find Chance watching me.

"I recognize that look," he said. "So we're clear, I asked you out, so I'm buying. No expectations other than a good meal."

I raised my eyebrows. "You recognize that look?"

He leaned on the table. "I did say I wanted to change your perception of men. We aren't all 'like that.'"

"Clean slate," I whispered to remind myself.

"Exactly," he said. "I like you, Elle. And I'd like to get to know you better. It seems we have things in common that aren't... common."

Like seeing spirits. I nodded.

The waitress arrived.

"Would you like to share a bottle of wine?" he asked me.

"Cabernet?" I suggested.

He nodded at the waitress, and she left to place our drink order. Chance set his menu down. "Why does this feel strange? We've spent a lot of time together over the past couple of weeks without struggling for conversation."

"If you've changed your mind..." I began.

"No. That's not what I meant. I want to be here, but now I don't know what to talk about."

The sommelier returned with our wine. He uncorked the bottle and went through the ritual with Chance, who nodded his approval. The sommelier poured us each a glass. Chance raised his in a toast. "To rectifying wrongs from the past, living in the present, and hopes for a happy future."

I touched my glass to his and we each took a drink. "I suppose we've spent a lot of time talking about Martin and the Lombards. Tell me more about your dad—about your parents," I said. "You told me why he took the job at Horned Owl Hollow, but how did he come to be a caretaker?"

"Well, the story goes he wanted to be a groundskeeper at Wrigley Field, but those jobs are hard to come by." He grinned. "In the meantime, he worked for a landscaper, and met my mother on a job. They dated, fell in love, got married—the usual. Bills were tight, and my mother saw the ad for the caretaker at the estate. She'd always had a penchant for the place and talked my dad into applying. The rest, as they say, is history."

His family seemed so normal, aside from the fact they lived in someone else's house. "I know you cared for your father after his stroke. How long was he ill?"

Chance toyed with the stem of his wineglass. "A couple of months. After the first stroke, I arranged to come home to Horned Owl Hollow and offered to take over his responsibilities while he recovered. At first my father was angry with me for walking away from the life I'd made, but I was tired of it. I missed working outside. With my father. Doing the day-to-day at the estate was peaceful, and it allowed me to care for my dad."

His voice grew strained. "That last day, I don't know how he managed to navigate the steps. He could barely walk. I'd gone to pick up his prescriptions, and when I got back, I couldn't imagine where he was." When Chance met my gaze again, his eyes were glassy. "He always loved the woods. He's the one who planted the bluebells and the jonquils that line the path." He swiped at his face. "He'd gone for a walk, fallen, and hit his head on a rock. If I'd been home, he wouldn't have gone out on his own. I miss him so damn much. Even when he was sick, he was my best friend. We spent our evenings talking over the chess board." He drew a shaky breath. "If he wanted to walk through the woods, why didn't he tell me? I would have taken him."

I reached for Chance's hands. "Maybe he knew it was his time and that's why he went out by himself when you weren't there. He died on his own terms, in a place he loved best."

Chance swallowed hard, his eyes red-rimmed. "I still talk to him sometimes. At the end of the day. Sitting over the chess board."

"Is he the reason you wanted to buy Horned Owl Hollow?"

"No," he answered quickly. "I love that old place, more than the Lombards do, I think. To them, it's an albatross. Norma loved it, though. She liked to talk about her father and her uncle and all the memories she had growing up there."

"Whatever happened to Darren's parents? How did they escape this whole trust situation?"

Chance took another sip of wine. "Darren's mother died of cancer about ten years ago, and Darren's father went within a couple of months of her. Norma worried about what would become of the estate. She knew Darren and Gloria didn't hold an attachment to the property. Darren wanted to update the trust to change the beneficiary, but Norma wouldn't hear of it. She insisted Martin would come home. Then when she died..."

I was flabbergasted. "How do you know all that?"

He chuckled. "Norma told me. She knew how much I loved the place. That's when I decided if the family ever decided to sell, I'd buy the place. When her mind started to fade, she was even more convinced Martin would come home. She made me promise to keep his room for him, and I did. After she died, Darren made it clear he planned to liquidate the trust."

"And then Martin came home."

The waitress returned to take our dinner orders. When she left, Chance raised a toast to Norma Lombard.

"I can't believe your mom was related to the Mansfields," I said.

He nodded, staring into his wine. "Have to say that was a surprise to me, too. What about your family? I've met your mother. What about your father?"

Considering all he'd told me, I decided I owed him at least that much. I took a long drink for fortification, and then a deep breath. "My father left us when I was twelve. He told my mother he couldn't abide her oddness a moment more, and the way she'd poisoned me to be like her. He threatened to take Laine with him, and my mother said if he even tried, she'd call all the demons in hell to chase him."

Chance laughed. "Could she do that?"

I shook my head. "I wouldn't think so, if for no other reason than the risk would be greater than the reward. Or, not, in my father's case."

"I'm sorry. I didn't mean to laugh." He lowered his gaze to his wineglass once more. "At least you have your mom. She seems to get it."

"Yeah. She and I have a 'different' sort of mother daughter-relationship. My dad always resented that. Heck, even Laine gets upset about it sometimes. Sure, I didn't always like being different, but at least knowing I was like my mother I didn't feel so strange. When you don't have someone to talk to about the crazy things you see, it can make you a little nuts."

"I've never told anyone about... you know. Like with Norma, and the rocking chair."

No wonder he became a recluse. "People tend to have a poor opinion when you tell them you've had a spiritual experience."

"Where do spirits go?" Chance asked. "Do you believe in heaven? Or hell?"

"I believe there is a place where they find rest. A well of souls where they reconnect with the people who have gone before—the people they've loved. Souls who have been waiting to be reunited."

"I like to think my parents are reunited." He thumbed the stem of his glass, and then met my gaze. "I'm glad I met you. And I agree. It's nice having someone to talk to about the crazy."

"At least the crazy seems to be finished at Horned Owl Hollow."

He leaned across the table. "When did you first know you were different?"

Good question. One I'd asked myself a dozen times. "I used to have dreams. A narrator, just out of sight, telling me what I needed to see. I didn't really understand when I was young that they were visions, or that other people didn't experience the same thing. I mean, everybody has dreams, right? The night my father left, I'd just told my mother about a dream I'd had. My father slapped the table, rose to his feet and said he'd had enough.

"I still didn't have a real sense of my weirdness until my last year of college, when my roommate's mother spoke to me in a dream. I told my roommate what I'd seen, and while I tried to laugh it off, my roommate started crying. She called her mother to check on her and discovered her mother had just died." I tensed, trying to forget that day. "When she ended the call, all she said to me was 'how did you know?' Then she shook me by the arms and demanded that I let her talk to her mother—her mother who had just passed." I drew a cleansing breath. "What about you?"

"I don't think I ever considered the possibility until I moved back to Horned Owl Hollow. I definitely noticed odd goings-on then." He held my gaze. "Do you run into this sort of thing every day?"

I sputtered, reached for my napkin and wiped my mouth. "You mean dinner?" I asked.

"Restless spirits."

Yes, I knew what he meant. "Not every day. More than I'd like, but the spirits at Horned Owl Hollow were certainly something I haven't encountered before. Thank heaven I have

279

my mother..." My breath caught. I wouldn't be able to call on my mother in the future. Not without putting her life in jeopardy again.

Our dinner arrived. Chance stared at his plate until the waitress left again.

"Elle, if you ever run across another situation... if your mother isn't well enough..." He sighed. "What I'm trying to say is..."

"I'll call you," I said. "And I appreciate that you're willing to help."

"We make a hell of a team, don't we? But it's more than that. I enjoy your company, and I hope this isn't our only date." He took another sip of wine.

I couldn't stop the smile from spreading on my face. "I'd say you're proof there's hope for the male of the species."

HORNED OWL HOLLOW

Story notes: On March 4, 1918, the USS *Cyclops* left Barbados en route to Baltimore with a cargo of manganese ore for munitions, pressed into service during the war to transport cargo heavier than the coal it had been built to carry. Overloaded and with a cracked cylinder, it disappeared in the Bermuda Triangle. On June 1, 1918, Assistant Secretary of the Navy, Franklin D. Roosevelt declared *Cyclops* to be officially lost, and all hands deceased. No trace of the ship has ever been recovered. It's believed a rogue wave swamped it to a watery grave at the bottom of the ocean. Wreck divers continue to search for it to this day.

Acknowledgements: A fond remembrance of teachers, most notably Arnold Bathje for infusing life into dull history lessons. To Audrey King at the Ellwood House Museum, a stately manor that inspired Horned Owl Hollow and which, to the best of my knowledge, is NOT haunted. Most notably, my thanks to Fran at *Whatnots & Whimsies* for sharing her time with me and stories from the antiques shop. As always, my work would not be what it is without the support of my critique partners, Terry Odell and Steven J. Pemberton, and my editor, Kelly Lynne Schaub.

Dear Reader:

Thanks so much for reading this book. If you enjoyed the story, I hope you will recommend me to a friend, encourage others by "liking" my books everywhere the option is offered, and post an honest review to the site where you bought this book. I love hearing from my readers, and am always eager to receive feedback to make each new book as good as it can be.

—Karla Brandenburg

Also by Karla Brandenburg

The Hillendale Novels
Family Alchemy
Unintended Consequences
The Hidden Grimoire
Interrupted Magic
Enchanted Memories

The Epitaph Series
Epitaph
The Twins
The Mirror
The Selkie
The Sculptor
The Garden

The Hoffman Grove Series
Being Neighborly
Breaking the Mold
Cookie Therapy
Return to Hoffman Grove
Living Canvas

The Mist Trilogy
Mist on the Meadow
Gathering Mist
Rising Mist

Other Novels
Heart for Rent, with an Option
While We Were Shopping
Coyote Legacy

Made in United States
North Haven, CT
22 July 2023

39405385R00161